D1073000

MURDER IN A COLD CLIMATE

Scott Young

FAWCETT CREST • TORONTO

A Fawcett Crest Book
Published by Random House of Canada Limited
Copyright © 1988 by Scott Young

ISBN: 0-449-21746-9

This edition published by arrangement with Macmillan of Canada, a
division of Canada Publishing Corporation

Printed in Canada

First Fawcett Crest Edition: July 1989

CONTENTS

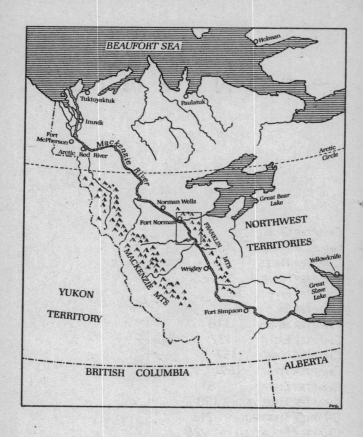

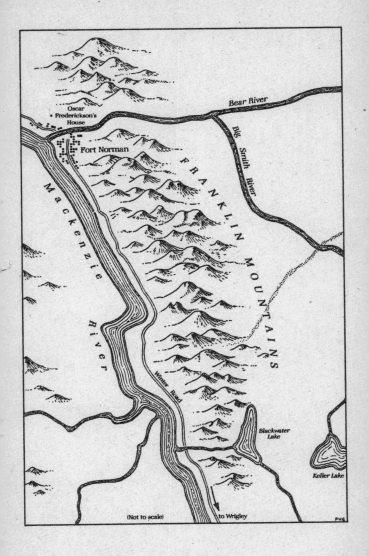

MURDER IN
A COLD
CLIMATE

AUTHOR'S NOTE

Although I'm not a Northerner, I've been drawn strongly to the North and its people since I was first there in the spring of 1955 researching a piece for *Sports Illustrated*. The topic was what seemed then to be a significant, even dangerous, decline in the great caribou herds. In Yellowknife I met a Canadian Wildlife Service biologist and a Wardair single-engined Beaver flew us to Fort Reliance on the eastern tip of Great Slave Lake. There each night after a lot of strong tea and fascinating talk I'd sleep on the floor of the Mountie detachment's combination home and office (three rooms in all). By day our pilot flew a grid pattern over the Barrens toward Artillery Lake and the Thelon River and beyond while the biologist counted animals below and I just sat there, I guess with all my senses open, because I remember the sights and sounds and smells to this day.

I kept that memory warm for years and in the mid-1960s returned. That time I chugged down the Mackenzie river by tugboat and barge from Hay River to Inuvik, stopped for a day at Norman Wells and for a cup of coffee at Tuktoyaktuk, and in Inuvik played in a baseball game, The Drunks versus The Bartenders, at 2 a.m. in the 24-hour daylight of June in the schoolyard across the street from the Mackenzie Hotel. This was research for a CBC-TV documentary about the Mackenzie (the river, not the hotel).

In 1969 as a Globe and Mail reporter I travelled with Governor General Roland Michener on a tour of the Eastern and High Arctic as far north as Alert, about 500 miles from the North Pole, and in 1987, researching this book, spent a few days along the Mackenzie again. Betweentimes I visited the Arctic Institute museum in Leningrad, one of the most interesting and little-publicized sites in that city. So though I'm not a Northerner, when I'm there I wish I were; which I guess is why the Inuk Mountie detective introduced in this book has been growing in my mind for years.

In that regard, I am deeply grateful for the help given me. Among those based in Inuvik I thank Cece McCauley, the woman who is Chief of the Inuvik Native Band and long ago was my first friend in the Arctic; Inspector Kelly Folk, officer commanding the Inuvik subdivision of the RCMP; Arctic consultant Dick Hill of the multi-faceted Hill Enterprises Limited; and Mike and Jackie McVeigh as well as Mike's Inuit, Dene and Metis students in the communications class at Arctic College.

I also thank RCMP Corporal Jim Herman and Wayne Irwin of Esso Resources, both at Norman Wells; Miles Shaw of Esso in Calgary; Don Wishart of Interprovincial Pipelines in Edmonton; oldtime trapper Gus D'aoust for his matter-of-fact writing about the North; Dr. Jules Sobrian for his encyclopaedic knowledge of firearms; Sheldon Fischer for his conscientious editing; and most particularly Barbara Heidenreich of Trent University and the Canadian Environmental Law Association, who worked for years among Native people from Labrador to the western Arctic and whose knowledge and cultural insights helped—plenty.

By all of which I mean: if there are errors, they are my own.

I have used actual place names in this book, but only refer (and that briefly) to one actual person, the redoubtable Chief

Cece McCauley. All others in the story, including the Mounties and their wives, are fictional, and all events and characters are solely products of my imagination, not resembling to my knowledge anyone living or dead.

Scott Young,
JULY, 1988

Scott Younce
[signature]

O N E

The air terminal at Inuvik has comfortable chairs and some nice Arctic art on the walls and usually a lot more empty space than passengers, so it is not exactly O'Hare, but it's not Tuktoyaktuk either. Which was about as profound an idea as I could manage on this particular morning, due to a kind of numbness that I sometimes get when I spend a couple of nights in Inuvik. It's not really a bad feeling: part Polish vodka for me and Hennessy (higher octane) for Maxine, part leaving her again, part talking most of the night when we might have been sleeping, part making love at a higher frequency than my norm (which still doesn't mean I set any world records).

But it was good, all of it. And when I'd stood at the window of Maxine's living room this morning and looked out into the pitch dark of 8:30 a.m., as black then as it had been at two or three when we were still awake, I had one brief pang of wishing that life was simpler again and that the Arctic was still my home. Then I came to my senses. What the hell, this was civilized Arctic: townhouses, pickups, roads, hot and cold running water. Not the Arctic I'd grown up in, with the shore in winter a tumbled line of great ice blocks

1

and komatiks and chained dogs howling and frozen seal bodies stuck upright here and there like popsicles for the dogs
to feed on. And out on the ice a seal hole watched by a hunter
with his rifle ready and his body warm in the two layers of
caribou skin that were his clothes.

While those thoughts were going through my mind Maxine had been running the shower. Over the splashing I could
hear her humming ''Bridge Over Troubled Water.'' Outside,
kids with their heads tucked into their parkas headed for
school. Across the dark street, the only Native thing about it
being the name, Kugmallit Road, streetlights showed two
ravens playing a con game on a dog. The dog was trying to
eat a scrap of something. As one raven dove at him so close
that the dog charged after it, snapping and snarling, the other
member of the raven team sloped in, bounced once, grabbed
the food and flapped away. A pick play. Maybe ravens in-
vented the pick play.

''Hey!''

I turned. Maxine, wrapped from knees to collarbone in
a white towel, was holding two cups of the fresh coffee
I'd just made. When I went to take mine I unhitched her
towel and she giggled and we fooled around a bit the way
people do when it's the fun and affection side of love and
somebody has to be off to work right away. Hardly spilled
any coffee at all. Then I wrapped the towel back around
her, patting here and there. I held her for a few seconds,
nose to nose with her black straight hair and almost black
eyes. I occasionally thought that the Scottish blood of her
father must have got lost somewhere in the Slavey blood
of her mother. In the twenty years we'd known one another
she'd become a little dumpy in the figure, as I had. Falling
asleep in each other's arms as we sometimes do, and did
last night, a guy doesn't notice the changes the years have
brought.

CBC Radio, where she works in news, isn't far from her
townhouse. She was due at nine. Anybody who saw us
clumping along a few minutes later in our kneeboots and

baggy pants, parkas trimmed with wolverine fur around the hoods, reflective tape across the backs for safety in the dark, would just be seeing two short, stocky natives heading God knows where; not knowing we went back all those years to when I was a special constable here for the Mounties and Maxine was emptying bedpans and changing beds at the hospital, both jobs the kind of no-hopers that were all a Native could get when she and I were younger. We'd gone on a long time and had a lot of partings like this one. We never knew when we'd see one another again, but it always happened. Or always had so far.

As we walked our breath made little frosty clouds that blew between us as we walked. There wasn't much to say.

"Minus thirty-five, according to the radio," I said.

"Yeah, but not a bad morning. No wind."

"Hope things go all right with Gloria this time."

"Me, too. It doesn't look too good to me."

Gloria, Maxine's sister, was twenty-three, strikingly pretty, strikingly dizzy when it came to men. Twice, at nineteen and again at twenty-two, she'd been to Edmonton expecting to get married. "That's how dumb she is," Maxine had told me once, laughing. When anything involving white people goes wrong, from a mechanical device to a love affair, laughter is a fairly common Native reaction. A white guy always *expects* an outboard to work, a snowmobile to work, a love affair to work, and is puzzled, even angry, when they don't. It's like a betrayal. But Natives *know* deep down that when they're involved with whites hardly anything works, for them anyway, so that side of life is really more or less a running gag. With Gloria, both times it turned out the guy already had a wife and what he really had in mind was a shack-up in a cheap hotel.

A couple of nights ago I'd seen Gloria for a while. She dropped in to Maxine's place with a guy from Fort Norman, William Cavendish. He was the son of Morton Cavendish, a big-deal Slavey involved in just about every major committee or Council in the North. I'd never met William before but Morton meant a lot to me. Twenty years ago his support had helped convert me from a Mountie "special," lowest of the low, into the Force's mainstream. Every promotion I'd had since—to corporal, sergeant, staff sergeant, inspector—was followed by a note from Morton saying in one way or another, "Way to go, Matteesie!" So I wanted to like William. It wasn't easy. He was burly, with black hair in a ponytail, droopy moustache, scraggly beard, and was rather drunk at the time, but he also struck me as being uptight, even scared. He couldn't sit still. In a few minutes he got up and jerked his head at Gloria with a brusque, "Let's go."

Later that night he'd been in his father's room at the Mackenzie Hotel when Morton suffered a severe stroke that had left him in critical condition. "A matter of pure luck that William was there to call the ambulance," the CBC news reader had said the next morning, when we'd first heard about it. Gloria lived with Maxine but her room door had been open and the bed unused that morning. I guess at the time we were assuming that Gloria had something going with William Cavendish, although we both were aware that for a while she'd had something going in fairly complete privacy with William's father, as well. Maxine had told me that William seemed to be not a bad guy; at least his decent upbringing usually showed, despite the way he'd acted the night I'd met him.

It was black dark yet, as we walked hunched against the cold past the municipal offices and the firehall and got to the main street by the library. At this time of year, the end of January, the sun wouldn't be up until nearly 11:30, meaning that early lunchers could watch a sometimes glorious sunrise along with their musk-ox *ragoût*. Still, that was better than the real dark days, a full month ending January 6 when the sun didn't make it above the horizon at all.

We stood inside the CBC building's door for a few seconds. Maxine said, "I might get to the airport at the last minute to see you off, if I can get a ride.'' She had the northern Indian's lilting way of talking.

"If you can, we could have a beer.''

We pressed our cheeks together in parting. What we had didn't require the reinforcement of big showy farewells.

A little way along the street I bought a couple of yesterday's Edmonton newspapers at Ted's News, a convenience store crammed into what looked like an old mobile home. Then I went back to Maxine's and made breakfast and drank more coffee. The papers had been published too early to have more than a brief item about Morton Cavendish's stroke last Sunday night. I phoned the airport about eleven when the first hint of dawn was appearing on the southern horizon. I was told that the daily Canadian Airlines plane from the south, due in at one to leave at two, was nearly three hours late. I called Maxine and told her about the delay, if that would make any difference about her getting to the airport.

"Don't think so,'' she said. "I'm busy as hell with the Morton story and that missing aircraft.'' The missing aircraft story, short on details, had been on the morning radio news, along with an update on Morton Cavendish's condition.

After the stroke Sunday night Morton had been conscious once or twice but not able to talk. Maxine was concerned more than usual because she knew Morton well—they were both from Fort Norman originally.

"Now it's fairly sure he's going to be flown out to the stroke unit in Edmonton,'' she said. Then, suddenly, "I have to go.''

"I'll call you from somewhere and hear how it all comes out,'' I said. Little did I know.

I read and slept a little. About three I called Inuvik Taxi and paid the standard twenty dollars to get to the airport. The plane had just left Norman Wells and would get to Inuvik about four, and leave on the return trip south before five. That meant waiting around, but I didn't have anything better to do.

At the airport I had a beer in Cece McCauley's Cloud Nine café, which occupied one corner of the building. Cece was a friend of Maxine's and mine, chief of the Inuvik Native Band and one of those northern women who could do anything from debating native rights to skinning a wolverine. I asked one of the two perky old waitresses if Cece was around and was told (with a hint of pride in the old girl's voice) that she was in Ottawa at a conference.

One beer by myself was enough.

Back in the main part of the terminal I slouched in an armchair thinking about Maxine's sister and her unerring faculty for hooking up with guys that made trouble for her one way or another. Like, even on such short acquaintance, William Cavendish. But I was also developing an uneasy feeling that had nothing to do with Gloria. There was nothing I had heard or seen to account for it, really, except maybe seeing Morton Cavendish's son William playing a jittery, drunken prince.

This was usually a time when I felt pretty good, relaxed. I'd spent a few days with my mother, a Kanghiryuakmiut from Victoria Island, near Holman. I took that trip every year no matter what, on the grounds that she was eighty-eight and couldn't live forever.

But now I could feel something unpleasant in the air. Maybe I don't bat better than .300 on premonitions but a couple of times winding up still healthy instead of maybe even dead has something to be said for it. I mulled over the last few days, looking for clues—O'Hare last week after a Chicago conference on aboriginal rights, airplanes to Winnipeg, Edmonton, Yellowknife, Inuvik; across the Amundsen Gulf to Holman, the nearest landing strip to where my mother lived; a brief stop at Tuk on the way out; now heading back to Ottawa for a few days before going to Leningrad. An orderly life. Hard to hit a moving target.

When I looked around the pleasantly modern terminal, built in the early '80s but tiny by southern standards, I could see the usual. Government types stood in clumps that sometimes overlapped clumps of oilmen or of the ever-present environmental partisani. The other red eyeballs, besides mine, mostly belonged to construction or oil-rig workers from farther north, up on the islands or out in the Beaufort Sea. Most of them had work contracts that provided a free trip out every few months. They tended to use Inuvik as a warm-up for the real industrial-strength fleshpots farther south.

A young Indian woman walked silently past my outstretched toes. She was carrying a solemn baby in a sling on her back. Two burly Americans sitting on one side of me were talking in low voices about an oil rig they'd just left on some ice island in the Beaufort Sea. One of them had the leather worn off the toes of both workboots, leaving bare the burnished steel of the safety toecaps. What could cause that? Did he have a snowmobile with bad brakes? Did he go around kicking blocks of ice?

I got up and strolled to the big windows facing the tarmac to watch a passenger Twin Otter taxiing to a stop, in from the milk run down to Arctic Red and Fort McPherson and over to Old Crow near the Yukon border with Alaska. The two Americans had come to the windows to have a look at the Otter as well. Burnished Toecaps murmured to his buddy, "My Daddy's got a motor home bigger than that."

I wandered back to the terminal entrance and looked outside where all the cars and trucks had their engines running, a habit in the north. The vapor from all the exhausts rose almost straight into the air. Six or eight snowmobiles were ticking over as well. When I was a kid it was all dog-teams in winter. I sat down and chatted with an old white trapper who only had one eye. He told me he was going to Calgary for his son's funeral.

"You use a snowmobile on your trapline?" I asked.

He pursed his lips over his few remaining teeth and shook his head slowly from side to side.

"Why not?" I asked.

"If I run out of grub I can't skin and eat a snowmobile."

We carried on a spotty conversation. There didn't seem to be a hell of a lot going on in that airport right then. It was only later I found I'd missed a few things.

However, I did notice one particular bunch near enough to me that I could hear what they were talking about: the missing plane. Apparently the noon CBC news, which I hadn't heard, had some details. It was from here, a Cessna 180 chartered from Komatik Air with (it was thought) two or three passengers, names unknown, and a pilot named Harold Johns. Nobody seemed to know where the charter was headed except, obviously, somewhere south. It had been heard near Fort Norman last night in a heavy snowstorm. I could imagine it, a few minutes of aircraft engines throbbing away in the howling wind and snow—probably pretty low or they wouldn't have been audible. Then fade. Then nothing. These guys were debating the chances of the plane being down safe somewhere.

Watching them and listening, I had the feeling I'd seen one of the group before. But when? Or even where? Not recently, anyway. The only time I'd been out yesterday was to the liquor store because Maxine likes Hennessy better then Inuvik's available fruit (three dollars per orange) or flowers (unobtainable), and I'd seen a few people I knew, but not this one.

He was slightly built and youngish, maybe thirty or a little more, with a lot of curly hair. In the old days when I was a special constable here I knew everybody, just about. The sergeant would say, "Go down and meet the plane, Matteesie." No further instructions were necessary. When the plane came I would be standing there in the old airport building, a frame job about as big as a small bungalow, knowing everyone who got on and off, who met whom and who brought whom to the airport. I would go back and report. In writing, if the sergeant said so. You never know when a little information might be useful. Sometimes my reports would be useful. Then, or later. Or never.

While I was thinking all this, a phone rang somewhere in the terminal. I could hear it faintly from back in one of the offices. Long ago in the old terminal a ground agent would have looked around to see if I was there and then yelled, "Hey, Matteesie! Phone!" But that was before the new terminal was built, with a desk for Canadian Airlines International, the major carrier, and all the smaller outfits. What happened now was a disembodied voice saying, "Attention, please. Will Matthew Kitologitak please pick up the white phone?"

Curious eyes turned my way as I walked a few feet to the phone, thinking maybe it was Maxine.

"Yes?"

"Buster wants you, Matty. Just a minute."

The voice belonged to the only person I knew who regularly called the Royal Canadian Mounted Police commissioner "Buster," that is, Buster's secretary, who herself is known around Ottawa headquarters as Old Ironsides.

Next voice was the commissioner's: "Matty. I need a favor."

I could imagine Buster at the other end of the line. He'd played football in college and still was all muscle, still had lots of hair, going grey, still had a fullback's shoulders and a jawline like a ten-pound iron mallet. He had served just about every place there was to serve, from Regina in Saskatchewan to Bonn in Germany to Yellowknife, NWT. I liked him mainly because he had never snowed me or in any way talked down to me, which your average Native in a country mainly full of white people is bound to find refreshing.

But a favor he wanted? Be careful, Matteesie, I told myself. Two years ago, give or take a month, he could have ordered me, but now there were other considerations. I was on loan to Northern Affairs, nominally out of his direct control. It had been a battle when the Northern Affairs deputy minister came after me on the grounds that what I knew about the North plus the university courses the RCMP had sent me on were too valuable to the country to be limited solely to police work. At the time Buster, fairly new as commissioner then, had given in with a few words that I remembered now standing at the phone in the Inuvik airport. "Okay, Matteesie," he'd said two years ago, "go ahead, you'll do that outfit good . . . but I might have to call on you once in a while."

So since then instead of police work I'd been going to conferences where I was usually identified in the program as an Inuk, or sometimes by the more specifically Western Arctic designation Inuvialuit, but often was introduced by white guys who either called me an Eskimo, or started to do that and then wound up with something like, "um, Matthew, um, Kitologitak, an Esk . . . um, In-you-it," almost invariably using the plural Inuit rather than the singular Inuk. The farther they lived from the Arctic the longer they took to get used to changes in terminology that had come with the Native rights programmes. Now Northern Affairs had me scheduled for something that really excited me—I was to represent the department in a meeting of northern countries at the Arctic Institute in Leningrad, so any favor done for Buster would have to be a short one.

"It's about those people missing south of Fort Norman," he said. "I'm told you don't have to leave for that Arctic Institute thing for a week. Could you poke around for me?"

I thought hard. "Poking around" meant police work. He knew better than I did that in other parts of the world, England and West Germany for two, the Mounties had anti-foreign-agent units that sometimes caused trouble for Soviet agents, to say nothing of vice versa. Mounties and the KGB might think alike on some matters but even after *glasnost*, they just weren't brothers in arms, united in maintaining law and order in a friendly way throughout the world, and that's all there was to it. If this "poking around" was something that brought much publicity, it might blow Leningrad for me. He knew that. But I was the one who had to bring it up: "I've got to keep in mind that it was sort of a victory that even a *former* Mountie was considered okay to sit in with their Arctic people. I'd hate to screw that up."

He just waited silently. He could spook some people with this technique of putting something on the table and just waiting, letting the proposal speak for itself. His long silence now showed he knew he was asking a heavy favor. But I was remembering that he had not referred to an "aircraft" being missing, but "people." Someone on the plane must mean something to him or to people who could put the arm on him. Because his concern was in the North, he was calling on me. I felt momentarily rebellious. He always thought I was a mighty shaman, or something, and could solve anything in the Territories just by mashing up some ice-worms with the hambone of a polar bear and reading them like goddamned tea leaves.

Usually, though, I was called in on murders. In which case, of course, I understood most crimes in the North better than would be the case with some white guy from Kingston, Ontario. For instance, I understood better why Native people sometimes did kill one another—one, to effect a change of home address for some female who was alluring to both killer and killee; or in the case of some still-nomadic Inuit it might be that some old and weak person who was a burden to the others and knew it, decided it was time to die and somebody thought the traditional way of letting such persons walk out into the tundra or onto the ice and freeze or starve to death somehow wasn't as nice as a bullet in the temple; or whatever.

If that kind of thing happened and was ignored, we, the Mounties, felt that it would cast a smirch on our reputation for always getting our man. The resultant cases usually were just exotic enough, being far away and involving no advertisers or their heirs or assigns, to make big headlines in papers that routinely covered your ordinary everyday city parking-garage murder in one paragraph under a roundup of other local briefs. In other words, in the world of northern crime I had become sort of a celebrity.

It got so I'd be working in RCMP headquarters in Ottawa, writing papers, making speeches, fending off women who thought I was so cute with my round brown face and slanty eyes and all, and something would happen at Grise Fjord or Gjoa Haven or Paulatuk and Buster would be on the line telling me to go at once, if not sooner. But that had been before Northern Affairs got me.

Taking everything into consideration, as the silence lengthened I thought, well, it isn't as if I'm in a big rush to get home to Ottawa.

"Can you give me any more on what I'm supposed to poke around about?" I asked.

"Yeah. To start with, the pilot, Harold Johns, is the son of the finance minister. Now, I don't owe the finance minister anything, but he called me because he thought I might have heard more than the media had. But I do know that the passengers might be guys we want, that we'd been watching there, or had been *supposed* to be watching. A bust was imminent. We have no intimation that the pilot had been involved, but that's not impossible either."

I could see through the big window that the flight from the south, a 737 with the big identifying *CANADIAN* on the side, was taxiing to a halt in front. Soon it would be unloading and then ready for us to board and head south with stops at Norman Wells and Yellowknife before Edmonton. Norman Wells was maybe fifty miles north of Fort Norman, where the lost aircraft last was heard.

I asked, "Would you have someone phone Lois and tell her I'm going to be delayed a few days?"

So I was giving in, actually at the same time that I was rerunning my parting from Lois a few days ago in my head. Her main lines were, "What don't you stay home once in a while? Chicago, Holman, Leningrad . . . and I thought police work was bad!"

"It's my job, Lois."

"Listen to God! What about me?" Then tears.

I could see her point. It was a lousy life for a woman. Lois and I were married in Edmonton. I don't always want to remember why, but I have to; it was due to some kind of mild conviction (which soon disappeared without a trace, if you don't count Lois as a trace) that marriage was important to be accepted in a white world. Five years with the police in Tuk and Inuvik on the mainland and a couple more at Sachs Harbor on Banks Island apparently had produced enough favorable reports from my superiors that I was targeted when some bozo high up at headquarters in Ottawa mused, perhaps aloud, "Before the human rights and equal opportunity people get at us, we better find some Natives good enough to take full police training."

Until then I'd been what is known as a "special." At the time that was really only police pidgin for an Eskimo, Indian or halfbreed who'd help around a detachment, translating, interpreting, cooking, catching fish or shooting caribou for dog food, or whatever, without getting in the way of anyone more upwardly mobile. The term still is police pidgin for Inuit (used to be Eskimos) or Dene (used to be Indians) or Metis (used to be halfbreeds) filling that role. In fact, many of the good Native specials, given the opportunity, decide not to play the mainstream game, preferring life the way they live it, among their own people.

Anyway, when I met Lois in Edmonton I was a constable, no longer a special, working "south" for the first time and trying to fight culture shock. None of my own people were around to impress on me that a beautiful and lissom fair-haired girl who didn't know muktuk from mukluks was one thing, and that her ardor might not last once the novelty wore off. But the God-given Eskimo advantage of being able to walk away from a troublesome woman, any time, was another thing entirely—to be valued more than gold, or mighty herds of musk-ox or stacks of polar bear skins. My father or uncles or one of my grandfathers might have thought to give this advice but they were 2,000 miles north at the critical time and anyway thought I must be pretty smart or I wouldn't already be such a distinguished policee. The end result over the years had been a disappointed and bickering wife from whom some day I might walk away.

Also, I admit it, if someone asked me in the middle of some stupefyingly boring conference, I might admit that I did occasionally miss police work.

"Sure thing!" Buster said. "Glad to phone Lois for you!"

I said, "Flight goes out in a few minutes. I'll get off at Norman Wells and call you from there." There was a police detachment under a corporal at Norman Wells. Presumably by the time I got there Buster might be able to tell me more.

"Good man!"

I put down the phone and went back into the growing crowd outside. A "bust" pretty well had to be a drug bust. The word was hardly ever used any other way. I noticed the guy with the curly hair again. When I was on the phone he'd been glancing at me and then away, glancing and then away. This continued while he used a pay phone. I could tell by the number of coins he used that at least one call was long distance.

Finally he came over. "I'm sorry to stare, but I heard you called to the phone. I used to see you here a long time ago. Are you still with the Mounties?"

"Do I know you?"

"Not really. Jules Bonner." He shot me a sharp glance.

Right away I remembered. Late 1960s. Joe Bonner, his father, a drunken assistant in the administration here, had taken to screwing every Native stenographer or clerk he could lay his hands on. In at least one case, he'd promised career advancement in return for sex. But had done so to the wrong person—Maxine. Enter the cops, including me. That's when Maxine and I met. Jules Bonner couldn't have been more than twelve or fourteen then.

"Where's your father now?" I asked.

Bonner shrugged. "Dead."

At that moment the flight was called. Bonner stayed with

me while I hoisted up my all-purpose traveling bag, big and black and heavy. I hate waiting for checked luggage, so I don't check any. I didn't think about it much, but my impression was that Bonner was on the same flight. Then an old Loucheux woman I knew spoke to me. She was with a well-dressed younger man whom I recognized from photos—he was her son, a lawyer connected with land claims negotiations. That was a reminder of how deeply buried in history were this Bonner's father and guys like him. They went back to the days when taking advantage of Natives was a way of life. Not any more. If any of those old fur traders came this way for the first time now with their glass beads and mirrors, they'd wind up picked clean, walking back to Montreal. We Natives had negotiators who were doing it year after year while the government people, especially the politicians, were here today and gone tomorrow with always some new guy trying to learn the ropes.

When I turned away from the old Loucheux and her son and shuffled into the line of people handing in their boarding passes, I noticed that Jules Bonner wasn't on the flight after all. He was standing outside the security area, again holding a telephone but not using it while he watched us board. That puzzled me briefly—there weren't any more flights out today—then he went out of my mind.

We straggled in twos and threes across the snowswept tarmac. Boarding was through the rear of the aircraft. Inside as we slowly climbed the steps a tiny stewardess with long dark-brown hair was repeating to each passenger, "Please keep clear the first three rows of seats you come to." This instruction was hardly necessary for the seats on the right side of the aisle. All nine—three abreast for three rows—had been folded down to form a fairly-flat platform. The three rows on the left of the aisle were being kept clear for no obvious reason. I took the aisle seat on the fourth row just ahead of and across the aisle to the left of the turned-down seats. It wasn't what I'd got in seat selection but on a half-full flight that wouldn't matter much. I was just curious.

When all the passengers were aboard there was a delay. Then, glancing from the window, I saw an ambulance rolling slowly around the nose of the aircraft toward the entry steps. Others were craning to look from windows on that side. The rear gate of the ambulance opened. Two attendants stood beside the vehicle's power platform as it slid out bearing a heavily wrapped stretcher.

The next hour or so I was to re-examine agonizingly in the next few days, weeks. But at the beginning there was nothing unusual. In the North many a normal commercial flight became a mercy flight of some kind. A doctor at Tuk or Sachs Harbor or Holman might judge that a patient urgently needed specialist treatment available only in Yellowknife or Edmonton. Hospitals were more suited to desperate human needs the farther one went south.

I stood up to watch. One of the pilots had come back from the flight deck. He stood near me. Others in forward seats wandered back to look but kept out of the way. The ambulance men, one backing up, negotiated the steps and laid the stretcher, a long tapered shallow aluminum basket, lengthwise on the sort of platform formed by the folded-down rows of seats. I couldn't see much of the man on the stretcher but what I could see was enough. Part of his face showed, his nose, forehead, and a good deal of white hair; his eyes were closed. Morton Cavendish. I felt a deep pang of sadness to see him so helpless, the man who had helped so many in the North. Including me. He was lying on his right side, his cheek on a pillow, his legs seeming to be slightly bent at the knees. A plump, dark-haired nurse put a heavy satchel on one of the empty seats across the aisle from the stretcher. A tall young ground agent edged past her, glancing at the stretcher's burden.

"Okay," he said to the ambulance men, dismissing them, then spoke to the stewardess with the long dark-brown hair.

"Seat-belt extensions?"

She nodded, her eyes briefly intent on his. From an overhead compartment she handed him several strips of sturdy webbing eight or nine feet long. At each end the webbing had two straps, one bearing a seat-belt fastener and the other a socket.

"That enough?" she asked.

"Yeah."

He laid one extension diagonally lengthwise from left to right across the blankets covering the stretcher, another in a criss-cross from right to left. He fastened all four ends to the regular seat-belt receptacles, tightened all straps, then laid another strap across the middle of the stretcher around the hips, fastened it at both ends, pulled it snug, and stood back.

"That should be okay," he said.

The stewardess gently tested the stretcher for play, found little, and nodded.

"See you," he said to her over his shoulder as he turned quickly to the exit.

The plane took off. I sat back thinking about the phone call from Ottawa and wondering who was on the missing aircraft, whether I knew any of them. When the seat-belt sign went off I got up and sat on a chair arm to have a good look at Morton Cavendish. If he was sometimes conscious, this wasn't one of the times. He was motionless except for the rise and fall of the blanket as he breathed. His breathing was regular but seemed somehow faulty. With each intaken breath his blanket would rise slowly an inch or so, then drop like a stone as he exhaled. He never changed position in the slightest, except for his breathing. The hefty nurse reached across the aisle, removed soggy face tissues from beside his mouth and moved in some dry ones.

I didn't want to distract the nurse but when the dark-haired stewardess wheeled up with the drinks cart I jerked my head at the unconscious man. "Where's Morton going?"

"Edmonton."

I thought of the tragedy of it, a man who seemed in his prime, late fifties, on the verge of seeing huge improvements in the lot of his people, improvements that he had helped to bring about. Father of the drinking man I'd met at Maxine's two nights ago. I'd liked him the many times I met him, cheerful and human, waving off thanks, disarming his opponents simply by being honest and consistent even when negotiations were at their toughest. He'd always been respected, more than ever now when victories had been won and others were in sight.

The nurse felt under the blanket at his midriff. I thought at first she might be checking to see if he had wet himself but then briefly saw his motionless right forearm as she held the wrist and glanced at her watch, taking his pulse.

After adjusting the covers again she reached into her satchel and took out an oxygen bottle about eighteen inches long, with a mask attached. She put the mask over his mouth and nose and adjusted a strap around his head to hold the mask in place. Then she tucked the oxygen bottle securely under the webbing at his waist. His breathing seemed to me exactly the same as it had been without the oxygen.

The first stop, Norman Wells, was about an hour south of Inuvik. In flight there'd been more light, especially at 33,000 feet, but as we landed it was nearly dark. When the aircraft taxied to a stop, people hurried past me to line up for the exit. Everybody always seems to want to be the first out of the door. Let 'em. I was in no hurry. There were always a few extra minutes between passengers getting off and others getting on.

The doors opened. As the aisle cleared I leaned over to haul my bag out from where I'd jammed it under the seat in front. When I straightened up, reaching for my parka and fur hat on the empty seat beside where I'd been sitting, I had my back to the exit steps. Add to that the matter of planting my hat firmly in place as a safeguard against the wind blowing outside, and getting one arm into my parka.

Then as I turned, reaching for the other sleeve, I saw a man coming aboard, fast.

In the instant when I was thinking that people boarding

aren't usually that quick, he pulled off one of his big mitts to reveal a black-barrelled automatic pistol. Without a moment's pause, he fired three rapid shots point blank into Morton Cavendish's head.

As I flung myself at him, he straight-armed the little stewardess flat on her back across the screaming nurse, both blocking the aisle in front of me. I jumped onto the seat behind mine and used its back to swing myself over the two women, then leaped down the steps, too late.

T W O

Corporal Charlie Paterson of the Norman Wells detachment was a big guy, towering over me. And right now he was extremely agitated. The two of us were in the mildly graffiti-scarred men's can at the terminal building. The corporal had locked the door behind us. "It's the only goddamn private place short of kicking the airline people out of their effing office," he said. He knew my face and name from when I had been full-time RCMP but thought when I went to Northern Affairs it was final. To him I was a civilian again. No doubt that made him feel free to act naturally, such as swearing a blue streak in a way he normally would not have in the presence of a superior, even one with brown skin and almond-shaped eyes, five feet six of sheer Native guile.

What I knew about him was that he was an officer on the way up, having been commended during his previous posting at Fort Simpson, especially for community work at the time of the Pope's visit there. I can only assume that the Pope never heard Charlie let fly when he was mad. He'd seen Morton's body. He knew how the murderer had gotten away. Charlie had been no more than a few hundred yards from the airport "and driving like a mad bastard," according to his own testimony, when the fatal shots were fired. I could see he felt sure that without those few hundred yards he might instantly have taken his place among the storied Mounties who always got their man.

His luck had been all bad. An Ottawa call instructing him to meet me at the airport had come in while he was out hunting rabbits. "Every effing Tuesday we go out, me and the doctor and a guy from the oil company, hunting, fishing, having a few drinks, whatever!"

He looked defiant. "It's community effing relations, you know!" But he didn't even like that excuse himself. Furiously, as if looking for something to punch, he flushed both toilets with a crash and gurgle unparalleled in the history of plumbing.

"A really bad break," I said, trying to soothe him.

"That's not all! My effing duty constable left word with Nancy to tell me to call the office but she didn't."

"Nancy?"

"My wife. Of course, she didn't know what the call was about, but anyway I got home and was cleaning the rabbits in the sink when right away she came into the kitchen and started yelling she'd just cleaned the sink, and I yelled did she think I was going out into minus thirty-five weather to clean some effing rabbits and she forgot the call, and . . ."

I'll summarize the remainder. When the rabbits were bagged and in the freezer the corporal and his wife went to a choir practice adjudged to be urgently needed because of special Easter services some weeks away. The practice had been called for 5:30 p.m., with potluck supper and euchre afterwards. They were just warming up in the joyful, "Christ is Risen!" when Constable Ned Hoare appeared at the back of the church and without waiting for a break in the music roared, "Charlie! Call from Ottawa! You're supposed to meet the plane! It's coming in right now!" and Nancy said, "Oh, God, Charlie. I was supposed to tell you to call the office."

"God damn it all to fucking hell," the corporal groaned, apparently having forgotten to use the more genteel "effing." "If I'd been here I might have been able to do *something*. Chase him, shoot him, whatever. The one day in the fucking week when for half an hour I'm away from the phone and this happens."

I was fresh out of appropriate responses. "What do you sing in the choir?" I asked.

"Lead tenor!" he snapped, and then, less forcefully, "Okay, now fill me in."

I told him what I knew. The murderer had used what looked to me like a Colt GM (for Government Model) .45, which in one form or another has been used in wars, revolutions, police actions and murders since about 1911. I own one myself. He had escaped on a Skidoo Elan, a machine I knew because it is a favorite among trappers—light, powerful, easy to handle and easy to fix. He (presumably he) had left it with the engine running on the tarmac about seventy-five feet from the aircraft steps and a little south of the terminal, toward the Okanagan Helicopters Limited hangar. I'd seen the murderer running for the machine as I charged down the steps scrabbling for the gun that was at home in Ottawa in my bed-table drawer and which I hadn't worn for two years. In seconds he was revving into high speed across the foot-deep snow, then across the main runway, last seen as a red tail-light dwindling to nothing in the dark and blowing snow. He'd been out of sight before anybody with a machine to make chase with could react, if that anybody had been of a mind to, which is never entirely certain when one man is armed and a prospective pursuer is not.

Going back to the airport I'd pulled a blanket over Cavendish's head (he was dead), told the pilot I was RCMP and would take charge for now (he seemed relieved), and told everybody to get off the plane but stay in the waiting room, which is where they were now.

Or most of them, anyway. Someone was trying the door of the toilet and complaining pitiably about the desperate state of his bladder.

The corporal barked, "Go outside and do it in a snow-bank," but the guy didn't go away.

Wishing him well, and knowing that at least he wasn't a Native or he wouldn't have had to be told to do it in a snow-bank, I went on. Before I left the aircraft I'd questioned the nurse, whose name was Hilda. She didn't know much so I summarized drastically for Charlie. But the full account of my couple of minutes with the nurse went like this:

I'd asked, "When was it decided to fly him out?"

"Sometime yesterday. This was the first flight we could catch."

"Do you know what kind of shape his son was in when he brought his father in the night before?"

"I don't know. I've been on days."

Then I came to the important part. "Who knew that he was being flown out on this flight?"

"Oh, a lot of people. People at the hospital, and people from CBC news who checked every few hours, and the girl reporter for the paper, *News North*. She came around—I mean, she's stationed in Inuvik by the paper and I guess she'd been phoning the story in, he was so well known. So there'd be people in the paper's Yellowknife office who would know, plus everybody who heard it on the radio."

Her voice trailed off and she compressed her lips. I think delayed shock was hitting her. She faltered, "The doctors, you know, at the hospital, they said he was in and out of consciousness and tried to talk but couldn't be understood, so even today when we were getting him ready, well, it was bad but certainly not hopeless." She drew a deep breath, "Not like now."

I still didn't have the answer I was looking for. "Did anybody call looking for details that made you wonder?"

"What do you mean?"

"I mean, made you or anybody else suspicious about their questions? Like, exactly when he was being flown out?"

"Not that I took. I wouldn't know about calls last night or calls the doctor took."

It had been about that time in our conversation that Corporal Charlie Paterson came bounding up the steps of the plane, loudly lamenting his fate, then instantly charged back out to order Constable Hoare to get out there into the bush on a borrowed snowmobile, musing aloud as that tail light disappeared into the murk, "As much chance as a snowball in hell. That bush has more snowmobile tracks than rabbit tracks."

I looked at him. "But we'd look real funny if we got helicopters out in the morning and found that the machine broke down or hit a tree or some damn thing half a mile away."

"No kidding," he said sarcastically. "I never would have thought of that on my own."

Touché.

The fact that the murderer's or anyone's snowmobile had been left running out in the open wasn't noteworthy. Half a dozen snowmobiles were sitting around right now among the pickups, taxi vans and two police cars. More were arriving every few minutes as word spread around town. Every vehicle had its engine running. In the North that was winter habit, like long underwear. Anything not left running would be too damn cold to get into and also might not start. The temperature outside right now was minus thirty-eight. In these parts in mid-winter, minus twenty is considered a heat wave.

When we were pretty well caught up on background the corporal unlocked the door. An old white guy, one hand with a tight grip on the front of his pants, groaned, "Thanks a lot!" and shuffled past. Civilization at the crossroads.

A few feet along the passage to our right the area in front of the airline counter was maybe twelve feet by eighteen feet with a bench along the outside wall. An opening led to another squarish room where a nice-looking woman, about thirty, held a metal detector while blocking the door to the tarmac where the 737 was sitting. Both rooms were crowded with people in parkas and big boots, the air blue with cigaret smoke. Some were sitting on benches, some standing.

The buzz of voices fell silent. We stopped by the door of the small office off the check-in counters. Outside to our right the cars and pickups sat with motors running, the exhausts pluming in the frosty air. Lights could be seen moving on nearby roads. Down beyond the main road was the Mackenzie River with its more than 200 oil and gas wells, many in the river itself on artificial islands. The oil-town settlement of more than 600 people spread for miles along the river, the glow from burn-offs at the main Esso installations barely visible from where I stood. I somehow didn't think the murderer had been from here, but there was no way of knowing yet.

"I think one at a time, whaddaya say?" the corporal asked.

"Sure."

He faced the crowd. He didn't have to ask for attention.

"No one leave the airport until we have names and addresses," he said in a carrying voice. "This can be speeded up a lot if anybody knew the guy with the gun, positive identification preferred, of course, but even a suspicion we'll listen to. Anybody with anything to say that might help, step right up."

I watched the faces in the growing silence. Even when they'd been filing past me out of the plane I'd been thinking of things I wanted to know right away. Never mind motive. Who could even guess that, yet. Somebody had had to know, and let the murderer know, that Morton Cavendish was on this flight. You couldn't load up a Colt GM .45, figure out how to shoot some poor unconscious man strapped onto a stretcher, back it up with an escape plan and then start meeting every flight on the off chance. It crossed my mind that I wasn't really supposed to be here for a murder. My assignment had been a missing aircraft bearing someone that Buster was concerned about.

The corporal had waited a few beats. Nobody had stepped up.

"Okay. Come in to this office behind me one at a time. First, airport staff, then plane crew, then the rest. This all has to be done before the flight can go on. If you know anything at all, be sure you tell us now, not two days from now.''

The two of us went back into the little airport office. The corporal sat behind a desk. There were two chairs. I took one. Through a window I could see the silently waiting 737, gusty snow visible against its lighted windows. Beyond it, snow and ice particles could be seen in the runway lights blowing thick and fast. Beyond that was blackness entire, the impenetrable Arctic night.

A second constable was inside the aircraft. Having taken photos of the body from every angle he was supervising the cleanup.

Whether the body stayed here or went on to Yellowknife had not been determined, but when we were finished here the inspector at Inuvik, commanding the big RCMP subdivision that included Inuvik, Norman Wells and other surrounding territory, would let us know.

Just before the first person, the woman from the airline counter, came in, I asked the corporal, ''Any word about that missing aircraft?''

He looked at me as if I'd gone nuts, asking about a missing plane when we had a murder on our hands.

The counter agent had streaky, fair hair and a very pale face. Before we even asked, she burst out, ''There was a guy came in on the flight this morning that I didn't know. A big guy. No luggage. I noticed him because he had one of those parka hoods that pretty near cover the face, and he went right out and took off in the taxi before anybody else left at all.''

She said that waiting for the flight to come through tonight she was sure the guy she'd seen this morning hadn't been around. There'd been no one in the terminal except the few boarding passengers, nobody who had asked any questions in person or by phone about the incoming flight and whether it had a stretcher case aboard. We quizzed her but that was all she knew. When we figured she'd told us everything we could find out right then, we started on the others.

An Esso Resources guy said that the chain-link fence that fanned out from both ends of the terminal building ran along this edge of the airport to restrict access to loading and unloading areas. Several private concerns along the airport strip, Okanagan for one, also had to be entered through gates in the high fence. Theoretically no unauthorized person could get through one of those properties to where the murderer's snowmobile had been parked, perhaps not for long. But the Esso guy also pointed out that the fence only ran along one side of the airport. Charlie obviously knew that. I had thought of that too. The other side, and the ends, were wide open. The man could have driven in unseen from the open bush and waited in the dark, watching the aircraft taxi in and then making his move.

Through the rest of the questioning, I just sat and listened. The corporal was thorough and well-organized. The profile that emerged pretty well matched my own recollection from the few seconds I'd been aware of the murderer at all.

The two baggage handlers, dressed for their frigid duties outdoors, had been getting their cart out to unload luggage when the man ran for the snowmobile and took off. The dark-haired stewardess who'd been closest to the action had a bruise on her right cheek from when she'd been flung out of the way but said nothing I did not already know. She said rather shakily that she'd been lucky to get off with a bruise, she might have been shot, too.

A young Metis woman who'd been among the boarding passengers, with a ticket to Yellowknife, said she had seen the snowmobile move slowly up as the plane was taxiing in, but had thought nothing of it.

Around seven the inspector in Inuvik called. The corporal filled him in and was told that the body should go on to Yellowknife when we were finished, and the nurse had better go, too, to be handy for questioning.

When the thirty-second and last person had filed in and out, at nearly eight, the pilot stuck his head around the office door and said, "When do you figure we can leave? We've plugged up the one hole in the aircraft as best we can. Any draft we didn't get we can say is air conditioning.''

The corporal shrugged. "I guess go when ready." He glanced at me. I nodded agreement. "I think we got the only two bullets that stayed inside. Find any more, let us know."

"Will do."

As the pilot lingered there was a moment of thoughtful silence between the three of us. A man had been killed and we could only get on with our jobs. When the pilot turned away he could be heard saying to the woman who did the security checks, "Okay, they can move out now."

Paterson and I looked at each other. "Not much?" I said. "Not much."

Then for the first time I mentioned that my original assignment, the reason he'd been supposed to meet me, was the missing aircraft and the request from Ottawa that I nose around.

He was surprised. "You mean you're still on the force, sort of?"

"Sort of, is right. Really just as a favor, but when the commissioner asks a favor . . ."

"Do you think the business between you and Ottawa could have anything to do with this?" Meaning, the murder.

"All I know is that I'm to nose around—for what, I'm not sure even yet until I check back. I thought you might know."

"I don't." He sounded slightly hurt. "But I don't like the idea of them feeling we need help in something before we've even had a chance."

I really didn't mind Charlie Paterson at all, rather liked him. Still, it always sort of amused me when a *white* man in the North got his itsy-bitsy dignity injured.

"Well, you did sort of screw up today," I said.

I was rather glad that, after a sharp glance, he laughed. "And I always thought you Eskimos were supposed to be nice guys, kind, for Chrissake! But I'll tell you one goddamn thing."

"What's that?"

"I've just resigned from that effing choir."

So I rode over to the RCMP office with Corporal Paterson. It was about five minutes away. Hoare still hadn't come back from his chase job. The office was just off the main street in a small building standing by itself, nothing else around. Paterson unlocked the door. A sign on the door gave the hours when the office would be open, and a phone number for emergencies.

The other constable was at work, typing his report about what he'd found inside the aircraft. I took one of the chairs while Paterson paced, thinking. He tended to think aloud, and loudly.

"What a goddamn break!" he groaned. "There's been snowmobilers out all day up hill and down bloody dale on the off chance that Cessna came down north of Fort Norman instead of south, like most people think. Not only me and the doc and the Esso guy are out shooting rabbits, but the bush is full of volunteer good guys, you know the mix—the serious ones out to serve suffering humanity and the guys who'll take any excuse to get away from the wife. There'll be so many snowmobile tracks . . ."

He let it die there and I had a mental image of the maze of snowmobile tracks through the bush looking like the string games we used to play as kids.

Something had been nagging at me. "That snowmobile wasn't carrying anything that I could see. No saddlebags, no extra gas, nothing. As if he either makes one fast run somewhere, and doesn't need any gear for living in the open, or . . ."

"Or?"

"Or he had fuel and other stuff stashed where he was going to hole up," I said.

"Or stashed a few miles out where he could pick it up on the way to God knows where."

"Yeah. All of those. Another thing, you probably thought of this"—behold the ancient Native custom of buttering the white man—"is that wherever he's going, if it's far at all he needs gas. Maximum on that machine with a five-gallon tank is sixty-five to seventy miles. About forty, if he has a three-gallon tank. We could telex to everybody, notice boards, post offices, schools, whatever, that if anybody loses gas or gas cans they should report it to you forthwith.''

He nodded, sat down, and started to type. "That's one thing we can do right away. Jeez, I like that word, forthwith.'' He grinned. "It's *me*, know what I mean?''

The phone began to ring. The corporal answered it and handed it to me.

"Ottawa,'' he said. "Who's Buster?''

I listened for a minute and then said, "Yes, I was on the same aircraft.''

Listened again, then: "Corporal Paterson will be reporting what we know to Inuvik in a few minutes. It isn't a hell of a lot more than you've got. Yeah, we can ask them to copy it to you. Now, can you tell me more about the other thing, what I'm supposed to be here for?''

Buster instructed me to stay clear of the murder, that was regular police work, the other was what needed my touch. My touch! I didn't reply directly to that piece of official advice. I had my own ideas. I listened for two or three minutes, taking notes, then said, "Okay,'' and hung up.

"That the commissioner?'' the corporal asked, impressed. He was at the counter, lighting a cigar, peering through the smoke.

I nodded.

"Anything you can tell me?''

"Yeah, there was just a flash on the news back east about the murder. About the other thing, the guys on the missing plane, the pilot's father is the finance minister. The other two or maybe three are suspects in a drug deal supposed to be worth about half a million bucks. Our drug people think they have been paid and have the money with them.''

Paterson slammed one hand on the desk. "This pisses me off! How come all this happens on our own turf and we don't know a goddamn thing about it?''

"Ottawa's tip came from Edmonton."

"Shit! Half a million bucks, out there in the snow someplace. Any names?"

"Harold Johns is the pilot. Apparently he came out here a couple of years ago after some trouble in Ontario, flying Ontario government aircraft. He punched some reporter he'd been drinking with. This happened during some minister's special trip by government aircraft to open a hospital up north, and sort of clouded up the political publicity side of the thing, as far as the media coverage went, so he was fired."

"We get quite a few like that, trying to lose themselves up here. They're not usually any more trouble than anybody else. How about the others?"

"No names yet."

"So what are you going to do?"

"Make some phone calls and then maybe get the hell out of your hair."

He grinned. "Just when I was starting to like you a little."

"We got an aircraft around here?"

"Not our own. We can call one in from Inuvik or one of the other bigger detachments when we need it. Or charter. What have you got in mind?"

What did I have in mind? A good question. Coming in here tonight, I'd been thinking of going on the fifty miles to Fort Norman tomorrow to get in on whatever search was going on by land. There'd probably be snowmobiles out to have a look and back up the air hunt by Search and Rescue, which Buster had just told me on the phone hadn't found anything today. Tomorrow's forecast, he'd been told, was very iffy in the way of flying weather.

But now, to me, whether I had official sanction or not, the murder came first. Everybody else might be working on it, sure, but I was the one who'd *seen* the murder, seen the murd*er*er, and had also seen William Cavendish only a few hours before his father collapsed. I wondered at what point in the evening William had left Gloria and gone to see his father. And if he'd been right there when his father collapsed.

I wondered where she'd been for the rest of the night and if she knew anything I should know.

"You know a William Cavendish, originally from Fort Norman?"

"Yeah. We've booked him once or twice, nothing violent, not a bad guy. Mainly drinks too much."

I told the corporal about meeting him the night Morton Cavendish had collapsed and my curiosity about what happened next.

"So?"

"So I think I'll go back to Inuvik and see what I can find out, not only about this but the other thing, too. Like, names of the other guys. After all, somebody's got to know something." I thought a minute. "That Canadian International 737 goes north through here about noon tomorrow—anybody flying sooner that you know about?"

He thought a minute. "Maybe. You might try Northwest Territorial, they have a sked, and there are others in and out. Buffalo Air, Aklak, Nahanni—any of them on charters probably would take you if they're going that way and have room. Best go to the airport first thing in the morning and see what's flying."

I thought about it. Obviously there was no better way. "Is there a cot here I can use?"

"Yeah, a rollaway in my office. But Nancy and I got room at our place."

"Thanks, but I'll be on the phone a bit and maybe getting some calls back in. Cot'll be fine."

He got to work on his report. I picked up the phone, but didn't learn much. The RCMP duty officer in Inuvik said that they'd found the charter on the missing aircraft to be rather irregular. The Cessna was owned by a three-plane outfit called Komatik Air, flying a Beaver, the Cessna that was missing, and a single-engined Otter. Whoever was in the office became the office staff. This Harold Johns had just left a note saying a sudden charter had come in for a flight south, he didn't give a destination. He'd left the pre-paid fee in cash but not the name of the booker. Inuvik thought maybe it had been a guy named Albert Christian. They'd had Christian's name in connection with a drug deal they were watching and he didn't seem to be around today. They had a man out trying to learn more.

I phoned Maxine and asked if she knew anything about the people aboard. She said Gloria knew them, they were friends of William Cavendish. Maxine didn't know their names, but could ask Gloria when or if she came in. I thought of Maxine in that big chair she used all the time, beside the phone, in front of the TV.

That was about all I could think of to do at the moment. The corporal finished his report. The constable had gone home. I wasn't ready for the rollaway yet. I had a big forty ouncer of Glenfiddich in my bag. I'd bought it duty-free in Chicago but it had lasted.

Normally I drink Mount Gay rum and Schweppes Ginger Ale, but I didn't have any of either with me.

"You feel like a drink?" I asked the corporal.

"I sure as hell do. What've you got?"

"Some Glenfiddich."

"Jeez, you rich or something? That stuff costs about fifty bucks up here."

"Twenty-three dollars in the duty-free," I said, hauling the big triangular bottle out of my bag.

He rinsed out two glasses in the bathroom just off the office. When he came back I handed him the bottle. He poured a fair drink. I did the same while he read the label, "Single malt, what the hell does that mean? 'Produced by the fifth generation of an independent family company.' Hey, how about that, eh? Having booze right in the family."

We both took it straight, although it's okay with a little water, too. After a couple of sips I said, "You glad to get away from Simpson?"

"Hell, no, I loved it there."

"But a lot of trouble from time to time. In a lotta towns

in the North you hear the people saying, 'We don't want to wind up like another Simpson.' ''

"Well, yeah, but . . . ah, I lived there, you know, just a kid. My father managed the Bay store. I never quite got over thinking about it that way, even with all the changes."

It was all very low-key, leading nowhere, but it was companionable.

"Like, when were you just a kid there?"

"We left in the early '60s. Back then, you know, there were Native families living right where the government buildings are now, including the jail and our headquarters."

I didn't say anything. So he'd been there when the population was about one third of what it is now, and more than half at least seasonally nomadic. I'd been there once when I was a special. In those days most of those Indians and Metis worked traplines in winter not all that far from town. Very handy. Then in spring around breakup of the two rivers— that's where the Liard runs into the Mackenzie—they'd shoot muskrats for the skins and after the ice went out they'd move to summer quarters on one of the rivers and fish and hunt until freeze-up. They had their houses handy to the rivers then and sure as hell didn't have booze and welfare problems, at least not like now. But like in some other northern communities the easy way of doing things was all shot out from under them by the town planners. The authorities needed buildings to be authoritative from, including a new combined jail and RCMP headquarters, and the best sites, the planners decided, were all taken up by the Native homes. So naturally the Natives were moved to a part of the community that wasn't handy to anything. In Simpson the highway from the south, brought in to serve mainly the purposes of oil exploration and other developments, did the rest. Now it was the place nobody wanted to emulate.

We finished the drinks. He declined another and rose. "Sure you won't bunk in at our place?"

"I might be back before you know it," I said.

"Good."

While he was doing a few final things I make up the cot. The sheets were clean and ironed. The corporal was amused at my pajamas. "I thought you guys just stretched out in the igloo with a few branches and stuff covered with caribou skins on an ice shelf, or something."

"Yeah, well, this is the way civilization hurts a guy."

But I had a restless night. It was that line about the igloo. I got thinking of when I was a boy, forty years ago. Up on Herschel Island the first igloo I remember was built of driftwood. White people always thought igloos were built of snow blocks, like our inland people do, but the word *iglu* just means house and along the Arctic shore in some places a lot of driftwood floated in on the Mackenzie and Yukon rivers and my people naturally used it. We built some snow igloos when we were out hunting, but not when we were home.

Half awake in the cot in the corporal's office I remembered a lot of images of after we moved across the Beaufort Sea to the mainland—the lines of kayaks on the shore when the white whales were coming in and we'd go out in the kayaks and get beyond them so we could drive them into the shallows and kill our winter's food, we hoped. I thought of the big umiaks that we used when we were moving on the water as a family. I thought of all the families I'd lived with as a small boy after my father drowned out hunting and my mother took another man and he left her and she took another.

Once I had been loaned to another man and woman, supposed to be for a few weeks. It turned out to be two years before I got back to my own mother again. That sort of thing was not unusual. I thought of my grandma, who had bad sores on her feet and legs and had to be pulled on a sled wherever she went, winter and summer. I stayed with her on and off, several times.

I thought of school in Inuvik, like a barracks, all the other kids, like me, brought in by air from remote settlements to be educated. It was there that I learned to swear, as part of learning English. There are no swear words in our language, Inuktitut.

It was fun sometimes except when I went back to my mother in summer and it would take a while to get used to eating nothing but flesh again, seal, ducks, geese, muktuk, if the whale hunt had gone well, fish, once in a while a caribou.

One winter away from home I'd set snares for rabbits. Once when I was nearly starved I'd killed and eaten a white fox.

THREE

Gloria looked like hell, for once. I have seen her after some nights that would have killed me (booze, sex and more sex, little or no sleep) when she still looked fresh and dewy-eyed. Her hair, which was much lighter than Maxine's, worn high off her forehead and fluffy around the sides of her face, would look as if it had just been washed, nice and soft. Her face would look as if she'd never had a drink in her life; no baggy eyes, no lines, good white teeth, and only when you looked into her eyes could you see the trouble, whatever it was that made her live on the edge the way she did. In her late teens she'd changed from an easygoing kid to one who seemed the same on the surface but couldn't let a good-looking guy go by without looking at him the way some men looked at sexy girls.

Today the smudgy charcoal-grey skin around her eyes made her look as if she'd used too much makeup, but closer inspection showed she had none on at all. Her hair was stringy, brushed only cursorily or not at all. On one side her hair was in that kind of tangle that comes from sleeping on it wrong. We were in a fake English pub called the Caribou

Arms, of all things. It's a wonder it wasn't called the Duke of Inuvik.

I'd caught a ride up in the morning with Nahanni Air, took a taxi in to the CBC, went to the newsroom, and asked Maxine if she knew where I could find Gloria.

Maxine shook her head. "I've been phoning home. No answer."

We both knew that Gloria had had, or was having until yesterday, or checked into on a part-time basis, the most discreet affair in the history of the North. With Morton Cavendish, who was thirty years older.

"How did she take it?" I asked.

"As if she'd been hit by a bullet herself. I'd got home and we were listening to the news when it came on about him being killed. After she stopped crying she was like a sleepwalker. Put on her clothes and went out and didn't come back."

The phone was ringing. Maxine answered, listened, made a note. On the staff list at CBC-Inuvik her title was news assistant, a job she'd got after getting high grades in the communications arts course at Arctic College. The idea behind the course was that some day Inuit and Dene would do most of the reporting and announcing jobs now done by non-Native imports.

In a big city her job would have been handling weather warnings, traffic foul-ups, slipping an on-air guy notes reporting something like, "Tractor-trailer jack-knifed on the Richmond ramp. Police are on the scene." Here she kept track of scheduled and unscheduled flights, taped people who wanted to send messages to outlying settlements, typed up notices for meetings (in Inuvik, there was actually a hobbyist type of dog-team club that had outings on weekends), manned the tape machine for voice reports from local correspondents about anything from a polar bear sighting to a homicide during a weekend party at Paulatuk.

At my invitation for a beer she quickly tidied her desk. "Good idea. Gloria's maybe at the Mackenzie." It was only one minute's brisk walk away, but Gloria wasn't there. Several other people we knew were. We were invited to grab empty chairs, but didn't. Nobody asked me directly about Morton Cavendish but there were questions in a lot of eyes. We said maybe we'd be back. We tried a couple of other places before finding her at the Caribou Arms.

She was alone and wouldn't speak. Just sat there. Maxine sat next to her and put her arms around Gloria's shoulders and said, "Listen, sweetie, look, we both know what you're going through. Let us help."

Gloria just looked at her.

I asked if she knew where I could find William Cavendish. Her eyes might have indicated she knew, but she didn't reply.

"When you left Maxine's with William Sunday night, did you go with him to the Mackenzie?"

Finally, she spoke. "No, I wanted to, but we went to the Eskimo Inn and he had a couple more drinks and told me to wait for him there."

"And he went to the Mackenzie?"

"He must have, because he took his father . . ." she paused and took a deep breath . . . "took Morton to the hospital, didn't he?"

The Caribou Arms used to be a restaurant called the Raven's Nest. It had served good food, some of the best in the North, Arctic char and musk-ox and caribou steaks, great french fries, strong coffee, but eventually it had been closed due to some dispute about the building being sold, a new owner having different plans. Not much more than a year ago he had re-opened. He sold hamburgers and steak-and-kidney pie and the place was decorated like every other ersatz English pub in Canada. Apparently you could buy the whole deal in Edmonton, fake beams and fake velvet wallpaper, fake hunting prints and old maps of London on the walls and an expert in fake English pubs to put it all together until presto, it was the Caribou Arms. A can of English beer, Double Diamond or Bass Ale or Newcastle, cost $7.50.

"How long did you wait for him?"

"It seemed like forever."

She was wearing pants and a jacket of that stuff called acid-wash, blue with white streaks. Her blue parka with Arctic symbols on the fringe at the bottom and wolverine fur on the hood was thrown over a nearby chair. She had been drinking a vodka on the rocks, which was almost finished. When I was ordering she asked for a Coors Light. I really wanted to ask her in detail about her relationship with Morton Cavendish. Maybe if Maxine hadn't been sitting there looking so worried, I would have.

Gloria watched me as I took a swallow of Double Diamond.

"I didn't know you drank beer."

"I don't, much. But order a drink here and you have to get a triple or you can't taste it."

Gloria said with a faint smile, "You can feel it, though."

"Okay," I said. "So you were waiting for William and he didn't come back. How long did you wait?"

"I don't know. Long. I was just thinking to hell with it, I'd go home, he could find me there if he wanted, when Jules Bonner came along and told me to come to his place, that William would be over later, so I went with him."

She paused briefly. "I had the impression that William had called Jules, or even gone to his place, and asked him to get me over there. When we got there Jules told me there'd been a big fight, William and his father, and Morton had collapsed and had to be taken to the hospital."

"A fight about what?"

"I don't know, but Jules still thought William would be along any minute.

"I got sleepy and Jules gave me a blanket on the couch and next thing I knew it was morning and the news had just come on the radio that"—again she paused and swallowed hard when she came to Morton Cavendish's name—"Morton was in real bad shape and might have to be flown out. I felt like trying to see him, but I didn't. Then I just stayed there.

I felt rotten. I kept thinking I'd hear from William but I didn't."

I pressed a little.

"About the big fight Jules mentioned. Did he give you any idea at all what it was about?"

"No."

"Any ideas?"

Deep breath again. "Every time William and his father got together they argued."

"What about?"

She shrugged, opened her mouth, closed it, didn't answer for a minute, then said, "Morton always wanted to know where William was getting money to live on, stuff like that. They just plain didn't get along."

"Was William violent with you when he was drinking?"

"Never."

"Do you think he and his father ever came to blows? I mean, physical violence?"

She didn't answer.

I said, "Either of you happen to know what doctor was on duty when they brought Morton in?"

Maxine nodded. "Bob Zimmer. He was quoted on the news."

I asked Gloria if she had seen William at all since then.

She was back to shaking her head.

It suddenly occurred to me that I hadn't seen him at the airport, either, where you might think he'd have gone, despite the fight with his father. He would have known that his father was being flown out.

"No idea where he went after he was at the hospital?"

Then it came in a burst, tears brimming in her eyes. "I tried all over, all day Monday. I couldn't get Jules, even. A couple of other guys who hung out with the two of them a lot flew out that day on that flight that went down—you know, Harold Johns, well, he wasn't really with them that much but I couldn't find Albert Christian or Benny Batten either, because it turned out they'd gone with Harold, but of course nobody knew that until yesterday. Albert's girlfriend, Julie, was the one who told the police who was with Harold on the flight. She was mad as hell."

"What about?" I asked.

"Albert had taken her car without telling her and just left it out by the Komatik Air office where Harold took off."

That was the first I had known that Johns didn't take off from the airport. But that wasn't unusual. These bush flying outfits often had riverside locations. That was handy in summer when they were using floats and when they switched to skis they'd do business out of the same locations. Saved money on airport office space, too. The river wasn't solid ice everywhere right after freeze-up in the fall but now in January it would hold anything, let alone the kind of light planes Komatik Air had. I still figured Gloria knew more than she was telling me but maybe I could get it elsewhere.

I got up and said to Maxine, "See you later."

She reached up soberly and patted my bum. "Take care."

It was broad daylight when I left the Caribou. Three weeks ago, the month of dark days when the sun didn't show at all had ended, and now there was about five hours of daylight. I walked down the street in sunshine and found Dr. Robert Zimmer, MD, in his office not far from the Inuvik General Hospital. In his waiting room were two little old Inuit ladies with wrinkled brown faces and toothless smiles. One was smoking a pipe. Both wore bright gingham shifts over the warm skin clothes beneath. These old ones and some of the younger Inuit, too, made the shifts themselves. They fell to about calf length and had fringed bottoms. I always think they look colorful on the street, neat and individual, dressed-up town Inuit.

The doctor looked surprised. "Matteesie! Come in." He spoke a few words in the Inuit tongue to the old ones that meant he'd see them in a minute and they grinned and nodded. He'd been here twenty years and had a twenty-three-foot launch with fish-finding gear that amused the locals. He also hunted caribou and polar bear and had a dog team;

everything but a wife, who had left him years earlier to go back to Kitchener, Ontario.

He closed the door, went behind his desk, gestured to a chair and looked at me.

"It's about Morton Cavendish," I said.

"Somebody said you'd been around but took the plane out yesterday, Matteesie. I thought of you when I heard that terrible business. It was on the radio that you'd been right there beside him. You back in the police?"

"Sort of. I guess I never really left."

We both laughed. It really was pretty ridiculous, but it hadn't taken long for people here to decide I'd gone civilian, moving to Northern Affairs.

At that thought I had a momentary flash of what kind of language I could expect from Buster when he found out what I was doing. Every once in a while, too, I thought of my superiors in Northern Affairs and how they'd dither over how the Russians would react if it came out that this certified Northern Affairs man, police work all behind him, was back getting involved the way I was.

But I couldn't do anything about that now. Maybe it would never make the papers. A cop, without portfolio. The search for the downed plane was stalled today. Bad weather a few hundred miles south, which meant Norman Wells, Fort Norman, and beyond. I'd kept track on the radio. The weather was okay for the bigger aircraft but no good for tree-hopping while looking for something on the ground. Even without being able to fly, I got the impression from the radio reports that the searchers couldn't figure out why they hadn't found anything or heard anything. They'd assume that the pilot would have tried to come down on an open space and if anybody was alive they'd put out colored markers and run a homing device. As far as I knew nothing yet had been seen or heard. But as soon as something was, I could get there in a matter of hours. I was keeping Buster's orders in mind, but meanwhile—a man was entitled to a hobby, right?

"What I wanted to know," I said, "was what kind of shape Morton was in when you first saw him at the hospital."

"Well, to start with, he must have had an angina attack before the stroke. He'd had angina before, you know, enough that he carried nitro pills with him. In fact, he still had some nitro clutched in one hand when he was brought in. But then sometimes he ate the damn things like peanuts. He must have either taken some, or been about to take some, when he had the stroke."

"Was he conscious?"

"Not when I first saw him. Slipped in and out several times later. He tried to speak. Seemed desperate to tell me something. I tried to get him to write it, but he couldn't hold a pencil."

"Would he have come out of it?"

"Well, you can never tell, sometimes the first stroke is just the start and if followed by others—but I did tell people that I thought the chances were not too bad, if we got him to a good facility, like Edmonton. Might take weeks of therapy but sometimes it's quite amazing, a guy seems totally gone, but over weeks or months, he'll come back."

"Anything else you can tell me? About him, or William, or whatever?"

"When Morton was brought in the son was a little loaded, I'd guess. Smelled of booze, anyway. Scared, but then who wouldn't be, seeing his father's eyes rolling around like a pinball machine when he tried to speak? Morton had a big bruise on his forehead. I asked William about it and he seemed to be trying to think when it had happened, but he didn't answer."

"Was it consistent with a fall?"

"Could be."

"Or being hit? Slugged?"

"Well, hell," the doctor said slowly, "yeah, I guess so . . . ." He looked at me more sharply. "Yeah, I guess so. I guess that's all pretty academic, now. From what I hear, I guess the bruise wouldn't show any more."

When I left there I thought I'd better check in at RCMP headquarters. The RCMP "G" division covers the whole North, with about 240 men in four sub-divisions and thirty-nine local detachments, mostly headed by a corporal or a sergeant. The Inuvik sub has something close to sixty officers, being one of the busiest subs anywhere. The inspector was an old friend, Ted Huff. Damn near a foot taller than me. Very straight-ahead officer. But when I walked in to the ground floor of the two-storey headquarters building and three or four officers had finished making heavy jokes about me and the civil service, I found out that the inspector had taken the police Twin Otter over to Banks Island that morning for the christening of the first child of the corporal in charge of the Sachs Harbour detachment.

"It's sort of a mercy flight," one constable said. "Young Lester over there, his wife had a bad time giving birth and her parents down in Kingston were all worried. They tried for weeks to get her to fly back to civilization with the baby, I guess they figure Kingston is pretty civilized. She's a good type and stood them off. But it is lonely at Sachs, you know, her in the North for the first time, more housebound than ever because of the kid. I think the inspector just figured it was a nice day and he'd go over there and show that the brass cares."

He'd be back in an hour, they figured. I said I'd be back about the same time. In front of the Mackenzie Hotel a couple of taxis sat with their engines running.

"Know where Komatic Air hangs out?" I asked the first driver.

"Sure do. Hop in."

I got in the front seat. In the North, a passenger is thought to be from Toronto if he chooses to ride in the back seat when he could be up with the driver.

This one looked at me closely. He was middle-aged, originally German, and had been here since 1962 that I knew of. "Hey, you're that guy used to be the special, eh? Matteesie, got to be famous since you left, eh?"

I try not to let it go to my head.

He made a skidding turn to head west on Distributor Street toward the river, back past police headquarters and Arctic College. He turned right at Franklin and soon was in streets I'd once known well from taking drunk girls home and picking up guys for beating up wives, and so on. Once or twice a murder. Natives like to be by a river. This area by the riverbank had become their part of town, Slavey and Loucheux and Eskimos. Sometimes in those early days there'd be ten to a one-room shack, and like as not some girl who had taken secretarial training and got a government job would get up in the morning and have to step over the sleeping people to dress and then walk a mile or so to work, where she'd compete with white girls who only had to walk through a heated tunnel from their subsidized apartments to get to the office. Sometimes, too, when these same Native girls faced going back to the crowded shack at night they went to the beer parlor at the Mackenzie instead. It had been a great system for transforming eager teenagers into twenty-seven-year-old hags.

Komatik Air's office was in an old prefabricated building called a 512 because that was their square footage. A lot were shipped in when the town was created in the early 1950s. Yellow light shone faintly from a window. A pickup truck stood by the door, with the engine plugged in to an electric cord leading to an outlet on the building's outer wall.

A weather-worn Beaver was out on the ice near the shore, with a tarpaulin draped over its engine like a tent. There'd be a heat-pot in there to keep the engine from freezing up. The pilot like as not would have an old felt hat tucked away inside the cabin for straining gasoline when he had to gas up from some cache of a few dozen barrels on the shores of some frozen lake. I told the driver to wait, and knocked on the door.

A voice called, "It's open."

The man behind the desk was an Inuk, about my size, five feet six, and with a face that lit up like a beacon.

"Matteesie!"

"Thomasee!"

He came around the desk a little shyly because I'd been gone a long time and he wouldn't be as sure as he once had been. He stopped a few feet from me. "I haven't seen you since the time I picked you up with that old trapper away out on the Barrens south of Paulatuk! Him and his furs and that Loucheux woman he lived with, dead as a white girl's ass." Abruptly he looked stricken. "Jeez, I'm sorry, Matteesie. I forgot your wife is . . ."

Then we hugged one another. Thomasee Nuniviak. About my age. Born around Letty Harbour on the Arctic shore and raised like I had been, more muktuk than caribou. We'd been at school here together. He'd gone to Yellowknife for the engine course and worked for others around aircraft and then got his pilot's license. He ran water into a kettle and plugged it in. We caught up. It was a little while before I asked, "Heard anything about your aircraft?"

He shook his head. "Not a damn thing. That what you're here about? I heard you're with Northern Affairs now. You hear anything?"

"No. But I'm interested." I told him why, the Harold Johns connection. "I'm told he didn't say where he was going."

"Damn right he didn't. I'd like to ask him why."

He busied himself with mugs and teabags. The water boiled. He poured mine first and politely shoved over a can of condensed milk that had two holes punched in the top. I added some to the tea.

"Did he, uh, goof off like this often?"

"Never before. Good pilot. No problems with Harold at all." He paused. "Policee been down, too, asking the same. The only thing I can think is he didn't know exactly where he was going to end up. Like maybe this Albert Christian comes in and says he wants to go to Arctic Red and somewhere else from there, he'll let Harold know at Arctic Red, so Harold would figure he could phone when he got there and tell me what was going on.''

"But he never called.''

"No, but hell, you know, where he got to, if it's south of Fort Norman, there ain't many goddamn phone booths! Anyway, all I can do is hope.''

"You know the guys he took, Batten and Christian?''

He pursed his lips and let out a long hiss of air. "That's what bothers me. I don't know Batten except to see. But Christian had done one or two trips with us before, down to Wrigley once, another time to Old Crow. Don't know exactly what for. But we don't generally ask. A guy's got money and wants a flight, we take him, maybe bring him back. You know how it is.'' He grinned. "That girl whose car Christian left here, she was some mad. She would've killed him. Didn't plug in her car, didn't leave a note, nothing. They must have been in a hurry, is all I can figure.''

"How far could they get without refueling?''

He didn't have a useful answer. "You know, depends on flying conditions. But he knew where the gas caches are.''

Obviously that was the least of his worries. It seemed he trusted Harold Johns.

"The police think Christian and Batten have been bringing in drugs. Maybe even on one of your flights.''

He looked anxious. "The policee who was here asked questions that seemed to lead in that direction. All new to me. But it worries me. For sure.''

"How about survival gear?''

He answered as I expected. It was in every plane. A guy could lose his license if it wasn't. The standard pack was a two-layer tent, primus stove, axe, snow knife for making an igloo, one Arctic-grade sleeping bag per passenger and pilot, watertight match container, candles, dried food, extra parkas if passengers didn't have their own, a rifle. If you're not hurt when you go down, you can hang out safely as long as you stay put. The cold wasn't as bad as the wind but basically you had to stop loss of body heat. A tent or an aircraft cabin would be shelter enough. Even a candle will heat up an enclosed space.

At least I knew a little more. And the contact might somehow help later. I finished my tea and told him I was going to Fort Norman and I'd phone him if I learned anything important. He regretted that I didn't have time to sit and talk. I was regretful, too. I was getting to be so damn efficient, no longer operating on what some people call northern time. Meaning time doesn't mean anything. Have to watch that.

"Next time," he said as I was leaving, "stay longer. I'll always drive you back uptown. You don't have to have a taxi waiting like a white man." I accepted the rebuke.

It was past four, the sun getting low. "Inspector Huff is back," the receptionist called as I headed upstairs to Ted's big office on the second floor. He crushed a few small bones in my hand to indicate that he was glad to see me. We went back a long way, all the way to basic training in Regina. We were friends but not like the "Matteesie!" and "Thomasee!" of a short time earlier; the same rank, but in my head I deferred to him because while I had always been as close to a lone wolf as an officer in the Mounties can be, he was officer commanding five dozen good, or mostly good, people. I still thought of myself as plain Matteesie and thought of him as The Inspector. He knew none of this. I didn't envy him but I think sometimes he envied me.

Now, while his secretary brought coffee, Ted enthused about his trip to Banks Island. The corporal's wife had been so pleased at his surprise visit that after the christening he'd taken her out in the Twin Otter to see some of the musk-ox herds he'd seen on the way in only a few minutes from Sachs Harbour. "Never saw so many! Every place you look—musk-ox! It's old stuff to you and me but when we'd fly over a herd and they'd get scared and get in a circle facing out to protect the young in the middle, it was something new for that young lady. Glad I went."

Then he waited for me to open the bidding.

I didn't really have to specify what I was there for. He

knew that Buster had called me originally about the missing plane. My involvement at the time of the murder, he knew as well. I got right to it.

"I don't want you to think I'm meddling," I said.

He laughed. "Once a cop . . ."

I filled him in on who I'd talked to, and then: "I'd really like to talk to William Cavendish." I was hoping he'd know more about William's whereabouts than I did, and I was right. To a point.

"So would I. Last night after we got word about the murder we tried all the bars, eating places, people he knew. Everybody said they hadn't seen him. Of course, some of them must have been lying. He had to be here somewhere. In hindsight, we should have put a man at the airport. He flew out on Nahanni this morning with a ticket for Fort Norman." Ted looked at me with a grin. "I guess this is all on Northern Affairs business, eh?"

"Oh, sure," I said.

He didn't ask any more questions, but I did. A suspicion suddenly began rattling around in my head looking for a way out. It had been born as abruptly as Ted saying where William had been heading that morning by Nahanni Air—the same place where a plane carrying his friends might have gone down without sending out any emergency signals.

"Do you think there's a connection between what happened to Morton Cavendish and those guys that took off in that Cessna that's down?"

"Same old Matteesie," he said. A compliment, I'm almost sure.

"Well?"

"Maybe not directly," he said. "But William was thick with the two guys Johns flew out of here. In fact, if they were making a run for it with their bankroll as Edmonton tells us, I was surprised that William wasn't with them. Hours after they flew out we got word that would have had us pick four of them up. But of course they actually left two guys behind, at least so far. So we held off."

"Left behind William and who else, Jules Bonner?"

He winced. "Jesus. How'd *you* know about that poisonous little bastard?"

I told him about Bonner being sent by William to look after Gloria the night Morton was stricken, and being in the airport making phone calls the day I left. I knew they might have been nothing, might have been to a girlfriend or somebody not connected at all to the rest. But somebody had had to line up a hit man, even if only on spec, and later let him know what flight to do it on. I wondered if the phone company could help. Didn't think so, with a pay phone, but worth a try.

There was something else I wanted to think about further. I'm not usually secretive, even about theories, when I'm dealing with someone who might need only a shred of fact or fancy to fit into other facts or fancies and get nearer to an answer, but for now I'd gone about as far as I wanted to go.

"You got any theories about the murder?" I asked.

Ted shook his head. "Morton had enemies, of course, people who think he sold out on land claims here and there, or others who think he's been too inflexible. But as far as we know they're only people who go to meetings and argue. Not dangerous. As far as I can gather there was nothing he'd done to anybody that would get a professional hit man sent in from somewhere." He paused. "Well, and there's this. Women liked him. That's one thing we're following up, looking for jealous husbands or whatever. There'd been stories about this conference or that, people with a lot in common being together for several days, doing a little drinking at nights. Things do happen, like people getting so friendly they go to bed together."

"It's got a lot of ragged edges," I agreed, rather redundantly.

But women? I knew the reputation. Handsome widower, well known, popular issues, I'd seen him surrounded by some pretty good-looking women around the Chateau Laurier at Ottawa conferences I've been at. I suppose some people would think that he was a womanizer. Either that, or a lot of the women he ran into were manizers, if that's a word, and it probably should be.

I didn't mention Gloria yet. If anybody was going to question her seriously, I wanted it to be me.

Ted shrugged and picked up what he'd been saying. "But that's just guessing. Until we come up with a motive, what we seem to have is a murder, period, plus a coincidence that some drug dealers his son had been thick with have gone off without taking the son along, maybe even doing him out of his split. Maybe William was being double-crossed, maybe Jules Bonner was, too, but how is that going to get his father killed?"

At that point, looking thoughtful, he picked up a pencil and made a note. I couldn't read it.

We sat for another minute or two. I was thinking again about Bonner and his phone calls from the airport. The only other key I could think of was William Cavendish.

"I take it you're fairly sure that the guys who flew out had their bankroll with them?" I asked.

"I don't know what else they'd do. We know a deal was made. We knew the money came in and the drugs went out."

That line surprised me. Drugs going out? Before I could ask, Ted gave the answer.

"Unfortunately we didn't know how it was being done until it was done. The tip actually came from Texas, if you can believe it. We've got some of our people in the US now, as you probably know, working with the US Drug Enforcement Agency. It seems a guy flying an oil company long-range executive jet was loading a shipment of assorted illegal substances, as they call them now, mostly hash, a little cocaine, for a flight he regularly made up here, and he got busted along with one of his suppliers. One of the ground crew apparently got religion and blew the whistle. This had been going on for at least three trips, flying a lot of stuff north, setting down on a remote landing strip to drop the stuff where it would be picked up by the gang working this end.''

Easy to see it all happening. Our border is like a sieve. There's no way every aircraft of executive size or smaller can be kept track of every inch of its flight plan. I thought right away of the old Canol road. When the Americans got worried in 1942 that the Japanese would shut off the coast as a supply route to US forces in Alaska, they'd built this highway and pipeline starting across the river from Norman Wells and leading through the mountains to Whitehorse in the Yukon. The Canol project was abandoned when the war ended and is pretty near impassable now, except for hikers in summer and all-terrain vehicles in winter. But it had lots of small air strips that could be cleaned up enough to land for a few minutes, transfer the contraband to a light plane or ATV and take off again for the legal destination. Maybe even one like Inuvik, with a customs office.

''Once in the North and safe,'' Ted went on, ''anybody could take it south in planes, trucks, boats, whatever the hell you've got. They'd turn it over for cash in Edmonton, Calgary, Winnipeg, then come back here with the money for the next shipment.'' He grinned. ''Nobody sniffs or searches baggage when a guy is going from Norman to Edmonton.''

The idea of the North supplying the south with drugs struck me as pretty ingenious. And also a little funny. ''Who ran the show?''

''Seems to have been Albert Christian. He's the really smart one of the four, one of those guys people instinctively like, or can be influenced by. Call it charisma, if he'd been a politician. Makes friends and influences people. Seemed to have money. Talked about looking for a place to set up a fly-in hunt and fish camp or some other tourist-oriented business. But if so, was still looking.''

''Where's he from?''

''He said Winnipeg. We're checking that now, because Winnipeg was one of the drug destinations from up here.''

''What about the pilot?''

"We just don't know. A cut above the other guys in education, manners, if that means anything. Early thirties. I know about the trouble he was in back east. But he's been clean as far as we're concerned."

"And the other guy that flew out with him, Benny Batten?"

"Used to be a football player. A centre, mostly. Had a shot with Green Bay about twenty years ago, just out of college, but mainly played for Canadian clubs, including about two games with Edmonton ten years ago before they cut him and he came here to work in construction. He did take work—usually as a big equipment driver, bulldozers and so on. Same as William. We had Batten once for punching out an American geologist who called him a no-talent palooka. I think he'd be mainly just muscle. Bonner did casual white collar work—clerking at the Bay and elsewhere. We think Bonner did some of the thinking and handled some contacts along the line, maybe he and William together. Actual dealing up here would be nothing. Too risky for their main operation. Not enough drug users in the Territories to support much of a drug operation. The known dribbles in Inuvik, Yellowknife, Norman Wells were mostly connected to whites. Our drug people used to figure any drugs we came across were being brought in mostly by users. Now it's obvious the big money was in getting major stuff flown in here the way I've said, and then shipping south."

It all sounded reasonable. If true, it explained why the downed aircraft hadn't put out markers and radio signals. It might even explain why Christian and Batten had taken a powder so suddenly: that they'd suspected strongly, or been tipped, that the police were closing in. If that was true and any of them were left alive, they'd know that a rescue would send them right back into the arms of the RCMP.

But unless there'd been a police leak, what could have scared them to the extent of feeling their only hope was to get the hell out of here somewhere and split up and try to lose themselves down south?

"So why do you figure that only half the gang went out with the money?" I asked. "Or three fifths of the gang if Johns is in on it."

"You got me," Ted said. "One possible theory is that they fought among themselves over something, maybe even over who could have been responsible for blowing the whistle on them. Another could be that at the last moment there was something left to be done around here."

"Such as bumping off Morton Cavendish?"

"Could be. But I sure as hell can't figure out where he'd be mixed up in the thing at all."

"Would NorthwestTel have any way of checking if Bonner phoned long distance from the airport and if so, where to?"

Ted grinned, picked up the piece of paper he'd made the note on, and held it up so I could see. "Check NorthwesTel. Question Bonner Re airport calls."

There was a silence. Like Kansas City in the song from Oklahoma, we'd gone about as far as we could go.

Then he looked at me with a twinkle in his eyes. "So where does your Northern Affairs business take you next, Matteesie?"

F O U R

"Well, well, the wandering minstrel!" Corporal Charlie Paterson said on the phone, and sang in a reedy tenor, *"A wand'ring minstrel I, a thing of ra-a-a-ags and patches. . . .'"*

I wondered if he was always like this in the morning. The time was eight a.m., the day Thursday, about thirty-six hours after Morton Cavendish's murder. I'd called to let him know I was back in Norman Wells and to ask if there'd been anything new overnight.

"Did Ottawa get you?"

"No, were they trying?"

"Trying, Jesus! The commissioner did everything except offer a reward and have dead or alive posters put up in the post office. The guy from Northern Affairs wasn't so bad, but amongst all the umming and ahing I got the idea he wants to talk to you too. Where the hell've you been?"

"Maybe I better call Buster first."

He pleaded, "Just tell me where you are, in case, ah, the superior officer you refer to gets me before you get him."

"I'm at this Esso place, Mackenzie House."

"Mackenzie House! Wait'll the dirty muck-raking newspapers find out about yet another civil servant accepting favors! A guy with beaucoup opportunities to influence major environmental decisions! On the dole from the oil elite!"

"Holy God, Charlie," I protested.

"Okay," he said. "Better make your calls and call me back."

It was a few minutes past ten in Ottawa. Buster came on the line.

"I understand you've been trying to get me, sir."

He was calmer than Charlie Paterson. "Yeah, a few things happening. I hear you were in Inuvik yesterday but I missed you. What I wanted to say was, I told you originally to nose around about that missing aircraft. But now the *Globe*, the *Star*, the *Sun*, the *Citizen*, the *Gazette*, and every goddamn body else in the media business is making a big deal out of you being on the plane when Morton Cavendish got it. They've raked up every big case you been on. First, do you think there's any connection between those drug guys taking off so fast, and Morton Cavendish being murdered?"

"Could be."

"Were you working on that basis in Inuvik?"

"Partly."

Drily, "Jeez, I'm not used to these long, comprehensive reports. . . ." Then, "But if that's the line you're taking, keep right on. Hate to think that Johns guy is part of it, but . . . Anyway, I don't want you to think that I'm pushed by the newspapers, because I'm not, and they know that you've been with Northern Affairs the last couple of years and are supposed to go to Leningrad, but the fact is a lot of people are fighting mad about this murder and we just can't figure on pulling you out until there's an arrest or at least some answers. I've been onto Northern Affairs, not to consult but just to tell them that you're Inspector Kitologitak again as of now and until further notice."

"Is that an order?"

"Yes."

"Okay," I said.

"Damn it, Matteesie!" he said. "Thanks! We can talk about Northern Affairs again when this is over."

"And sir, I should say one thing."

"What's that?"

"It simplifies matters a great deal."

Meaning, now I didn't have to be doing one thing while he thought I was doing another. I wasn't just playing good dog, roll over and be scratched. Ever since that shot was fired into Morton Cavendish's head, I'd been a Mountie again. I owed him, and I knew that better than anybody.

I phoned Bert Ballantyne, my superior in Northern Affairs. This was a big switch in my head from Buster with his jutting jaw and straight talk. I could see in my head Bert Ballantyne as he answered his phone: slim, short haircut, black horn-rimmed glasses, necktie in a Windsor knot, suit by Holt Renfrew, every inch a guy ready to move upward in the civil service. I told him respectfully that I'd just been talking to the RCMP commissioner.

"Yes," he said. "Well, the bad news is I don't think we can hold the Leningrad thing open. I'm sorry about that, but I hope you understand."

I told him I did and would see him when this was over.

Then I made one more phone call. It was a mad impulse, or maybe intuition that right now there was one other phone call I should make.

"Lois," I said. "It's me."

I had rather expected an immediate complaint, but what she did was ask where I was, and when I told her, she asked, "Are you all right?" and without waiting for an answer, rushed on, "Oh, Matty, when I heard about you being on that plane when Morton Cavendish was shot, and what you did trying to stop the murderer, maybe taking a chance you'd get shot, too, I felt just terrible . . ."

She paused a few seconds and continued somewhat tremulously, "Ever since, I've been thinking about us, and about all the bitching I do when you're home." Another pause, a tremulous laugh, "And sometimes when you're not."

I simply didn't know what to say, but I had to get something out. "Well, we can talk about that when I get home."

"I'll try to be better. Be careful. Come back to me."

I hung up and thought of how Lois and I used to be. Couldn't get enough of each other. For years now the opposite had been true. We could get enough of each other, sometimes in a matter of minutes. Yet marriage persisted. It's a conundrum many face, men and women, and I didn't have any more answers than I ever have.

Then Charlie Paterson was hammering on the phone-cubicle door and saying, "For God's sake, time's a-wastin'!"

I pulled myself together and pushed open the door. He didn't use up time asking questions, commiserating about the Northern Affairs thing, making fatuous remarks about life is like that, and so on. What he did was fill me in, which is what I needed to jolt myself back to what had become once again my real world.

As I knew, yesterday there'd been no air search for either the murderer or the lost aircraft. "Weather today'll make it two in a row. Still no radio signals. Also, no murderer." He'd organized six local volunteers for a snowmobile search that had covered a fair amount of territory and found nothing significant. "But there is *something*. Maybe plenty. I'll tell you about it while I'm showing you what there is to see. Get your clothes on and I'll pick you up in the parking lot near the front door."

In Inuvik the day before I'd gone straight from RCMP headquarters to the airport in the same German guy's taxi. Travel in the North depends a lot on either planning well in advance, or getting lucky. I got lucky. An Esso Resources Citation, cruising speed 400 miles an hour, equipped to carry eight or ten passengers, flew north from Calgary three mornings a week and back in the evening. Usually the plane laid over for the day in Norman Wells. But as I walked into the Inuvik terminal an Esso flight was being called.

At the moment I could see only one guy, youngish, heading for the door leading to the tarmac. I called, "Pardon me!" (not an old Inuit saying, but one year the Mounties had sent me on a course to Princeton, you know). He stopped. Yes, he was with Esso. He could have modelled for one of today's keen young oil execs in a Petroleum Council of Canada commercial. Bright-eyed, clean-shaven, short hair. Also courteous, as oil company people long ago conceded is good policy in the North, especially when talking to anyone with dark skin, some with eyes set at a slight angle.

"I'm with Northern Affairs," I said, producing a card that testified to that side of my identity. "I have a watching brief for the department on the air search for the aircraft that's missing and urgently need to get to Norman Wells. I wonder if . . ."

Watching brief. Maybe I'd been in Ottawa too long.

"Matthew Kitologitak," he read from my card, and then smiled at me. "Not with the police any more?"

I'd hate to be trying to travel incognito with some carnally intensive blonde in this part of the country.

"Anyway, the answer is yes, we can take you," he said. "Glad to." He stuck out his hand. "I'm Milt Lawton."

Turned out that he'd been the sole reason for Esso's flight extension to Inuvik today, here for a meeting with some administrators and elected officials from a group of northern communities. He was an adviser in the company's public affairs department. Keeping up with the times was his business.

The pilot, grey-haired, tall, fit-looking, was standing a few feet away. We were introduced. He looked at me, appraising, and nodded. Then the three of us tucked our heads into our shoulders and leaned against the bitter wind and ground drift snow walking out to the aircraft.

This Milt Lawton had a very good grasp of how to conduct public affairs. With me, at least. I was tired and thirsty. We were scarcely airborne before he reached behind a seat and opened what looked like a cupboard door, muttering, "Wonder what we got here . . ."

What they had included my favorite rum, Mount Gay. He chose vodka. We poured good ones, which seemed to get the talk going. His university degree was in geography. He wanted to know what I did normally at Northern Affairs. I thought it wise to mention vaguely the Arctic Institute in Leningrad as one of my concerns. A lot of people I run into, immediately on hearing that sometimes I deal with Soviet concerns in the Arctic, tell me what some junior hockey player just back thinks of the food and accommodation. Somebody should tell those kids that not all the world's cultures are based on that of Swift Current, Saskatchewan. But this guy, even though it turned out he had played hockey, said, "I envy you. Never been there."

He went on to say that he was just back from two years working in Saudi Arabia. I'm always learning things about the world that I had never suspected and this was one: in common with some other oil people assigned to Saudi, where restrictions on normal Western lifestyles can be rather severe, he and his wife had lived in Cairo during his Saudi stint.

"It was just easier for her there," he said, without elaborating. He'd flown to her there on weekends.

He mentioned the Morton Cavendish murder, saying earnestly the truth, that it represented a great loss to the North. He'd known Cavendish and went on to talk about him with affection. I recognized that this was no patronizing knee-jerk reaction, being pretty fine-tuned to that brand of white talk.

He didn't know I'd been there when it happened. I didn't tell him. There are advantages to being where the media is either no factor at all in daily lives, or has none of the unavoidably pervasive impact it has in big cities. We had our drinks and the hour passed quickly. When we were coming in to land I looked from the window nearest me. Lights along the Mackenzie at Norman Wells came closer and closer, twinkling like a mighty daisy chain against the snow-covered ice that ringed the drilling islands. The river bends west slightly here while keeping its general south-to-north course.

The bright burn-off flare from the main Esso site marked the northwestern limits of the community's seemingly careless space-eating sprawl. Dimmer lights from homes and cars and various business installations stretched for what seemed like miles, and probably was. As we touched down and rolled toward the terminal and stopped near where Cavendish had been murdered, Lawton said that his wife would envy him meeting Matthew Kitologitak. Imagine that. The world is a funny place.

He wasn't getting off. "Gotta keep my seat by the bar," he grinned. "Where're you staying tonight?"

I said probably in a cot at the RCMP detachment.

"I think we can do better than that, if you want," he said, glancing the question at me. I guess my expression said yes. He wrote briefly on a notebook page, which he tore off and handed to me. "Tell the cab to take you to Mackenzie House and hand this to the guy in the office by the door. They usually have some spare rooms."

I had done as he instructed and was delivered by taxi, actually a nine-seater van, to a largish two-storey building near the centre of town. From the outside it was unexceptional; looking not unlike a spartan kind of hotel, which in a sense it was—living quarters mainly for Esso people coming to Norman Wells temporarily.

But it was spartan with a lot of differences. To the left of the main entrance a grey-haired man in a stylish cardigan sat at a desk with today's *Edmonton Journal* spread out in front of him. He read Lawton's note, signed me in, gave me a meal card and room key, told me that breakfast was served from seven to ten, and pointed toward a nearby room where he said I could find coffee and snacks twenty-four hours a day.

I carried my bag along a corridor past a bank of pay phones, then past a big lounge where some guys were playing pool on full-size tables and others in easy chairs were watching a hockey game on television. Another lounge room that I passed, empty, had an assortment of newspapers and magazines spread out on a table, plus, thoughtfully, an alternative TV set. Not everyone in Canada is addicted to hockey. I continued through a door, up some stairs, along to the end of the corridor and put my key in a door.

The room was narrow, utilitarian, industrial transit-house gothic. It was complete with one bed, three well-thumbed paperbacks, a well-worn pair of Greb boots a previous incumbent had left in a closet, a shower stall, towels, soap and a sign giving the rules of the house—which informed me that drinking alcoholic beverages in Mackenzie House was okay, but to keep the noise down because people on different shifts might be sleeping.

Accordingly, I was quiet. Decided not even to go get some ice in case it would clink too loud. I hadn't realized until I had that drink on the plane that I was very tired. I took the Glenfiddich from my bag, poured a stiff one, added a little water, very little, and stood by the window looking out at a large open space of snow and not much else. The clumplike tracks of rabbits. The straight-line pussyfooting of a fox. I hadn't eaten but as I stood there and sipped the drink I didn't feel like going out again to find anything.

No food, and a second drink, might have been responsible for my uneasy night. I'd had nights like that before when I was on a case. I hadn't really been on a case for a long time, but as I drifted in and out of sleep I was out in the bush with three other men in a blizzard. We had made a shelter against the wreck of an aircraft. It was damn cold. The other three were arguing but I couldn't hear what about. Even while still half-asleep I was thinking this certainly wasn't the kind of thing I needed to consult Dr. Freud about: I was hunting for three guys in a crashed aircraft, what else would I dream about? If I'd dreamed that I'd just scored seven straight goals to give the Montreal Canadiens a 9–8 win over the Edmonton Oilers, that *would* have required professional interpretation. After all, I'm a Toronto Maple Leafs fan.

I awoke to sounds of doors closing and boots clumping. I showered, dressed and, very hungry, found the dining room simply by following the crowd. While I moved my tray along the food-laden hot tables of bacon, sausages, ham, scrambled eggs (and a guy who'd cook eggs any other way you ordered), breaded fish, English muffins, hot cakes, French toast, hash browns and French fries, I ate a smoked sausage with my fingers. Then I was among the Danishes, muffins, every known packaged cereal, juices the same, coffee, cream, milk, hot water, tea (loose as well as bags).

I took my loaded tray to an empty table by a window and as I ate, watched as men moved along the line. They'd serve themselves grandly, meagrely, or in between, then look around for company and carry the tray to this table or that. Some glanced at me but none came to mine.

There weren't many Dene or Metis that I saw, but that didn't mean much; Norman Wells was about eighty percent white, I knew from someplace. Not like Fort Norman fifty miles south, which was almost all Dene and Metis. Maxine had said once, "In Fort Norman we got about two hundred and fifty people. No goddam"—smilingly—"Inuit at all, maybe twenty white people at the most."

Some of the men, after eating, filled paper bags with fruit, doughnuts, muffins, cartons of fruit juice and milk. These must have been for between meals, because on a table at the end of the food line other well-filled bags were labeled with names, obviously pre-ordered lunches. I thought that if I was ever out of a job and hungry I would try to get on with Esso Resources at Norman Wells.

Finally so full of food that I could think about murder again, I'd made my phone calls and then Corporal Charlie Paterson was hammering the phone booth door. I went back to my room and zipped up my down vest, pulled on my parka, placed my fur hat squarely on my head with the ear flaps hanging loose. It was still a couple of hours before daylight. Outside, Charlie was waiting. I climbed into the van beside him.

"How about something to eat?" he grinned.

Ridiculous idea. He must have known.

As we pulled out of the parking lot the headlights of a line of school buses came the other way. I hadn't noticed the Territorial school across the street the night before, just seeing another dark building. But you couldn't miss it now, with all the life, bundled-up kids yelling and horsing around, kids leaping down from the buses to mingle with those who probably lived close and therefore were arriving on foot.

Charlie honked his horn and wound down his window to call, "Hi, there!" to a boy who looked about twelve.

"My kid," he explained. "Good kid. Takes after his old man."

"I don't have any kids," I said.

"Yeah, you told me."

I hadn't told him, but that didn't matter. Early in marriage I had cared, but got over it.

Snow mixed with sleet was rattling against the van's roof in gusts. "Great goddamn search weather," Charlie said. As we reached the town's main street he turned right for a few yards and then left into the closest thing Norman Wells has to a commercial plaza. The parking area was a square of hardpacked snow and ice. Several cars and pickups and snow machines sat with vapor rising from the running engines. The lot was flanked on three sides by buildings set in the form of an open U; coffee shop, Bay store (traditionally groceries and everything else from parkas to felt boot liners), Northwest Territories office, Canadian Imperial Bank of Commerce, Norman Wells Inn and others whose signs I couldn't read in the dark.

"What are we looking for?" I asked.

"Just showing you the lay of the land. A guy fitting the general description of your buddy the murderer was here the day of the shooting, so he could be the guy the ground agent told us about who came in on the northbound flight. He started out with coffee and something to eat over at"—jerking his head in that direction—"the Norman Wells Inn. Sat by himself. After a while, not long, the waitresses say, maybe thirty minutes, he went over to the pay phone, which rang a couple of minutes later and he answered it.''

"Waiting for a call at a specific time, right?''

The corporal looked at me. "Don't know what I'd do without your Native intuition,'' he said.

"I'm famous for it.''

"So I've been hearing—anyway, after the call he left. Nobody could say what he left in, as far as I could check. Or which way he went. But what seems to have been the same man arrived maybe fifteen minutes later at the Mackenzie Valley Hotel, which sort of sits by itself farther south along on the road you take to the airport. He had a double Scotch, then more coffee. After a while, same thing with the phone, he took a call on the pay phone there, again as if he'd been waiting for it. It was only a short call, the guy on the desk happened to notice.''

That might have been about the time Jules Bonner in Inuvik made what I'd thought must be a long distance call, from the number of coins he used.

"After that call,'' the corporal went on, "he left. The desk clerk, a lazy bugger, did stroll to the window and notice that the guy was driving a Skidoo Elan. That's the model you thought it was, remember? Lots of pep. The clerk noticed because he's got one the same.''

I asked, "If it's our guy and he's not from here, where would he get the snowmobile?''

"Rented, for Chrissake,'' the corporal said with what sounded like a tone of disgust, but not with me. "Somebody early in the day phoned the dealer here saying he was from Esso and wanted to rent a snowmobile that afternoon. The dealer thought it was a local call but probably it wasn't. The guy showed up just a little while after the plane from the south came in, gave a name, no doubt phony, Esso tells me they have no record of a John Williams, paid a one-hundred dollar deposit, seventy dollars to be returned when he brought the machine back, and took off.''

"And never brought the machine back,'' I said.

"You got it. Oh, yeah, and the dealer tells me it has a five-gallon fuel tank, meaning more range than the three-gallon jobs. Anyway, seems like it's the same guy we traced until he left the Mackenzie Valley Hotel with the clerk watching. He said the guy turned right as if he was going back into town but a few minutes later an Elan went by in the other direction and he could've sworn it was the same guy. That time he definitely drove out of town."

"Where does that road go?"

"If he went a bit and turned left, which we gotta figure he didn't, it goes to the airport. If he keeps on going, it's called the D.O.T. road. I'm going to show you."

He circled the van to get back on the main road and turned left. A few minutes later he slowed at a driveway where a sign read MACKENZIE VALLEY HOTEL, a building whose lights we could hardly see through the snow and dark of a little after nine a.m. Then we drove on until we saw a sign pointing left, reading AIRPORT. He drove past that without turning and continued a bit until we came to another intersection. To our right a road sloped gently downhill toward the river. We turned left, away from the river.

"Now this road," he said as we were driving along it a couple of minutes later, "can you figure out where we are right now?"

Best I could do was guess, but I did know the airport runway would take 737s, which meant it had to be close to 6,000 feet long.

"We must be on the edge of the airport, maybe close to the end of the runway."

The van, just crawling along, stopped.

"Right. Now, if the guy on the snowmobile kept on going this way he coulda been heading for Nahanni Air's float base, but there's nobody around there in winter. Past Nahanni Air this road goes to the stone quarry where the oil company's contractors get the stone to make the artificial islands they drill from. But nobody in his right mind goes up to the quarry just for fun. In winter, anyway. Which means there's no reason for a guy on a snowmobile to go up this road by himself.''

"I have a feeling you're going to say, 'However . . .' " I said.

"Smart bastard. *However*, if he came this far, right where we're stopped now, and turned left off the road he could go through that bit of bush''—we both looked that way but couldn't see much except blowing snow—"he'd come out on the airport with the fence no problem because his end run had taken him around it. Then he could cruise along without lights to get so close that when the flight came in, all he had to do was move up a little, wait for the steps to come down and the people to come out, then run over and do it.''

"Yeah," I said. I could see the whole sonofabitching thing in my head, plainly. Too plainly.

"If," Charlie said, emphasizing, "that's all *if* the guy we're talking about wasn't just some other guy who might not have come this way at all, but just kept right on going along the D.O.T. road to some shack out in the bush, into the arms of some husky dusky maiden.''

"Let's pretend we're talking about the murderer," I said. "It's more fun." It also supported the idea that somebody masterminding this thing had arranged for him to come in here either from Edmonton or Yellowknife on the morning flight, and had phoned well ahead of time to arrange a snowmobile rental.

He started the van again. "I want to show you something else.''

We went uphill a few hundred yards further. Now I could see great chunks of windswept stone ahead and to the right; obviously, the quarry. Before getting there he turned left on what wasn't more than a rough trail, deep ruts in the snow, the kind of place only a four-wheel drive vehicle like this one could go and hope to get turned around and out. Charlie went along that trail maybe a hundred yards, then braked and reversed into a sharp turn so that the back end of the van headed uphill and we were looking downhill.

Even with the snow I could see that we were on a shelf overlooking the Mackenzie. Below and to our right I could dimly see the airport lights, blinking through the squalls. Between us and the airport, even though there wasn't much light yet, we could see a straight white line cutting through the bush like a chalk mark on a blackboard. It vanished in the distance in both directions. Everyone flying in the North along the Mackenzie sees miles of these straight white cutlines through the bush. Many were cleared originally in the 1960s for Canadian National Telegraphs but now were shared here and there by International Pipelines and in some places from about mid-January to mid-March, by the vital winter road. That's the only time when ice at the river crossings is thick enough to hold big transports.

I stared at the cutline, nodding, saying to myself, yeah, yeah. When he got that far after the murder, which way did he turn? I didn't ask it but Charlie answered it anyway.

"Ned Hoare picked up the guy's trail coming off the airport property," he said. "He could do that because nobody else goes across the airport on a snowmobile. But the farther Ned went, the less he could be sure he was following the right track. At the cutline, of course, it was game over. Snowmobile tracks in both directions."

These cutlines in summer are too rough to travel except on foot with a backpack. Winter is another matter. I knew the geography. If a cutline connects one community with another, like Fort Norman and Norman Wells, or even comes close, almost automatically it becomes a winter road. Transports large and small, normally limited by strictly local road systems, move supplies and equipment. Places that don't have a winter road, like Fort Good Hope a hundred miles north, downriver, near the narrow part of the Mackenzie where it runs between high cliffs called The Ramparts, sign petitions and beefs to their legislative members. They feel that civilization is passing them by.

"So which way do you think?" I asked.

"Hard to say. If you weren't trying to fool anybody, Fort

Norman would be a piece of cake. Can't ignore north, of course, but jeez that road north is tough. A truck slid off a cliff once this winter already."

Anyway, Mountie detachments along the river both ways had been alerted. Any stranger would be getting very searching looks.

I asked, "Did you manage to fly the cutline yesterday at all?"

"Got a chopper up for about an hour before the weather forced us in. Saw some snowmobiles towards Fort Norman. Pengelly from the detachment there came the other way on his machine and checked them out. All local. Saw nothing to the north. Like I say, can't rule north out, but if the guy went south, what time's the murder, around five-thirty, he could have been in Fort Norman by midnight, except that he wouldn't be that dumb."

We were on the same wavelength. The fugitive couldn't have expected to last long unspotted if he stayed in the open. If he ran without lights, which he probably did, he couldn't make good time. If he ran with lights, say toward Fort Norman, anyone out to intercept him could stop and turn out his own lights and spot anything coming.

"I don't think the guy would be heading for a settlement at all," I said.

"So where?" Charlie asked.

"Some hideout, even a place he'd specifically fixed up himself in advance."

"If he knew the bush," the corporal mused, emphasizing the if, "he could stick it out for weeks or maybe months. I mean, an experienced trapper could, easy. Some of them do. Go out after freezeup and come back starving, eating ptarmigan and their goddamn dogs and, well, girl friends—"

"Charlie . . ." I protested, although none of the possibilities he had suggested was unprecedented. The old barren land trapper in Inuvik who'd declared in favor of dog teams over snowmobiles on the grounds that he couldn't skin and eat a snowmobile had been making a fairly limited assessment of the disaster plans he might consider if the need arose.

I reran those few seconds frozen in time, the shots that killed Morton. "The guy was no trapper. Hell, I know trappers, how they smell, how they take half a day to decide to blow their nose. He was a killer, a guy with a plan. Now, what kind of a plan *could* a guy have to make sure that he got away fast and safe?"

"You tell me," the corporal said.

I opened my mouth and then shut it again. I'd had the idea first the day before in Ted Huff's office and hadn't mentioned it, and still didn't want it to sound like *the* solution until I'd thought about it more.

But the corporal was reading my mind. "Out with it," he said. "When you get an idea you do everything but throw your arms in the air like a goddamn hockey player and do a little dance."

"And here I thought I was pretty inscrutable," I said.

"Out with it."

I'd been hoping that he wouldn't insist, because even while I'd been talking the idea had been developing some more.

Suppose the Komatik Air flight now listed as missing, but which had taken off with no stated destination, had been supposed to land somewhere not far from here and wait for a murderer arriving by snowmobile. Of course, that would mean the murderer was absolutely part of the drug gang on the run.

I said, "This guy would have had to have a lot of help, even on the basis of what we know of him. He knew he'd been seen, so no alibi would stand up for sure."

"Yeah, go on."

"So he'd have to have a deal where he'd get to a lake somewhere or someplace along the river, fast, and be picked up."

"No goddamn plane is gonna land and take off in the dark!"

"It doesn't have to be dark," I said. "A plane could have been out there waiting for—hell, twenty-four hours. There's hundreds of lakes and ponds. Maybe thousands."

The possibilities didn't really have to be spelled out. Charlie got the Komatik Air connection, or possible connection, right away, the one plane we knew of that had been down this way a day before the murder and maybe wasn't missing at all, just misplaced.

"Shit," Charlie said. "That's too far-fetched."

"You got a better idea?"

"No." After a while he said rather respectfully, I thought, "So tell me more, oh shaman."

"We ask the rescue people to go on with what they're doing, as soon as they can fly, except to keep in mind that maybe these guys don't want to be found. That would explain the lack of radio signals. Along the same line of thinking, if they landed on purpose rather than crashed, they might have camouflaged the aircraft with trees, snow, sheets, whatever, to make it less visible from the air."

"Jesus," Charlie said. "And I could be missing all this if I hadn't resigned from the choir."

"That's not all," I said. "Just in case the bunch from Inuvik isn't in on it at all, maybe we should ask up and down the river if there's any pilot who is, or was, supposed to meet somebody at a certain spot."

With most trappers carrying two-way radios these days such pickups are common for a wide variety of reasons, from death in the family to a suddenly unbearable case of hemorrhoids to which the owner wished to bid farewell.

"That makes sense," Charlie said. "Let's get on it."

He put the van in gear and started back down the road. By then it was near ten and there was a pre-dawn lightening of the landscape, a greying of the snow-filled overcast.

We rode in silence until we got to the police office and sat a moment outside. I was thinking, what's next? So was he.

"I'd better go to Fort Norman," I said.

"Anything particular in mind?"

"Well, it doesn't seem fair to have two great brains in the same place, where some places haven't got any at all."

Grinning, "Too true. But what do you really have in mind?"

"Somebody has to find William Cavendish."

It had been confirmed by the Fort Norman detachment that William had landed there Wednesday morning. Then he seemed to have vanished. Of course, he was on his home turf, relatives and boyhood friends sometimes being willing accessories to this and that. It wasn't certain, either, that anyone would talk to me. The farther you get south the farther you are from Inuit country, and although we and the Dene got along a lot better than we had in olden times when they felt they ought to kill us because we looked different, and we thought we should kill them first, to avoid that fate, we still don't always bend over backwards for each other.

"Nothin's flying," Charlie said. The radio weather forecaster had been droning on about the weather getting worse before it got better. Charlie waved a hand at the windshield bashing sleet and snow as evidence.

"Can you let me have your snowmobile?"

"Better you than me. But I can't spare anybody to go with you."

"Did I ask?"

I looked off to the south to where now, ever so faintly, I could see more signs of dawn. "Let's get moving. I can use all the daylight I can get."

That was good enough for him. "I'll drop you at Mack House first and then go check for phone calls and load the snowmobile," he said.

In my room I unpacked and got out the stuff I didn't use unless I needed it. I needed it now. Stripped down, I regarded with regret my little brown pot belly. "The great lover," I muttered aloud. I pulled on thermal longs, a thermal top, heavy socks, a wool shirt, then the wool pants I'd been wearing. My kneehighs were the best, leather with rubber soles and felt liner. Down vest. In my parka pocket I

tucked goggles and a new face-mask I'd bought, better than
the old-type woolen balaclava. Designed much the same,
with eye slits and a mouth-nose opening but made of some
material that didn't absorb moisture and fitted almost skin
tight. Some things I didn't have to worry about. Helmet,
rifle, snowmobile tools, spare parts and other equipment
would be in the machine or available. I packed the rest of my
stuff in my carry bag. I might be in and around Fort Norman
a while.

I felt no foreboding, only excitement. For a long time, it
seemed, I'd been with people, most of the challenges, if any,
cerebral. Now I was going out on my own where the challenges were the kind that come at you out of the blue. It had
been years. I missed that.

The van was waiting outside for me, the detachment's
snowmobile loaded on its trailer. Before getting into the van
I climbed onto the trailer. Charlie watched me with a little
grin as I opened the snowmobile seat and made my inspection; a flashlight, pipe wrenches, spare sparkplugs and flashlight batteries, spare drive belt, pliers, screwdriver, airtight
container of matches, a light block-and-tackle with nylon
rope and pulleys with which I could pull myself out of trouble
if I had to and could find a nearby tree, stump or rock as an
anchor. A spare fuel tank, full, was strapped on the sled
hitched behind along with canvas saddlebags containing two
Thermoses and some plastic containers of sandwiches. Held
by clips alongside the right side of the machine was a loaded
rifle.

The corporal watched me during this check.

When I nodded, he nodded.

''There's a two-way radio under the sandwiches,'' he said.
''Use it once in a while. Tell me what's happening. I'll run
you out to the cut.''

On the way mixed sleet and snow fell more heavily, drifting in spots. A snowplow was working the main road. Charlie told me he'd learned nothing new on his trip to the office.
The weather was going to continue bad, canceling search

flights, so on the missing aircraft front, nothing. G division headquarters in Yellowknife would know as much about what was going on as I did. Or more. They or Ted Huff would be keeping Buster informed in Ottawa.

When we stopped on the road where the cutline came in at right angles, Charlie tipped the trailer into its unloading mode and I backed the machine and trailer-sled off. I pulled on my face guard and over it the crash helmet and goggles, keeping the engine at idle so I could hear what Charlie was repeating to me, raising his voice: "Pengelly will meet you a few miles out of Fort Norman."

I nosed the machine off the side of the road, down the steep bank, through the ditch, and gunned it up the other side. Then I waved and was gone.

The mind is not greatly involved in a trip like that. The daylight was meagre, no sun showing although it was supposed to rise up there in the murk somewhere at a few minutes to eleven. When the wind blew snow into brief whiteouts, I'd slow to a crawl. I hardly even glanced at the trails that led off into the bush. This close to the town there were too many to worry about. Anyway, this was Charlie's territory. They'd be combing the bush on snowmobiles, their own and volunteers. On my mind all the time was my guess about the guy maybe heading for a place where a plane could land and pick him up.

But it would be tricky. The plane had to find the pre-arranged spot. Then the guy, not from these parts, had to find it. And it had to be where no one else was likely to stumble across it and screw up everything. The North for thousands of square miles was littered with small lakes, most of them unnamed. If one of them was in the plan, wouldn't it have to be a lake shown on normal navigation maps? But wouldn't that increase the chance of discovery?

I was assuming that the guy would stay on this, the east side of the Mackenzie, but why, I didn't know. From the map I had in my mind I knew that the prospect nearest to Norman Wells was Kelly Lake. Farther south and closer to

Fort Norman was Brackett Lake. Both okay for aircraft, but no cinch for a snowmobile because reaching either would mean getting through the Franklin Mountains. It seemed more plausible to me that there'd be someplace easier to get to but not obvious, meaning it would be known mainly to those who knew the area intimately. More and more, there were reasons to find William Cavendish.

As I bumped along, a feeling of peace gradually came over me. Much of my life, both before I signed on as a special and after, I'd spent time out in the bush or the tundra with snow machines or dog teams. On long trips I might have an objective many days away but the important thing was always just to get through the next few hours before night and food and sleep. On such a trip the mind roams free. I hadn't felt this good for a long time, leaving behind conferences, memos, reports, the trying to convince others that this policy was good and that bad, being polite with deputy ministers and deferential with the political ministers who came and went like migrating geese.

The snow continued. Sometimes in a whiteout I would steer by the straight lines of bush on either side of me. I was in no rush. I had six or seven hours of light to go fifty miles. Easy.

In places the track left by other vehicles, trucks and snowmobiles, was drifted over, only to become visible again where it had been swept by the wind. Animal tracks showed as blurred dents crossing the trail in some patches of snow, leading to other places where they had been snowed over altogether.

A little more than three hours out I figured I must be approaching halfway. The snow had changed again to sleet that rattled against my goggles. I stopped and turned my back to the storm, happy that I was alone, out in the bush, nothing between me and God but the wind and the snow. I had seen no living thing since leaving Charlie. Just to hear my voice, to reassure the storm that I harbored no hard feelings, I said aloud, "Time for a coffee break."

And then, suddenly, I was shown how free I was feeling. A raven flapped out of a gust of snow, saw me, came back for a look, then headed heavily away again, and I yelled at it, my voice tiny against the vastness, "Raven! Raven! Why art thou forsaking me?"

The raven came back and sat in a tree, probably not because of my appeal but on sober second thought realizing that where there was man there would soon be garbage, something to eat.

I conversed with the silent raven further as I drank strong coffee from the Thermos and ate two good salmon salad sandwiches, heavy on salmon, mayonnaise and butter on thick firm bread. Red salmon cost six bucks a small tin up here, but Nancy Paterson had spared no expense. The raven was still waiting. I pushed the transmit button on the radio and said, "Kitologitak here. All clear. Over."

Charlie answered in seconds. "Roger. Go man. Over and out."

I left half a sandwich for the raven, stowed the food and drink, and climbed aboard. As I started up I looked back and saw the raven flapping down to pick up its share of the lunch.

About two hours after the social event with the raven I glimpsed something ahead. A northbound transport passed. Then through a break in the snow gusting across the trail I could see another machine coming toward me. I stopped, watching, conscious of the rifle there beside me. The other machine also stopped. I could see its pilot pull out binoculars and have a look before he waved and came on. When we got close and stopped there was not much to be seen through his face-mask, but he stuck out his hand. "Corporal Pengelly, sir. Fort Norman detachment. Everything okay along the way?"

"Just like a Florida beach."

He laughed. "Yeah, really!"

"Any sign of William Cavendish yet?"

"Not a whisper. The thing is, with his father dead and all,

no murderer caught, the people are a bit hostile where we're concerned. He's got to be in somebody's house, but nobody is saying.''

"You mean he's pretty well-liked, then?"

Pengelly nodded. "More by some people than his father was, as far as I can see. It seems to be one of those situations where the locals feel that Morton went high up and left them all more or less behind, especially William." He shrugged. "That's the idea I get, anyway. But we haven't really pushed hard. No house searches. Couldn't justify that."

All very interesting, but the light was beginning to dwindle. Sunset was an hour or so away. Probably so was Fort Norman.

"So let's get out of here," I said. "You lead. I'll try not to ram you from behind."

I could see Pengelly's teeth as he grinned under his face-mask. "I'd appreciate that."

Back aboard waiting for him to turn around, I was contrasting his easy manner with the uptightness I'd known as a constable his age. If I'd been faced with an inspector, even a former inspector, in these circumstances I would have been yes-sirring like crazy.

He was no hot-rodder. I could see him glance back once in a while to make sure I was still with him. I drove almost automatically, thinking about William, an unreadable guy whom I'd met drunk and abrupt, even rude. Anyway, fairly objectionable. Could there have been something bugging him about lusting after Gloria even while maybe knowing that his father had beaten him to her? Did he really know that? If so, what would that do to his relationship with his father?

I simply couldn't think of him as a man who would help others plot to kill his father, no matter what the provocation. That was instinct and I thought it was accurate. But against that I had to put the way he had acted. He had not visited the hospital at all after the night he'd taken his father there, had not been at the airport when Morton was being flown out, was not to be found anywhere the police in Inuvik had looked for him after his father had been murdered.

And his subsequent actions didn't clarify anything. He'd have known at the very least there'd be questions. Such as, did he and his father come to blows that night? What was his explanation of the head bruise the doctor had noticed? When Morton collapsed, how long before the ambulance was called? Had William let anyone else know?

After that line of questioning, sooner or later it would have to come down to his connection with the drug ring. Did he know that Christian and Batten had taken practically no luggage, but half a million dollars? Did he know where they went? Did he have any idea, even a suspicion, of who had killed his father?

As the questions went in circles in my mind, we putt-putted across the ice at the mouth of the Great Bear River and into Fort Norman on the Mackenzie. The buildings didn't show their age all that much. It had been two centuries since fur traders of the old Northwest Company decided that where two rivers joined, there should be lots of business. Maybe I'd buy some postcards.

FIVE

A big guy who I later discovered was a cousin of William Cavendish came to call on me late that night at Bear Lodge. He didn't bother to knock, just pushed the door open and stood there. I was sitting on the edge of the bed with the last of my Glenfiddich in one hand and a glass in the other, about to pour what, after the day I'd had, I badly needed. He was close to six feet tall and was built a little like William, except William's stomach hung over his belt and this guy's didn't. But they had the same look around the eyes and the same kind of black moustache, the kind that turns down at the corners, providing a modified Charlie Chan effect. His hair was black and pulled back into a short ponytail.

"Come in," I said.

"I am in."

"That's what I mean."

He got it, all right. People of the North are almost invariably polite. Some of it even rubs off on the whites.

"I'm Paul Pennycook, William's cousin. What do you want him for?"

"To talk about the fight he had last Sunday night with his father in Inuvik."

80

Startled, "What'n hell are you talkin' about?"

"Ask William."

He looked angry, then thoughtful, his eyes holding mine. I think he was doing the arithmetic: last Sunday night was when Morton had his attack, and William had been with him at the time. I hadn't risen and didn't plan to, as that would have put my nose just about at the level of his shirt's top button, not good for my confidence.

However, I had shaken him a little, put him off balance.

So much so that he sounded somewhat less forceful than his actual words when he said, "We don't like slant-eyed Eskimo bastards around here." Funny thing, him saying that. Until I was about twenty I always thought our eyes were the proper shape and it was just too bad about all those white people. Once in a while now they even seemed a potential asset, as in a coolly appraising Toronto woman in a low-cut dress a couple of years ago opining that I was real cute, "with your slanty eyes and all."

However, with this guy I wasn't taking.

"That's odd you don't like slant-eyed Eskimo bastards," I said. "I don't object to tall, skinny half-breed bastards."

"Metis!" he said automatically.

"Inuit," I replied.

Of course, this puerile debate was based, however distantly, on the historic fact that in our aboriginal state Eskimos and Indians had bumped one another off, or tried to, on sight. Which means that in the old days maybe Maxine and I never would have got together. But then, in some societies even today adultery itself, never mind the ethnic mix, is punishable by stoning unto death. A comforting thought is that if such a thing ever happened in North America, the continent would run out of stones in less than a week.

Anyway, here I was, and at least I was in touch with someone who might possibly admit to knowing where William was.

"We know you're a Mountie," he said. "You should be out catchin' the guy that killed Morton, for Chissake, right?"

I said mildly, "It just plain might help a lot if William would talk to me. For instance, tell me his ideas on who disliked his father enough to kill him."

Then I went on, not quite so mildly. And suddenly the way I felt gave me a momentary flashback to a guy named Harry, forget his last name but he was president of an American drug company and would rather hunt and fish in the Northwest Territories than sell aspirin. He and I used to hunt geese sometimes when I was a special in the Holman detachment. Just after dawn he'd go off with his roll of toilet paper, the hunter's best friend, and soon he'd come back looking happy and chortle, "Well, Matteesie, I got the plug out."

When I got the plug out now with Paul Pennycook it did my mental health a lot of good. As I said, I started out mildly but in a matter of seconds I was on my feet yelling, "Ever since I got here I been running into dead ends! What the hell's the matter with you people? Don't you want the murderer to get caught? You all afraid to help the police for once, even when it's one of your own people got killed? God damn it all anyway! Then you come in here and start telling me what to do, you asshole!"

I started toward him. If he'd so much as put up his hands to defend himself I'd have been on him, and he might have killed me.

But he didn't move. He just looked at me, as if pondering, and then he pronounced judgement.

"William's fuckin' business is his own fuckin' business," he said, and nodded slightly as if listening to his own words and finding them gratifyingly profound.

Then he left, quietly closing the door behind him.

I poured the last of the Glenfiddich into a glass and sat back trying to think cool thoughts, which wasn't all that easy. I went back over all the dead ends I had run into in the last few hours of knocking on doors all over Fort Norman. The whole damn lot of them, men, women and children, weren't especially impolite, they were just implacable. Even the ones that offered me tea. Something of substance was being hidden from me because nobody would say where William was. It was even possible, I had to admit, that no one I talked to did know where he was. If so, that line from the guy I'd just yelled at, about William's fuckin' business being his own fuckin' business, had something to it besides a pleasant ring. What could I have done differently? Could I have got myself asked someplace for dinner and hope that a drink or two from my trusty Glenfiddich might produce some loose talk?

But in the end I'd decided on Arctic char in the Bear Lodge dining room, and that I needed thinking time.

Bear Lodge had been my choice of hostelries for two reasons. One was bold print. When I checked through the sixty-eight telephone numbers listed in the Fort Norman section of the NorthwesTel directory, looking for the Cavendish name and not finding it, Bear Lodge was listed in large letters. In the Yellow Pages a boxed ad read:

6 DOUBLE ROOMS
CENTRAL BATH AND SHOWERS
DINING ROOM
*Overlooking the Mackenzie River at the Junction
of the Great Bear River*

Sounded scenic.

The second reason was that the only other listing for a possible place to stay was something called Drum Lake Lodge. Upon enquiring from the trusty Pengelly which was the better of the two he said he couldn't really say from personal experience because Drum Lake Lodge was about 175 miles west on the other side of the Mackenzie.

So Bear Lodge it was, with its central bath and showers and some good no-frills cooking in its dining room.

Even though there were no other Cavendishes in Fort Norman, there were cousins and in-laws and other connections. Pengelly and I had chewed it over at the RCMP office after

I'd knocked on enough doors to get myself known as that slanty-eyed bastard who was trying to find cousin William.

"I'm beginning to think he might not be in town," Pengelly said, at one point. "God knows there are places up and down the Bear or the Mackenzie where he could have got to by now, and we wouldn't know unless somebody told us. But the thing I can't figure out is—why? I mean, if he's hiding something, what the hell is it?"

The question exactly. If he had anything to hide, it was what had been happening between him and his father when Morton had the angina attack, and whether that had anything to do with the other guys taking off. It might be significant that they had taken off just about as quickly as anyone could arrange it after Morton was taken to hospital and found to be in critical condition. Almost as if there had to be a connection. Something they knew must have made them vamoose while the police were tapping their fingers and waiting for the time to be right to close in. It was a riddle that I couldn't think of anyone better than William to answer.

A stray thought struck me now, back in my room. William was really the only true Northerner among them. Harold Johns was from the East, spoken well of by my old and true friend Thomasee Nuniviak, his employer. Maybe Johns could be ruled out on all grounds. Maybe he just got attached to the thing as an innocent bystander. I had a feeling that would please Buster, if so, but it wasn't necessarily true; just a mildly supportable guess. Albert Christian at least said he was from Winnipeg, apparently one of those guys who used the North for whatever he could get out of it; tax-free dollars being the backbone of the drug trade. Benny Batten, the old football player, seemed on the evidence to be the foot soldier type usually found in the lower echelons of any bunch of hoods. That left Jules Bonner, who'd spent part of his life here but was still a transient and (in the opinion of Ted Huff) poisonous little bastard, and William Cavendish, who seemed intent on keeping from us exactly where he belonged. But if there'd been a battle within the gang, it might have been split along lines that hadn't occurred to me before.

I didn't figure William was any pillar of Northern virtue, but he had been brought up here and could have been the odd man out. How could Morton have known any of that? Still, if Morton had some inkling of the drug side of William's life, couldn't that have been why he was angrily hunting for William just before the explosion between them? Leaving the question, what could I do here that I hadn't already done?

What I did was get up and go out, on the grounds that sitting still was rarely productive. I met the glances of a few people lounging around the lobby, pulled my parka zipper tight around my neck, pulled the hood up over my fur hat to keep the snow from driving down my neck and faced into the frigid, blustery night.

Snow was swirling around the few street lights as I clumped along past the Bay store, the Pentecostal church, the Roman Catholic mission, a few government offices. All were dark and uninviting, suggesting no answers. Still, my way of doing things, whether on my home turf of the Arctic shore or down here on the Mackenzie where I felt somewhat out of my element, was to keep turning over the known facts in my head, challenging each in the hope that something would turn up.

So.

Morton Cavendish had been in Inuvik looking for his son, who was drinking part of the time with Gloria but later went to meet his father at the Mackenzie Hotel. During that meeting Morton Cavendish had an angina attack and then a stroke, perhaps helped along by rage at whatever he'd wanted to see William about.

The next afternoon Harold Johns had flown the Cessna out of Inuvik either aware or unaware that he was carrying two men who might have known that their drug operation was on the ropes. No one now available knew the flight plan. The Cessna's engines were heard a couple of hours later during a bad storm near Fort Norman, and the plane had then vanished, at least from public view.

The following day, Tuesday, Morton was being flown out to the strokes facility in Edmonton when he was murdered. Reason, unknown. Almost certain guess: to shut him up about something.

Wednesday: I go back to Inuvik, find William had avoided police Tuesday night after his father's death, but had flown to Fort Norman the next morning.

Thursday, right now: I'm in Fort Norman trying to find William.

Conclusion: be my guest.

William's coming here could have been natural enough. There aren't any funeral directors from Inuvik to Yellowknife, so funerals in smaller communities are generally arranged by the family. William would be it, in his family. However, right now it wasn't even sure when the body would be released for burial, or where it would be buried. Pengelly had checked both local sets of clergy, Roman Catholic and Pentecostal. Neither had heard about funeral plans.

Neither had the government offices, where William might have been expected to call or appear for a particular northern reason, that reason being that in much of the Northwest Territories grave-digging doesn't alter much in form from one season to the next. With the permafrost so close to the surface, the only way a proper grave could be dug winter or summer was with a jackhammer, which the government office routinely supplied without charge. And they don't even bill Medicare.

My mind was traveling up and down those various blind alleys when, through the swirling snow, I saw something that at first looked like just an overturned sled, larger than a kid's sled but not more than half the size of a komatik. As I walked closer I could see a lot of threshing around, and hear some fervent cursing. Someone on the sled was trying to get it back upright again. Then a grimy, frustrated face peered up at me.

"Hey, I'll give you a hand," I said.

Wondering why he didn't get off and do it himself, I leaned over and caught the edges of the sled and heaved it back upright again. Then I saw why the man now mumbling thanks hadn't done the straightening out himself. He had no legs. He wore a parka and pants, but the legs of the pants had been folded up so that they disappeared beneath the skirt of his parka. The parka hood was up. Under it he wore a leather cap with earflaps. He wore big gauntlets and in each hand was a short length of what appeared to be poplar sapling, sharpened at the end. Still watching me, he dug these into the snow and moved the sled a few feet and then stopped and looked back at me, searchingly.

He had a deep, melodious voice. "I hardly ever seen an Eskimo before," he said.

"Inuk," I said.

"What's your name?"

I told him. He didn't seem hostile, which was a nice change.

"Mountie?"

"Yes. I'm trying to find out something about why Morton Cavendish was killed."

His reaction was total jaw-dropping, eyes-bulging shock and a wordless cry. Dropping his sticks, he flung back his parka hood and stared. "Morton killed? Where? How? You're crazy! He can't be!"

I felt a surge of excitement. "I'm sorry. It's true."

We're standing in the middle of the storm in beautiful downtown Fort Norman, an Inuk Mountie and a man who had no legs and pushed himself along with sticks. The snow fell on his upturned face, full of anguish.

"How come you didn't know?" I asked. "I mean, it's been on the radio, everybody talking about it."

He told me he'd been out on his trapline. I couldn't believe it.

"You run a trapline without legs?" I blurted. It had been a long time since I blurted anything.

"What the hell else I gonna do?" he demanded sharply. "Morton encouraged me. He said, 'Hell, George, you ain't finished yet unless you let yourself be finished!' He was workin' on gettin' me some legs!"

I just stared. I might have thought of something else to do or say if I'd had time, but he gave me no time.

"Jesus!" he said. "I gotta find out about this!"

As he spoke, he grabbed his two short poles and in a few swift strokes moved away from me, zooming along the street and out of sight. I started after him but changed my mind and went to the RCMP office instead. Pengelly was off duty. The special, Nicky Jerome, lived in a room behind the office. Nicky was a Slavey and the classic special; sturdy but small, bow-legged, with button-like eyes, happy in his work (I'd noticed earlier), and happy in his play—his feet now in felt boot liners resting on a footstool as he watched "Knots Landing" on television. The room was blue with tobacco smoke from his pipe, which I noticed was an Ontario-made Brigham, the kind I smoke myself. On the table at his elbow was a mug of steaming tea and a can of Erinmore mixture, which I smoke when I can't get John Cottons Mild. A pretty classy special. Maybe he'd make inspector some day.

"Sorry to disturb you," I said.

He waved that away politely, glancing back and forth between me and the TV screen.

"Anything new?" I asked.

His mind and eyes were on the TV show. "Abby's been thinkin' 'bout this guy from a long time ago, her first boy friend, and suddenly he shows up again."

"I mean, anything about William Cavendish?"

He laughed merrily. "Oh, sorry, I thought you meant . . ."

When I told him about meeting the man who hadn't known about Morton's death, Nicky kept on watching the TV but filled me in.

"George Manicoche," he said. "Don' drink no more, but three, four winters ago, got drunk and lay down in a snowbank and damn near froze to death. His legs were frozen stiff and they tried to save 'em but couldn't, had to take 'em off. Woulda lost his arms, too, prolly, but he had his hands tuck' in around his balls where it was warm and that's what saved his arms. Reason he wouldn' know about Morton, well, this time o' year he goes out two, t'ree days at a time, not very far from town. Got a little shack out there. Can't really go far but he gets rabbits, you know, and the odd fox and udder stuff. Got a marten this year a'ready. It was Morton got him goin' again. Kept kiddin' him that he was still young and strong and now that he wasn' drinkin' he had to do somethin' to fill in the time, so George built hisself that sled. He put wheels on it in summer so he can get to his boat.''

"Some guy," I said, and didn't mean it like a pat on the head.

"Some guy is right," Nicky said, snapping off the TV, which had gone into a mile of credits. "Ever'body knows him. There's another same name, no relation, up at Franklin, so aroun' here nobody call him just Georgie any more. No Legs, that's what he's knowed as, by most.''

I beat my way back through the storm to Bear Lodge. With my own whisky gone I went into the bar and ordered a drink. There were four others there, all sitting alone. They'd been calling back and forth between their separate tables when I came in, but not much was said after I arrived. That figured.

When I finished my drink I went to bed and dreamed once again I was near an aircraft out in the snowy bush; but this time the three men arguing were in the aircraft's fairly intact cabin. I was sure that they were arguing but looking on from outside I couldn't hear a thing.

The next morning about 8:30 I was lying in bed listening to the moan and howl of the wind when there was a tapping at the door. I got up and opened it. The man standing in the hall outside had been tending the desk when I checked in, and tending the bar when I had that drink. He was middle-aged and had white hair, a flattened nose, and suspenders with a black and white zigzag pattern on them.

He shoved an envelope at me. "Message," he said, and waited curiously for me to open it while he explained, "No Legs Manicoche sent a kid along with it when the kid was on his way to school."

I decided I would open it in private. Couldn't think of any reason why anyone else, even a neutral as this guy seemed to be, should be able to report what happened when I read it.

"When's breakfast?" I asked, still holding the unopened note.

"Being served right now. Coming down?"

"Maybe I better get my pants on first. Might scare the ladies."

"I doubt it," he said. "None around who scare easy." When I closed the door he was glancing back at me, moving away.

The note was on a sheet of blank paper that looked as if it had been torn out of the back of a paperback book.

I read it: "Sir. Thanks for help me. I here yer want William. I seed him. Come see me."

I hope Bear Lodge didn't wait breakfast, or they'll still be waiting. I went out a side door so I wouldn't look like Ben Johnson trying for a new world getting-through-the-lobby record.

At the detachment office Pengelly was holding the fort, as he put it, smoking a cigar and drinking coffee. I handed him the note and told him how I'd met No Legs.

"You'll probably find him where he and his sister live," Pengelly said, looking ready to stub out his cigar if such drastic action would be helpful. "Sounds like a break, eh?" Eagerly, "Want me to come along?"

"I don't think so."

He sighed and puffed his cigar alight again. "Okay. You know where the old fort is, and the old log Anglican church? Go down past that and you see a little white house with blue shutters. That's it."

I didn't know whether I should just walk straight there and

let everybody in town know where I was going, which might
not sit well if they figured No Legs was helping where they
had refused to. But I couldn't think of any other way, so I
walked out into the wind and snow again. Anyway, it
wouldn't be light for nearly two hours and in the dark nobody
but the school kids moved outside much. So the streets were
deserted except for some ravens flapping around, and some
chained dogs barking when I went by.

I found the house, which like a lot of northern houses had
a sort of small enclosed entry, like a vestibule, for containing
the worst blasts from the outdoors before the inner door was
opened. I tapped on the outside door. It was opened immediately by a pretty young woman. She had black bangs that
hung right to the straight line of her eyebrows, and below
that regular features, a slightly puggish nose, a wide mouth,
sharply appraising eyes. Her brightly printed calico dress fell
below her knees, where woolen pants led to felt boot liners
that throughout the North are used as indoor footwear. Hers
were scuffed and worn though at the heels.

Obviously she was expecting me. Without smiling, she
jerked her head, signaling me into the tiny vestibule out of
the weather.

I crowded in beside her. It was dark in the tiny area as she
closed the door firmly against the cold and snow but in that
few seconds I'd seen wall hooks festooned with heavy shirts,
parkas, scarves and headgear, the floor strewn with boots.
Then she opened the inner door into a warm kitchen smelling
of fresh bannock and frying fish. The room had a good feel
about it, made me feel comfortable before a word was spoken. A wooden table with its legs painted red and its top
covered with red-checked oilcloth stood in the middle of the
room. Sitting at one end on a battered wooden chair whose
legs were braced with twisted wire sat No Legs. The grime
of the night before was gone. He looked younger than I'd
thought. His face was thin, even ascetic, and his muscular
shoulders and upper arms seemed somewhat out of sync with
his slight build. You sometimes see that upper body devel-

opment in wheelchair athletes. His hair was in the standard ponytail.

"I got your note," I said, as his sister poured a mug of tea, set it at one end of the table and gestured that it was for me. There was a chair so I sat down.

Without a smile, "Yeah. I figgered you had or you wouldn' be here."

His sister put two big pieces of fried fish on a plate, hot bannock on another plate, and set it all in front of me where a place already had been set.

"I gotta ask you," he said, "what you wanta see William for?"

The North is not the place for skimming through the answer to a serious question, especially when the questioner's face could be remembered from not many hours earlier, full of torture and anguish.

I told the whole story as I knew it, starting with the bare bones of what I'd heard of Morton's collapse in Inuvik and my sight of him two days later when he was carried aboard the aircraft. His eyes were intent on mine. He shook his head and grimaced when I told of the shots, my vain attempt to do something, the instant death.

Obviously since our meeting last night No Legs had heard parts of this from his sister and maybe others. But some things he hadn't been told, including the murderer's escape by snowmobile, possibly heading this way.

Then, going back, I told of the part involving William, that he had been with his father but hadn't told anyone about what happened just before his frantic call for an ambulance. And also that some people William had hung out with had fled Inuvik the next day in an aircraft that might have come down around here in the Monday storm.

"I heard that plane," he said. "I was in my shack. It seemed low."

I said that maybe William couldn't tell me anything, but maybe he could.

"Like what?"

"An enemy that no one else knew about. Some trouble that no one else knew about. I don't know, but after he left his father in the hospital he didn't attempt to see him again. I thought that was strange. If he and his father had a quarrel that brought on the attack, which is possible, because other people told me that he and his father had not been getting along, I think"—feeling my way—"if they did have a serious argument, maybe even coming to blows that led to the father's attack, it might have had something to do with the other people getting the hell out of there, even though they left before William did. Only William knows some of those answers."

No Legs was silent, very still. It could have been only a minute or two but seemed longer. An old clock sat on a shelf near the stove. Its ticking sounded loud even against the only other sound, the moaning of the wind outside.

Finally he compressed his lips in a straight line and nodded. "William troubled Morton. Was there drugs involved?"

Nothing had been said between us about drugs, yet he'd asked the question.

"Have you got any reason to believe there might have been?" I asked.

A long blowing out of air, puffing his cheeks with his breath and then letting it out slowly. "Last time Morton was here, jus' maybe a week ago, he seemed worried. He didn' talk about William and drugs, but he talked about drugs, and that they were gettin' in somehow. At first I thought maybe he thought I was usin' drugs, or might have them offered to me, and was tryin' to tell me, don't. But I ast him straight out if that was it and he said, 'Hell, no! I know you got too goddamn much sense.' But I thought he knew somethin' he wasn't tellin' me. You know, those meetin's he was always goin' to, he picked up things. You never had to draw Morton a map."

I let the ensuing silence grow. I didn't want to be talking when I should have been listening. He still hadn't told me

when he'd seen William. I knew he'd do that when he felt the
conversation had reached that stage. I had the feeling he and
I both had spent parts of our lives sitting in silence for as
long as it took, so the opening would be there when there
was something to be said. His sister refilled my tea mug. No
Legs shoved the condensed milk can in my direction.

"So you been lookin' for William for that, to ast about if
he had a fight with Morton."

It was a statement, not a question.

"That's it."

"When I seen him was yesterday," he said. "It wasn't
long after the Nahanni flight come in, cause I heard it both
comin' and goin'. Anyway, I was on my trapline along the
Bear River there and was on'y about half through, I mean I
had the rest of the traps to check. He was on a Skidoo."

"Were you close to him? I mean, did you talk to him?"

He shook his head. "It was snowin' bad and I was two
hunnerd yards away, anyway, upriver from him so he wouldn'
even see my tracks. I hardly saw him for more'n what it'd
take a fox to cross a trail, he was goin' fast, but it was him."

I hardly knew how to ask, but I had to. "Could you really
be sure at that distance, with the storm and all? What I mean
is, one guy on a snowmobile looks a lot like another."

"It was his dog I reco'nized."

I noticed his sister's head move suddenly. Under the black
line of her bangs she gave him a sharp look. The doubt that
I thought I'd noticed from time to time in her eyes, as if she
had been weighing what No Legs said and what I said, was
gone. She went back at her knitting more slowly and raised
her eyes to me and then back to her brother.

"That dog, you couldn' mistake," No Legs said. "When
William was aroun' here all the time, before he starts spend-
in' most of his time in Inuvik, he had a dog team, an' that
was his lead dog, Smokey."

I know about lead dogs, the differences between the good,
the bad and the average. I've seen some of each, from a lead
dog one of my uncles owned that was so undependable that

the only thing my uncle could do was shoot him and buy another, to a lead dog another uncle had that would take you home from wherever you were in the worst blizzard ever to hit the earth.

"That dog o' William's, if I had a team, would be my pick of all the dogs I ever seen or heard of," No Legs went on. "I mean, William sometimes now does bad things, but if he never does another thing right on this earth, that lead dog would stand up. He picked 'im out of a litter when he was jus' a pup a month old."

Talking about dogs was like replaying my own boyhood, when dogs could mean life or death and were brought up carefully. To me dog talk was like remembered music, hourslong discussions of dogs by friends and relatives and people now dead or far away, dimly seen faces along the igloo's sleeping benches with wind battering the smooth snow walls outside; a woman listening while trying to coax a few willow twigs into enough heat to boil a kettle for tea.

"William let Smokey run with the team when he was on'y a few months old, just to build speed and be able to stick with the others. Morton was home then and he's the one taught William what to do, and when. Smokey was maybe a year ol' when William harnessed him aroun' the middle of the team so he'd learn how that part worked. I think he was near two when William began hookin' him in right behin' the lead dog, a good one but gettin' old, Morton had trained 'im. It wasn' more'n a few trips before Smokey learnt what a lead dog done. I remember the first time Smokey went on the lead himself. Morton told William, 'Take him out on a half-day trapline, with the old dog leadin'. Then when you come to head back, harness Smokey in the lead and see if he can follow the fresh trail back home.' And he did."

I broke in, couldn't stand not to, even though I knew it wasn't new to them, actually old, like it was to me, knowledge that's in the blood.

"It's all slow but sure," I said. "First the dog follows a fresh trail like that, only half a day old, and soon he can do one not so fresh and soon he's watchin' where he goes any-where, even a two or three day or longer trapline, so he'll know how he came and how to get back.''

I stopped and No Legs resumed. ''When William sold his dogs he could've got twice't as much if he'd let Smokey go too. But he wouldn'. Allus said if he had a dog team again he wanted Smokey for lead. He'd take him everywhere, everytime he went out, winter or summer. Trained him like he was a house dog. Say, 'stay!' and he'd stay. Say, 'go home!' and he'd go. Say, 'git in the boat, Smokey, and sit!' and he'd jump in and sit in the bows.''

His expression was one of pain, regret, maybe for himself or maybe for William, how could I tell?

''I could mistake William, but not Smokey,'' he said.

''There was that Skidoo, and there was Smokey runnin' alongside or out front, like showin' he could still do the job better.''

I had no more questions but we kept talking. Their par-ents, they told me, both were dead. This had been their house when they were children and their buddy William was in it a lot. We sat there another hour or so, I don't know why except that I had some dog stories, too, like one about how along into April when the snow sometimes got crusty out on the trail and would cut the dogs' feet, we'd make moccasins for them . . .

No Legs: ''What of?''

''Seal-skin or canvas, but seal is best because with canvas you'd be lucky to have it last a day.''

Then we both produced examples of how some hunters and trappers had the patience to teach a mediocre dog until he was some use, and others had no patience and would be whipping a good dog until he was no good. I told about my father, the one who drowned when I was young, and how people often told me he never bought a dog in his life; was given a male and female when he was fifteen and raised every one he owned after that, training them so good that people were always wanting to buy or make a good trade for breeding stock.

I finally stopped, realizing I had done an awful lot of talking, my reward being that they were easier with me, all stiffness gone.

"I didn' know Eskimos was such big talkers," No Legs said, and his sister giggled and looked to see how I would take it.

"Inuk," I said.

"You goin' after William? I don' know where he was goin' but he ain't back or I would know, or Cecilia."

I had been thinking about it even when I was talking. With the weather still too bad to fly, following him through new drifts by snowmobile wouldn't be any bed of roses. But somewhere in the dog conversation I'd had an idea. What the hell, there was nobody here to say, Matteesie, don't be a fool.

"Anybody still around here with a good team?" I asked. "Six dogs would be best but four might be okay, with a lead one that could follow William's trail even through this snow."

No Legs looked at me long and hard.

"How about it?" I pressed.

His smile was a lovely thing to see, like a guy who had come through a long hard night and was greeting a new kind of day. "There's a woman here with a team. She's a teacher. Useta be at Arctic College in Inuvik and belonged to the dog-team club they got there, goin' out weekends and stuff. Don' know how good her dogs are but"—laughing—"they go by me like the bloody wind sometimes."

That's when I had another idea, the kind that zooms into the head and out of the mouth all in the same breath, with no time left over for considering the ins and outs, the on this hand and on the other hand.

He would know the territory and he was friendly.

"If we can get them, how about coming with me?" I asked.

I hadn't seen a look like his before. It was like, through his eyes, without a sound, he was crying and cheering at the same time.

SIX

When I got back to the detachment a little after ten the grey dawn was breaking and the snow thinning out. Two phone messages were waiting. One was timed 9:05, a few minutes after I'd left to see No Legs. It read: Call Inspector Ted Huff RCMP Inuvik. The other, timed three minutes later, was for me to call Maxine at the CBC.

I decided not to take them in order. Except when I was at her place and she might call to say she was just leaving the office and was there anything I needed, Maxine had never called me before, anytime, anywhere. No long-distance chit-chats for her even though, as she once confessed in an uncharacteristic moment, she'd often hope I'd call her. Pursuing me as if we were married or betrothed or even something lower on the Richter scale was not part of her style. I could only hope this variance from the norm was because of some super good news she had to impart. I dialed the CBC number.

She did not have super good news. When she heard my voice she said fervently, ''Thank God!''

Before I had a chance to ask what we were thanking Him

for, she said, ''Gloria's got to talk to you. She started to try
to get you last night but . . .''

She sounded more upset than I'd ever known her to be.

''But what?''

''She didn't know where you were, exactly, so made the
call person-to-person figuring NorthwesTel could track you
down. When she was spelling your name for the operator I
guess Jules Bonner must have arrived outside our door. Next
thing she knew, he kicked the door open and yelled that he'd
heard who she was calling and grabbed the phone from her
and hung up. Then he started bashing her around, which is
about where I came in . . .''

Her voice sort of broke up and she was silent for a few
seconds except for a muffled ''Damn!'' as she got control.
''She told me they'd had an argument at his place a little
earlier. She'd told him that now Morton was dead anyway,
she wished she'd talked to you before you left. When she
said that, he threatened her and must have followed when
she left. When I got home from work I could hear this
Jesus uproar and when I got in there he was beating the
hell out of her.''

''With all the noise, wasn't there any neighbour or somebody who'd help?''

After a pause, she said, ''It wasn't necessary.''

''You mean you scared him off? Right away?''

''Not right away. The bastard had to come to, first.''

''Whaddaya mean, come to?''

''I knocked him out, or pretty near. Down, anyway.''

''Jesus! How?''

''I hit him with one of my skis.''

Maxine is about five feet zero. I'd never kid her again
about leaving her skis in the front hall.

''While I was trying to get Gloria back together he took
off. I didn't try to stop him. I wanted to call the Mounties,
but she was pretty well in hysterics and anyway said she'd
refuse flat to talk to them and pretty soon it didn't matter
much . . .''

Didn't matter much? I thought it but didn't say it.

"I was in the bathroom for just a couple of minutes and when I came down that new bottle of vodka you left was half gone and she was chug-a-lugging it. I had to wrestle her for it and then carry her to bed. But I phoned the inspector this morning from here in the office. He told me that they'd been looking for Jules on something else, he didn't tell me what, left messages and so on, but hadn't caught up to him."

"I sure wish we'd been able to get on this last night," I said.

She properly did not interpret this as a criticism. That makes her the opposite of the more common type, who live on imagined slights. I think of Maxine as lovable for this and other reasons. "Sure, but anyway she's okay this morning." Pause. "If being scared half to death can be called okay."

"What scares her now? Bonner'll know he's in trouble. He won't show up there again."

No joking now. "One of the things he told her while he was beating her up was that if she spilled her guts to you, the same thing would happen to her that happened to Morton Cavendish."

I felt the menace like a shiver.

"We could have tried harder or longer to get you last night, sure. But my life can't . . ." She abandoned that in mid-sentence. I was pretty sure she had started to say that her life couldn't be predicated on leaning on me, and then decided that would go without saying and therefore was better unsaid. "When we did try to get you this morning, Nicky Jerome told us to try Bear Lodge. The guy checked your room and said you'd gone out. Anyway, she still wants to talk to you. You having any luck with William?"

I said, "Not so's you'd notice it. Can't even find him. But I finally found someone who admits *seeing* him. Where's Gloria now?"

"At home with all the doors locked."

"I'll call her," I said. "I had a call from the inspector this morning but haven't returned it. Probably about the same thing."

"When you call her," she said, "let it ring twice and then cut it off and call again. Otherwise she won't answer."

I hung up, pondering. Bonner didn't strike me as the physical kind even with someone he outweighed, and a woman at that. He must have the heat on him hard. But where from? Could what Gloria knew be so drastic that even a career non-combatant like Bonner would be pushed into threatening her life?

Ted answered his phone on the first ring after the switchboard announced me.

"Matteesie, we got something going here," he said.

I told him that I'd been talking to Maxine and had heard about Bonner clobbering Gloria and threatening her life if she talked to me.

"What do you think she knows?"

"I don't know until we talk to her."

"She won't answer the phone or the door," he said. "What we've done after Maxine called is have a car parked outside the house, a plain car belonging to one of our people. There's a guy in it. If Bonner shows up we take him. We want to ask him about those airport phone calls, anyway. Couldn't find him, all day yesterday. If Gloria tries to leave we take her into protective custody."

"I'll call her and call you back."

"What if she doesn't answer?"

"She'll answer. She and Maxine have a code. I'll let you know what she says right away." I hung up before he could ask me what the code was. I could imagine him yelling, "Hey! Matteesie!" and then banging up the phone, maybe angry, but I could survive that.

The phone in Maxine's house rang twice. I cut it off and dialed again. When Gloria answered I could hardly tell it was her voice.

"It's Matteesie," I said.

"Oh, God, Matteesie," she said. "It's about Morton. I wish I'd been able to talk to you about that before you left."

"Why didn't you?"

She said brokenly, "I didn't have the guts. I hadn't put it all together."

I made my voice as kind and reassuring as I could though I didn't feel kind and reassuring at all. I felt close to something important, and wished I was there. Sometimes questioning someone who is near hysterics works if you can be there and keep everything calm, let it come out. While dialing, I'd switched on the tape machine to record the call. I didn't tell her that. I didn't want to spook her any more than she already was. The part of me that belongs to the police made that decision easy enough. I'd keep the tape myself until I figured out what to do with it.

She talked and I asked soft questions and she answered, sometimes slowly, but she answered. I had to fill in some parts from my imagination, but that wasn't hard. It all took a while because sometimes she wailed and stopped and couldn't go on. She wasn't a rock, like Maxine.

As we talked, Pengelly came in and looked at me curiously and then wrote me a note: "There's a woman teacher who sent a note to me, she's trying to get in touch with you. Something about a dog team."

He raised his eyebrows in a question.

I made the kind of a motion an umpire uses when he's signaling that a base runner is safe at first. It was the best I could do on short notice.

The tape kept on rolling. Words, silences, the odd sob, from her; from me mmmhmmmns, prompting here and there, soft questions. When I thought I had all I was likely to get I told her to sit tight, try to stay calm, Maxine would be home soon in her lunch hour, and also told her about the unmarked car standing by and that she was to phone me here at the Fort Norman detachment if she remembered anything more.

I gave her the phone number and in case she didn't write it down reminded her that it's also in the phone book.

She sighed at the end, "I feel better now, Matteesie. But I'm so sorry. Maybe I could have helped. Maybe I could have stopped something . . ."

She sounded as if she might be about to cry again but if so there wasn't much I could do.

As I hung up Pengelly and Nicky Jerome were hanging on my every soft word, trying to figure it out. They'd have to wait. I dialed Inuvik. "I talked to Gloria and got it on tape," I told Ted. "I'd better replay it for you so you can tape it."

"Give me the gist first. The tape I'll listen to later."

Right away I had to make a decision about Gloria's right to some personal privacy. But the stakes were high enough that I figured personal privacy didn't apply right now. "I don't know whether you were aware, but Gloria and Morton had been seeing quite a bit of each other—"

"You mean lovers? No, I wasn't aware."

Lovers was the term, all right, but I questioned to myself how serious Morton had been. Not as serious as Gloria, I knew that damn well, because as flaky as she was, she had this thing about being trusting and whole-hearted when she went to bed with anybody, seeing nothing but rosy futures ahead. I remembered that line of Maxine's about the two times Gloria had gone to Edmonton thinking she was going to be married.

"Yeah, lovers," I said, but still wanted to get in my slight cavil. "He insisted on being careful that they meet only in private, which—after all he's a widower—makes me wonder how serious it was from his side. We can't be sure exactly what kind of game he was playing with her, you know, lots old enough to be her father, if that matters, which it probably doesn't, but she thought the sun shone out of him, and that's what started this whole goddamn thing. In Inuvik, he'd get a room at the Mackenzie or sometimes the Finto or the Inuvik Inn, and they managed it without drawing attention. Also, a couple of times she'd go to where there was some conference that he was at.

"Last Saturday when he was there for some meeting or other, after it was over they met in a room at the Finto and when they woke up pretty early, after a while he started quizzing her about if she used drugs, and if so to cool it because he'd heard in Edmonton from somebody in the know that there was a big drug bust coming up in Inuvik."

"Shit!" Ted said.

"Yeah, so much for security. But to look at it another way, all he's doing is warning somebody he cared for. He wasn't going out and spreading the word in a way that might have blown the whole thing—"

"You mean even quicker than it was."

"Well, there's that. But one thing Morton didn't have was names."

"Thank God for small mercies."

"Yeah, but here's the part that'll kill you: when he's laying it on real thick about how she's got to watch herself, be careful who she associates with, because this ring is going to be smashed, etcetera, etcetera, she starts to cry."

There was a silence. Ted didn't need to hear more from me. "Oh, Jesus, no!" he groaned. "She knows who the guys are, or some of them, at least William, and thinks she should warn Morton?"

"Yeah. She didn't know any details, she told me, like where the stuff was coming from or where it was going, but one time when she was at Bonner's place and they thought she was asleep, she heard William telling Bonner that he wanted a bigger cut, and Bonner was to tell Christian that if he didn't get better paydays, to count him out.

"Anyway, knowing what a blow it would be to Morton when he found that William was one of the guys to be picked up, she thought she should tell him. She says she only told him about William, thinking he could maybe get William disconnected in time. But what did happen surprised her. The way she described it is that he went very quiet. They were in bed. He got up and put on a dressing gown and turned the lights on. He thanked her but did not kiss her—'I had to kiss him,' she said, 'but he just stood there, not mad, not unkind, just sort of gone somewhere' is the way she put it. He did ask her not to mention this to anyone, but said nothing more—nothing about seeing her again, seeing William, what he was going to do, anything.''

We both had ideas about what happened next. For all Morton's dead calm when he got the bad news from Gloria, maybe he hadn't yet taken it in and even when he did, might somehow have hoped that she had made a mistake. I don't know when it was that he decided to confront William and find out for himself, but that afternoon he called William's place and left a message on the answering machine telling William to come to see him at the Mackenzie Hotel.

"Gloria told me that," I said. "William had told her. Incidentally, Gloria was fairly good friends with William, but nothing more. She got a little indignant when I asked if she and William ever slept together, said there was no way she'd do that with Morton's son.''

"Maybe she saw herself more as William's stepmother," Ted said drily.

I laughed. Had to. She wasn't *that* flaky.

"But anyway, that afternoon, last Sunday, she and William had some drinks, at Bonner's place. A lot of drinks. Some time in there apparently William checked his phone messages—his apartment is only a couple of minutes away—and found that his father was looking for him to come to the Mackenzie.

"When I met the two of them at Maxine's around eight they were both walking pretty crocked but it was only later when they went downtown for something to eat and more drinks that William told her about his father's message and that he had to go and see Morton at the Mackenzie.

"She knew what it was likely about, but he didn't, of course, and complained that every time he and Morton got together they'd argue, especially when one or the other was half cut. He told Gloria he had half a mind just to ignore the message, say he never got it, and hope Morton would go away. But he didn't ignore it. He went.

"From then on, it's partly her guesswork, but you gotta figure she knew them both pretty well. William was drunk when he left her in the bar and it was late in the evening so probably Morton had had some, too. She figures that when William arrived, Morton probably just asked the question and then, however the answer went, there was a huge shouting match, maybe even some shoving, and sometime along there Morton collapsed. But meanwhile just his question, the way he'd have put it, drug gang and so on, would have alerted William. He must have been beside himself, certainly not wanting his father to die, but knowing that only a few minutes of consciousness could do a lot of damage to everyone involved if his father decided that way. We just don't know what was in the mind of either of them.

"From the hospital William went to Bonner's place. Gloria was there, but had passed out in a bedroom upstairs. She didn't even know William had been there, until morning. But I think we have to figure that William told Bonner right away, this would be sometime after midnight, that his father knew enough to blow the whistle on them. Then Bonner would get word to Christian—"

"And the balloon goes up," Ted said. "Goddamn."

I was remembering the news reports Monday saying that Morton, although conscious for brief intervals, was in critical condition. Doc Zimmer had told me that around noon Bonner called and was told in what would be the Doc's most reassuring tones, thinking it was going to be passed on to William, that even though Morton couldn't speak or write right now in his brief periods of consciousness, he might recover with the kind of care he could get at the stroke facility in Edmonton.

"That must have been when murder first got on the rails as a possibility," the inspector said softly.

Well, people have been killed for less; and probably with

less trouble, come to think of it. Christian must have known
exactly where to turn for a hit man. Serious drug guys have
that in reserve, just in case. They learned it from the Co-
lombians. God knows there are enough drug-related killings
to indicate that anybody in the racket must know where the
hired gun types are to be found, at short notice. I don't have
to put my collar on backwards to tell a continent brought up
on "Miami Vice" that the drug business isn't all nice guys
with ponytails and granny glasses listening to their old folkie
records. Even though anybody like Christian running drugs
from Texas to the Arctic and then back to southern Canada
would be fairly small potatoes, well below the enterprise's
chief executive officer, he'd have to be able to act when
threatened. Still, it had never really seemed likely to me
before that in the Mackenzie River Valley it could happen
this fast.

Now I did think of the simple logistics of lining up a con-
tract killer familiar with both handguns and snowmobiles,
briefing him in a fairly substantial way, and having the job
done between one night and the next. Central Casting would
have thrown up its hands and said, "You've gotta be kidding."

It would help if he knew the Norman Wells airport setup,
but it wasn't necessary: all the other four knew. And there
had been lots of money to offer. Fifty thousand, say, could
get many a nasty thing done.

Christian would have known that as long as Morton was
in hospital, bumping him off and getting away with it would
be just about impossible. But even on Monday noon everybody was being quite open at the hospital about Morton
maybe being moved. That would give Christian, if he was
calling all the shots, the idea that bumping him off at Norman
Wells was possible. But because he wasn't going to be there,
he would tell Bonner everything to do; to keep a close check
on Morton's condition, when he'd be moved, how, and when
to make the phone call to put into effect what Christian al-

ready had decided they'd do, maybe even making the arrangements on spec.

I'd been thinking all that to myself. This phone call had been like a conference, with silences. Now I said the obvious. "He must have known somebody to call who could get to Norman Wells Tuesday *before* the first flight that could carry Morton."

"Then as a safety backup," Ted said, "he decided he and Batten would get out right away, Monday afternoon, with the money, thinking it would be easy enough to come back if Morton died naturally, or if murdering him took the heat off. It all figures, even the part about leaving William and Bonner behind. Not a bad plan. They'd have no drugs, no large amounts of money, really not a hell of a lot we could hang a charge on. We had to catch them with evidence or there was no goddamn case. We didn't know then about the likelihood of half a million bucks."

We'd pretty well covered it all, except, as I put in, "The only hitch being that on the flight out they seem to have disappeared out in the bush somewhere, maybe dead for all we know. Or maybe alive, figuring out their next move."

I still didn't mention my theory that maybe they were waiting for the murderer to show up and then all go together.

A few seconds of silence ensued before he sighed, "Well, I guess that's it, Matteesie, except for finding the bastards. We can hold Bonner on the assault business with Gloria when we catch up to him. But until the search planes can get into the air again, which looks like tomorrow, from the forecast, we're up the creek on Christian and Batten. And what about William?"

The inspector's question was still hanging there when a woman came into the detachment office, shoving back her parka hood. She was young, fit-looking, somehow like one of those women who run, not jog, a few miles a day. When

I heard her ask for me, I had an idea she was the dog-team lady. She had a very determined expression.

I answered Ted's question about William. "Having trouble catching up to him, too. Keep you informed."

"Please do that."

I also decided not to tell him my dog-team idea right then, but hung up and went over to the counter, smiling my best smile.

She was smiling, too. I soon found that she almost always smiled. It had nothing to do with having a kindly disposition. "I'm Edie McDonald," she said. "I teach at the Chief Albert Wright School and have a dog team, as I believe you've heard."

I liked her looks. Good mouth, no makeup, curly brown hair cut short but not too short. A big nose. Once I read that people with big noses are almost invariably forceful and rather prying, which might be the derivation of the derogatory tone one uses when referring to people who stick their noses into things. Until I got to know Edie McDonald I thought that was probably just an old wives' tale, like women being the weaker sex.

I also soon found that most of the time, no matter how tough she was being, she smiled, putting people off guard and leading them to think of her as that nice Edie McDonald. Until they found out differently.

"That man with no legs came over to the school a little while ago and said you were interested in borrowing my dog team for some important police business," she said.

"That's No Legs Manicoche," I said, figuring she should know his name. Did I say I liked her smile? Nice big white teeth. She seemed very much the co-operative type. Might even think I was cute.

"No Legs. Very descriptive," she said, smiling at me winningly. "Imaginative, even. I used to know a man with only one leg, but they called him Stumpy, which I thought was not very precise."

I like chatty women. Actually, I know a lot of them.

"Anyway," she said. "About my dog team, the answer is, no bloody way."

I'm afraid I stared. I also spluttered. It is somewhat of a tradition in the north that people pull together, help one another, trust the police not to ask favors unless they are important. A stranger appears out of the blizzard and you share what you have to eat and drink.

Edie McDonald was not like that at all.

"This probably surprises you," she said.

"Yes, it does," I said. It was no trouble to look hurt. I *felt* hurt. "I'm here on a murder investigation. There's a man I have to question who has gone off into the bush south of here on a snowmobile. I don't know where he was heading so I don't know where to go to look for him. But I know that a good dog team has a lot of advantages in a search like that."

"They're a hell of a lot quieter than a snowmobile," she said.

"Right."

"And they tend to go where someone else has been. I mean, left to their own instincts they like to follow a trail if there is one, which there won't be much of after all this wind and snow."

I agreed with that, too. So I knew that any pitches I could make she already knew and didn't have to be told.

"A good man has been killed," I said, and even that seemed to come out lamely. "His son has disappeared and might be in trouble himself. I just thought you might like to help."

Talk about lame. I could catch out of the corner of my eye that Pengelly was trying to hide a smile. Nicky Jerome wasn't even trying to hide his. They must have run into Edie McDonald before.

"Let me tell you," she said, never ceasing to smile. "When I first came north, I didn't know my ass from third base. I also got bored to death. I almost even took up knitting so I'd have something to do besides drink and deal with guys making passes at me. I mean, I could have stayed in Calgary and done all that.''

I thought of remarking that I imagined she would be very good at it and no doubt, with her looks, would have lots of practice.

I might have said that to some women. But it would not be smart, I felt, to say it to this one.

Just as well. ''That was four years ago,'' she said. ''Then I decided, screw this. I'd always had dogs at home. Show dogs. Show dogs were no use here, some bloody husky would eat them, and then I read an ad in *News North*. Six-dog team for sale. Easy terms to responsible person. I went to have a look. They were skin and bones, they always cost a lot to feed, but at least the guy who owned them had done the best he could until he realized he really couldn't afford them, what with his wife having to stop work when she had a baby.''

There she smiled brilliantly. '' 'It's an ill wind' . . . anyway I bought them, along with some harness and a broken-down komatik.''

''And you got them in shape,'' I said winningly. Any compliment in a storm. ''What did you feed them?''

''Frozen fish. You can get them in Inuvik at a dollar per fish. Then I bought a good pickup in Edmonton and drove it to Inuvik over the Dempster Highway and fitted it up so that I had six dog cages in the bed of the truck. The fixed-up komatik rode on top of the cages. Took me months to get the whole outfit operative, dogs healthy and all. Then every winter weekend and sometimes in between I'd go out with the few other people in Inuvik who had dogs, and I had fun. But I got tired of Inuvik. Too civilized, too many civil servants. Guys I'd rejected before were making passes the second time around. So when the job in the school here came up I applied for it and got it. Last summer I put the whole outfit on a barge, pickup, dogs, dog feed and all, and came down here where there's more places to go that aren't full of people.''

It was a long speech but apparently she had enjoyed making it.

"After all that," she said, "you can understand my dogs aren't for loan or hire. I drive them myself; nobody else does. But I thought instead of just saying no, I should explain why, and that's why."

There are some people you can argue with and maybe convince. I had just about decided on the evidence that she wasn't one of them. Which meant, almost, that that was that. But then I had one final crazy idea. What the hell—I really didn't like the idea of going after William on a snowmobile. With him long gone by now, God knows where, I didn't think I'd have a chance.

"So what you're saying is that nobody but you drives your dogs, but you like getting out and around and doing interesting things."

She smiled. "You're a quick learner."

"Okay," I said, "how about we provide all the dog food and guarantee in writing return of your dog team and equipment in exactly the condition everything is in now, you to be the judge of that, and you come along and drive."

She looked at me piercingly. For the first time she wasn't smiling. I had an idea I was being summed up mainly from the standpoint of, could she stand my company?

"You know something about dogs?" she asked, and then the smile returned. "That's probably a dumb question."

I nodded. Twice, to cover both the question and the related opinion.

"You got a deal," she said.

Pengelly and Nicky broke up in the background.

"Right now," she said, looking at a big gadget-filled wrist watch she wore with the face of it on the inside of her left wrist, "I'm due back in school for one o'clock. We could get the outfit ready after school tonight and go tomorrow."

She was scarcely out of the door when the phone rang again.

"It's for you, I can tell," Pengelly said. "What you need is a bloody social secretary."

Gloria now had her voice well under control. "I remembered something," she said. "Last summer there was a big guy here. I remember him because he said he was from Nashville, but had never been to the Grand Old Opry, couldn't stand country music, liked hard rock better, like Black Sabbath. He was a friend of Batten's, they'd known one another in the States, and Christian seemed to know him, too. The three of them were drinking at the Inuvik Inn. When William and I got there and we were introduced the guy said that where he came from any woman who wasn't white would screw anything that moved, and is it the same with you, sweetie? William jumped up and there would have been a fight but Batten held them apart, and then we left.

"Anyway, his name was Billy Bob Hicks. One night a month or two later when Batten was high and happened to mention Billy Bob and William said he was an asshole, Batten told William not ever to say that to Billy Bob's face. He said that one guy in the world he'd never fool around with was Billy Bob, because he shot first and asked questions afterwards, and if he hadn't done that once too often he'd still be tending bar in Nashville, instead of Yellowknife. I just thought it was a lot of drunken Yankee bullshit at the time. Now"—she paused—"I'm not sure. Maybe I'm crazy, but I been thinking about him, and I can *imagine* him doing . . . that . . . to Morton."

"Tending bar in Yellowknife," I said. "You know where?"

"No, but people would know him. He's really tall. When he was here he had his hair cut long at the back and short on top and he has a long jaw, I remember his jaw. And he blinked a lot, as if he couldn't see very well. And he sort of slouched when he walked." She stopped and there was a silence. "Thought I should tell you."

I phoned Yellowknife and got a sergeant I know and said,

"I'm going to describe a guy to you, maybe from Nashville, southern accent anyway, maybe a bartender there, name might be Billy Bob Hicks."

I repeated Gloria's description.

"Well," the sergeant said, "that fits a guy who's worked for two or three places around town, but the name is wrong. This one's name is Dave something. I'll find out for you."

"Can I hang on?"

"Sure."

He was back in a couple of minutes. "Dave Hawkinsville. What do you want to know?"

"Where he was Tuesday and Wednesday."

"I'll call you back."

He called in about an hour. I was sitting by the phone eating part of Pengelly's lunch. Normally he ate at home, he said, but his wife, Bertha, worked two days a week in the Child Development Centre and Friday was one of her days. Bertha Pengelly's salmon salad sandwiches had more onion and mayonnaise than Nancy Paterson up in Norman Wells put in hers, but were equally good. It really helps to know guys whose wives are not above making good, or even excellent, sandwiches.

My sergeant friend in Yellowknife detachment said, "The guy I mentioned, Hawkinsville, flew to Edmonton Monday on Northwest Territorial's evening flight. They fly two a day to Edmonton, the morning one to Edmonton International and the evening one to Edmonton Municipal, so that's where he'd go, to Edmonton Municipal. Seems it was sort of a surprise to the place he worked, but people do decide things suddenly around here sometimes, especially when it comes to getting out in January. Told a couple of people he wouldn't be back, but to think of him lounging on the beach at Waikiki. His ticket was just to Edmonton, one way. People said he got a phone call at the bar around one or so in the afternoon, bought his ticket about two. Took all his stuff from the hotel where he was staying, so I'd guess he was serious."

"Thanks," I said. "And damn it."

"Take it easy, Matteesie."

About an hour later I called the sergeant back. "Look," I said, "this is a long shot, but it's on the Morton Cavendish murder and long shots is all we've got. You don't have a picture of that guy Hawkinsville, do you?"

"No. I checked. He's been clean here. Not squeaky clean, but no charges. A Metis woman complained he'd tried to do it to her, but there really wasn't enough to lay a charge on."

I said, "Know anybody who was on the Tuesday Canadian Airlines flight from Edmonton that goes through there in the morning?"

"I'm pretty sure I could find somebody. You mean the guy might have come back?"

"It's worth a check. Like I told you, a long shot."

But long shots do come in sometimes. The sergeant called back at four to say that a bank loans officer who knew Hawkinsville slightly from drinking at a place where he'd worked thought she had seen him on the Tuesday morning flight from Edmonton. "But she was coming off a holiday and was slightly hung over herself, she says, and walking along an aisle she was past him before she really took a good look, and then she figured she must be wrong. This guy on the plane didn't have a moustache and Hawkinsville did."

Of course, he could have shaved it off. Making at least two men in the world, him and me, with no moustache. "Know anything about his habits?" I asked. "I mean, interests?"

"No. What is it you're looking for?"

"A guy who's at home on a snowmobile and knows something about the bush and maybe has an interest in guns."

"Well, the snowmobile fits. He left his here with a dealer, for sale. I don't know anything about an interest in guns. You think he might be the guy who shot Morton?"

"I'm just guessing. A fairly flimsy tip."

"Better put it on a telex. Then more people around here can be watching, or might know something."

So I asked him to put it on telex to Edmonton, asking for

a check of the flight crew in Canadian's Tuesday flight north for anyone who might remember seeing a guy of the following description on that flight, or any Edmonton counter agent who sold him a ticket from Edmonton to Norman Wells or beyond for that flight, and to ask around for any other Yellowknife-bound passenger who might have noticed him.

His height, southern accent, slightly hunched walk and habit of blinking, as described by Gloria, could be Dave Hawkinsville or Billy Bob Hicks or both in the same skin.

S E V E N

Heading out of town the next morning a little before ten, the beginning of enough daylight to run by, lights still showed in most windows, falling in yellow rectangles on snow piled against the sides of houses. Edie's dogs belted along at a gallop, running fresh, the big, the small and the middle-sized, all of them mixed breeds with some husky here, some wolf there, and a lot between—including a black-and-white bitch named Alice that looked like a border collie. If any of the few Fort Norman people about were curious, none showed it. There weren't that many dog teams in town any more but Edie's was seen often enough to be glanced at and then ignored. The temperature was minus thirty-six and the sun wasn't due above the horizon until about 10:30, but was reflected in a growing rosiness on clouds to the south. Including the pre-sunrise half light now and twilight at the end of the day we'd have maybe seven or eight hours. If we used it all and hadn't found William, we planned to stay out overnight.

In some ways I was reminded of moves when I was a kid, except that our loads then were a lot heavier. Hell, we even used to pile stones on komatiks when we were training young dogs, to get them used to the weight they might have to pull when things got serious. No Legs and I didn't add that much to the weight. When we started, Edie was on the back, No Legs and his sled ahead of me on the komatik along with bedrolls, food box, primus stove, its fuel, rifle and a seven-by-seven nylon tent that weighed like a feather compared to the old caribou-hide jobs of my childhood.

I was having fun. Why not? So the quarry was maybe a murderer, maybe an accessory or accessories to murder, or at the very least clues as to the present whereabouts of same. I felt good, No Legs felt good, and I had an idea that Edie wouldn't be here if she didn't feel good. All in favor? Carried.

Up front Edie's lead dog, a half-husky, half-Labrador named Seismo, was straining into his collar in a manner that struck me as dedicated. Earlier when the dogs were being unchained for harnessing, No Legs kept catching my eye and jerking his head at Seismo and then grinning, one old dog man to another. Seismo had snarled and lunged at every dog in turn except his obvious favorite, the smallish Alice. Such behavior wasn't unusual in a good lead dog, the daily reminder: I'm the boss. Kicking and flailing with whatever she could grab, Edie would straighten him out.

But then he had showed another side: Seismo the comedian. When Edie was hooking him up and had the harness only half on, he rolled on his back waving his legs in the air like a puppy, his eyes never leaving Edie as he calculated how far he could push her. Her string of mule-team curses informing him that party time was over seemed to be as much a part of the routine as his fooling around, because then he stood like a rock while she completed his harnessing, and if any of the others so much as moved while they were being hooked up he'd snarl and plunge threateningly. Now on the trail he was out in front, leaning into his collar, belly close to the snow, legs pumping powerfully, his traces the tightest of all. Nose to tail behind Seismo, the others, good strong dogs, leaned hard into their collars and traces under the lead line that ran back to Edie.

Edie left her perch occasionally to glide along on her snowshoes when a slope ahead made the pulling more difficult. I started out doing the same in such situations. It's the decent thing to do, you know, saving the dogs. The first time we had a slope to climb I was off and running easily enough.

I had a new set of what are called trail shoes, just like Edie's, narrower and more tapered and therefore a little easier to run on than standard snowshoes. I felt real good in them the first time—for several minutes. Then I began to struggle. Somewhere over the years my old easy mile-eating gait had abandoned ship. Thighs and calves cried for mercy. Thank God for the komatik, on which I flopped, to wide grins from Edie and No Legs.

It didn't soothe my damaged ego to think what I'd shelled out for them last night at the Bay. Reminded me of Tom Berger's 1975 inquiry into environmental and social impacts of the Mackenzie Valley pipeline. Chief Paul Andrew of the Fort Norman band, testifying passionately in defence of traditional Native lifestyles, had detoured briefly into the white man's justice system. He called it, "A system which punishes Indians for stealing from the Bay, but does not pusnish the Bay for stealing from the Indians." The chief could have included Eskimos as well. The only alleviating element was that they were well-made, and by Natives of here, not of Taiwan.

Coming out of town we traveled along the south side of the Bear River until we got to where No Legs had last seen William. There No Legs stretched out an arm to point the way more or less south. At the signal Edie yelled, "Gee!" and Seismo wheeled abruptly right, into the bush.

No Legs had never stopped smiling from when I first saw him that morning. He was good-looking anyway, with deep-set eyes and a broad face now mostly covered by his bala-clava. He and Edie must have been about the same age and although neither was exactly Rotarian by temperament they were close enough to talk and did occasionally even after we set out, No Legs soon calling the dogs by name.

"I think that Seismo like that Alice," he called once.

She laughed. "You're not kidding. Marriage made in heaven. Don't think I'd even have to chain that dog as long as I chained Alice."

Bush isn't great for dog teams—they're better in the open—but this stretch we were going through now had been open enough for a snowmobile and was only a little more difficult for the dogs. After days of snow and wind, naturally there were few signs that anything except animals, whose tracks were everywhere, had passed this way. Yet what signs there were, we found. I came to have more and more respect for Seismo on the lead. He either sensed the course that William had followed, or was making the same decisions as William about which was the easiest way to go. Edie rarely interfered. Twice in the first fifteen minutes after leaving the river, we'd seen on open spots the unmistakable serrated tracks of a snowmobile, hardened and swept clear by the wind. Both times these were at the top of rises where the bush was thin.

It was a nice day, clear, no wind, no noise to inhibit conversation. Edie, seeming hardly breathless at all after running up the rise we'd just negotiated, was doing trapline research. She'd have to call to be heard, and he'd call back.

"What's the best day you ever had on your trapline, George?" she asked once.

"Nine," No Legs said. "Four beaver, three otter, two marten."

"Was this after you lost your legs?" Edie asked.

"No."

"Do you skin them right on the spot, or what?"

No Legs: "Depen's what time o'day it is, how cold, how much more trapline you got. If you're goin' to be out long they freeze and you can't skin 'em frozen, but in my shack I got a stove and if I got a frozen animal I put it unner my bed for the night. By mornin' it's thawed. I skin it then."

We had come to a down slope. Edie jumped back on the sled. I lumbered along off to the side, getting a little better with the trail shoes, watching for signs but not really expecting much right there with the snow deeper in a sheltered hollow.

"Do you ever find animals dead in your traps?"

"Naw. If they're there long enough, prob'ly somethin' eats 'em."

Somewhat startled, "What? I mean, what would eat them?"

"Usually wolves. Maybe wolverine. Anything that'll eat meat. One time I got sick and couldn' get on the trapline for five days and when I did wolves had eaten everythin' 'cept a fox who'd dug hisself away down in, two or three feet into the snow, and was dead. Maybe they didn' know it was there."

"I guess you'd feel bad when they get wasted that way."

"Yeah, I hate to lose anything."

I thought he realized she meant something else, that he'd feel bad about a trapped animal unable to hide or defend itself, but if so he decided to avoid that debate. Still, his answer could have been taken either way. Even about his lost legs.

"Ever trap a wolf?"

"Yeah. But I don't set that size traps no more. I used to rub beaver castor on the bait for wolves. They go crazy for it. They'd dig halfway to China to get at it. But now the size trap I set for smaller animals won't usually hold a wolf, okay with me. I've found traps sprung, bait gone, wolf tracks around." He paused. "You get out here with no legs and a 150-pound wolf stuck in a trap, you might just wish you was back in town, drawin' welfare."

They both laughed.

We went on, skirting clumps of bush, tough hills, as William's snowmobile trail did. An hour out, the day by now nearly full daylight, we stopped, unloaded tea Thermoses, and called Fort Norman by radio.

"Anything doing? Over."

Pengelly was on duty. "The rescue people are out, but they ain't finding anybody to rescue. Over."

"What's the word from Inuvik? Over."

"They found that Bonner guy and, um, *interviewed* him a little." I think he meant, interviewed him hard. "Decided to forget the assault charge for now and see if he led them anywhere on the main event. Over."

I had an idea. "This frequency we're on, like, if that downed plane is anywhere around, could it be picking us up? Over."

"Sure, wanta send a message? We only take personals. Over."

His kidding about personals was a reference to the highest-rated radio program in the remote districts, called the "Northern Messenger." Babies born, deaths, birthday wishes, broken bones, liquor charges, instructions on what pattern of china to buy or what a polar bear skin sold for; anything and everything is the show's stock in trade.

I didn't have a message to send to Christian, Batten, Johns and Company, but I couldn't help wondering if they were out here somewhere, listening. Or if the guy who killed Morton Cavendish could hear us, he couldn't be far away, either, wherever he'd holed up. Or even William—the whole goddamn bunch of them, huddling around their radio like fans listening to the final game of the Stanley Cup.

All along, we were getting just enough show of snow-mobile tracks, and once a plastic Baggie like those kids take to school holding their lunch, to keep us feeling that William had gone this way, too, a couple of days before. Apart from that, what we saw was snow and bush. A porcupine had eaten the bark from halfway up a tree. Tracks large and small were everywhere. Flocks of ptarmigan in their winter white burst out of cover now and again.

Once the Number 5 dog tried to take off after a rabbit and caused a tangle, plus getting chewed somewhat by Number 4 and Number 6 and a mean snarl and dirty look from

Seismo. Another time Number 4 took a chew out of Number 3 and right away there was a hell of a dogfight going on, mainly Seismo against the world, but before they could get the traces in much of a tangle Edie waded in with her whip and got them separated without much damage done. She ran her team as expertly as any dog-team driver I'd ever seen. Her commands naturally weren't in the language I'd heard most as a child, but had heard lots of since. She'd yell "Chaw!" for the lead dog to go left, "Gee" to go right, "Mush" for go and "Whoa" to stop. I've known dogs long ago who wouldn't know what the hell to make of that.

When I thought of William somewhere ahead I wondered what frame of mind he might be in, why he was out here, whether he was armed, and what he might think about being followed. My alertness on this score was sharpened somewhat by remembering last night's dinner at Pengelly's, after I'd met Edie at her place and quickly became convinced that she had everything well in hand and wanted no effing (as Charlie Paterson might say) interference.

Earlier, Bertha Pengelly had dropped in to the detachment in late afternoon to say that if I could stand caribou sauerbraten and dumplings I was welcome to come to dinner. At this, Pengelly had said he had some rum but no mix, so when I was buying my snowshoes at the Bay I also bought mix. We'd eaten the sauerbraten and dumplings and it was great, although Bertha said it was even better with musk-ox and told Pengelly if he ever got a chance to transfer to Sachs Island detachment, where the musk-ox were plentiful, to take it, and they'd have me to dinner again. Some woman. Anyway, we had eaten and we were drinking and talking.

"I had something last year like you might get ahead of you tomorrow, y'know," Pengelly said, glass in hand, stripped down to braces and shirt and pants in the comfort of his own home.

The living room was maybe twelve by twelve, and included a chesterfield, two big chairs, the TV set.

"I mean," Pengelly went on, "going out into the bloody

bush not knowing when a goddamn gun is going to go off and drop you bleeding in the snow.'' .

"Which is very white, and sets off the blood nicely," I said companionably. After the second drink, rum can be like that.

Bertha had been listening. She appeared in the kitchen doorway. She must have weighed 200 pounds but on her it looked all right. Her face was pretty, and cheerful, and she had nice hair. Whether this shade somewhere between off-white and golden was its original color, I have no idea, but it was fluffy and fell in curls over her forehead and around her ears, and besides that she had personality.

"Yeah," Pengelly mused. "You get these things sometimes. I sure as hell remember this one."

"Come on, Steve," Bertha protested. "You're not going to tell him *that* story, are you?" She turned to me. "It's all about how he got scared damn near to death."

"Well," Pengelly said, "since it's the only time I ever got scared since I used to be undercover in Toronto as pals with a lot of hair-trigger coke importers, I gotta tell it, don't I? It's all in the line that when you're hunting somebody you gotta be careful, what's wrong with that?"

The wind had died down outside, the sky clearing. We knew the search people would be in the air at daylight for sure, meaning that when my safari struck off with the indefatigable Edie and her dogs, we'd be checking by radio often in case everything got solved before we had to make some really interesting decisions about sleeping arrangements in our tent.

"Ah, well, what the hell," Pengelly said. "We just came here in the fall a year and a half ago, you know. So last spring I'm pretty green and I get a call, maybe six in the morning, that there's a body in a snowbank down by the old fort. The guys who found it had been out drinking, that seems to happen a lot when the days get longer and there's a lot of steam to let off, and when I get to the alleged body what I find is that it isn't really a body at all, she's not dead, just *damn near* dead, had hell beaten out of her with this guitar.''

I sensed that I was in the middle of events beyond my control but I had to say it. ''This guitar?''

''Yeah! This guitar! Actually, the guitar was very impor- tant in court later. What happened was there's this guy called Oscar Frederickson, an Icelander from Manitoba, lives with this Metis woman out on the other side of Bear Rock, near the winter road to Norman Wells, and he got a cheque for something, yeah, I remember, got an income tax refund from when he worked on the pipeline, and of course he and his lady—''

''That! God! Damn! Word!'' exclaimed Bertha, enunci- ating each word separately, for emphasis. ''Lady! Used to mean something. These days it means bugger-all! Except maybe somebody who gets laid a lot, if you ask me.''

''Finished?'' Pengelly asked, after a pause.

Bertha nodded decisively.

''Okay,'' said Pengelly. ''Oscar and his *woman* come to town with the cheque and start boozing and spending the money, and one of the things he buys is this guitar. That's what sets off the riot. Some of the evidence in court was that they're in this dining room at Bear Lodge and she throws a bowl of barley soup at him and some of it got *into* this guitar, which really pisses him off, and she's yelling that he couldn't even play a goddamn ukulele, let alone a guitar and him yelling that he can learn, can't he, if every goddamn sideburn in the world can play guitar, he can learn it, and so on, and the upshot is when they get out of there and start lurching around the streets looking for the way home he beats the shit out of her with the guitar. Smashes this new guitar all to hell. Trouble is, he thinks he's killed her. On the way home he meets a guy, in fact, and tells the guy he killed his la . . . pardon me, woman. The guy he tells is the second one who phones me about it, two calls in about five minutes, and then we all meet at the so-called body, which by then has come to and is really hurting, the poor woman.''

"If this was any other story, it already would be too long," Bertha said.

He sipped his rum and said, "So I get her to the nurse and she's got broken ribs and maybe concussion and for sure a broken nose, she's all beat to hell, so I've got to go out and bring Oscar in.

"So I go out there, it's April but the winter road is still in use, and I get as close as I can in the police van. I'm beginning to think a little about he's probably still drunk, maybe still drinking. Oh, yeah, it had snowed overnight, too. So I walk up his path in this fresh snow and I can see smoke coming from his chimney, so I know he's there. I mean, I think he's there. I go and knock on the door, and when nobody answers I open it. There's nobody there but there's coffee on, not even dripped through yet, which I take as being a clue that he hasn't been gone long. Then I notice that from his window I can see my van. So he'd seen me coming. Then I notice that in his gun rack there is no gun. Then I notice that the back door is slightly open. I have a look and can see in the fresh snow there's this one set of footprints, heading for the bush."

My drink was empty and I didn't even notice. "So you came back and got help," I said.

"That's what he should have done," Bertha said. "The stupe."

"I didn't even think about it, right away. I start following his tracks. When I get out of his clearing, there go the tracks off into the bush. That's when I begin to go slower and even stop and look hard at every bush or tree near where his tracks went, and suddenly I thought, shit, if he doubled back he might be fifty feet from me and I don't know it. I know he's out there, he's violent, he's got a gun and he thinks he's killed this, um, woman he's been living with. So what's he got to lose by shooting me?

"I can tell you, I was damn scared. Every step I took it got worse. I thought I was going to, well, you know, mess my pants, I was so scared. I'm even thinking how loud a bang a gun would make on a quiet morning like that. So you know what I done?''

"Did," Bertha said.

"What I done was yell as loud as I could, 'Oscar!'

"And from behind a tree not a hundred feet away comes this yell back! 'What?' he yells.

" 'She isn't dead! She's gonna be all right!'

"There was a pause and then he called, half crying, I could tell, 'You're not shittin' me?'

"So I said I wasn't, and he came out and got into the van with me and came back to the detachment to get charged and then I drove him and his, um, you know, home.''

Well, so much for that. It surfaced in my mind once in a while, helping me pay attention to what lay ahead. We came out of the bush and started along the ice of a smallish river. "This here's the Big Smith," No Legs called. "Runs into the Bear back apiece."

On river ice, out of the bush, the snowmobile track was easier to follow. In most places it would show plainly, fresh snow over the original indentation. By that time I was mostly riding, I wasn't quite in shape to snowshoe even as little as I had, and still have much in reserve. I was saving myself for the playoffs, if any. Just as I was thinking it would be a good idea to run until nightfall, we came around a bend and suddenly No Legs put up a hand, the stop sign. I scanned the horizon ahead for a reason and saw nothing. Edie pulled her dogs to a stop and they flopped down in their tracks, tongues lolling out, all except big Seismo. He sat imperiously on his haunches and stared intently ahead along the river course, ignoring the rest of us. Meanwhile No Legs was quickly maneuvering his sled off the komatik.

Then I saw why. We had just crossed very fresh animal tracks, couldn't have missed the animal by more than minutes, and if my first impression was correct it was an animal that some people who've spent a lifetime in the North have never seen. No Legs poled himself swiftly back to check even though he probably was sure anyway, because when we were all closing in on the tracks and Edie said confidently, "Wolf," No Legs and I said together, "Wolverine."

Edie obviously wasn't used to being contradicted, especially by two guys at once. "Sure looks like wolf to me."

"Five toes," No Legs said.

"Oh," said Edie in a smaller voice, looking closer.

So the three of us and a whole dog team are out in nowhereland looking for a guy who might know something about a murder that he hasn't told anybody yet, and we're doing nature study.

"It's easy to make the mistake," No Legs said gently.

"Not all that easy," I said, relishing the task. I liked Edie, but that doesn't mean I don't enjoy setting the Edies of the world straight once in a while. "All you do is keep in mind that the whole dog family, poodles, spaniels, wolves, foxes, coyotes and so on, has four toes. Everything in the weasel family has five—mink, marten, fisher, wolverine, ermine."

No Legs said, still gently but with a little grin, "So Edie, when some oil guy in Calgary gives you what he says is an ermine, count its toes before . . ."

He let it die there, holding back from finishing the sentence in what some guys might have thought was a good enough and inoffensive crack . . . "before you jump into bed." Maybe he was shy or maybe just shy with Edie, or maybe he instinctively knew, or at least believed, which is not the same thing, that even if a thing did have five toes, going to bed for an ermine was not Edie's style.

Which is how it happened that we were all standing there in the thin daylight, right out of it, reaching for Thermoses and the food box when far ahead, unmistakably, exactly in the direction where Seismo had been staring for the full two or three minutes since we stopped, all of us could hear the merest whisper of a distant snowmobile.

In the circumstances I don't take too much credit for it, but I did come to, first.

"The radio!" I said.

Watching the snowmobile grow rapidly from a tiny dot to

a larger dot, nothing between it and us but the snow-covered river ice, we raised Norman Wells.

"Whaddaya got, Matteesie?" Pengelly's voice crackled. "Over."

"Snowmobile in sight, coming our way," I said. "We're close to twenty miles south of the Bear, in the open, on the, ah, Big Smith River. Whoever it is will be here in less than a minute. Over."

"It's William all right," No Legs called.

"Better leave the radio on," said Pengelly. "Over."

I thought it was William, too, but couldn't be sure yet; there could be other burly guys out on snowmobiles, even here. Whoever it was maybe had seen us for as long as we'd seen him, but probably not; he was looking through goggles and a windscreen and we weren't. There was a point at which, I thought at the time, he did see us. The machine suddenly swerved, the kind of startled movement that might be natural in a lone man cruising along lost in thought when unexpectedly, even shockingly, he finds he has company. At first he steered at slightly less than his former speed on a course that would have taken him around us. All the while he was staring at us intently. His machine was at least a hundred yards past us when he slowed and stopped, stood up on the footrests, and pulled his goggles down to have a look with the naked eye.

With the helmet and face-mask I still couldn't be absolutely sure but No Legs was in no doubt.

"Hey, William!" he yelled, poling his sled a few yards into the clear and then hoisting himself up as high as he could to wave. William couldn't have heard the voice over his motor and a sudden chorus of howls and yodels from Edie's dogs, but he'd know there was only one man around who poled himself along on a light sled. He came in slowly. His snowmobile was a big old Arctic Cat. Behind him on a small sled were lashed two extra gas cans, bed roll, tent, food box. Enough for quite a long trip. No gun unless it was a take-down model stowed under the seat.

The snowmobile engine was ticking over as he stopped a few yards away. I'm not sure that he'd ever seen Edie before, probably not, but something about the situation stopped her from saying anything. There was no, "Hi! I'm Edie! You must be William!" manner to her at all. His glance skimmed her and went right by the smiling face of No Legs as well, although I could see how excited No Legs was. This was his old friend and he wasn't going to be denied. Not yet.

"Cecilia told me to bring you back!" he called, and I had another thought: maybe there was something between William and Cecilia. Which would be natural, growing up friends in the same town, about the same age. Or might have been before he took to what I guess we have to call, in the circumstances, the bright lights of Inuvik. Also, it occurred to me that whatever I was after, and however Edie had been drawn more or less neutrally into what was just a different kind of weekend to her, No Legs probably saw William's actions as understandable enough in a bereaved son, as so many others in Fort Norman did. But William didn't reply in kind.

He was staring at me, obviously badly upset, even though he didn't have the kind of appearance that usually gave such emotions away. Physically, now that he was out of the lighter clothing he'd worn when I met him first, he looked like a biker who had challenged me once in Edmonton, powerful sloping shoulders, hair that was parted in the middle (he'd taken off his helmet) and pushed behind his ears to fall from there to his shoulders. A small amulet or badge hung on a chain around his size seventeen or eighteen neck and he hadn't shaved for a few days, or was growing a beard to go with his droopy moustache.

But he only looked tough until you looked closer. Then his face was drawn, sleepless-looking, and I thought there was a hint of fear in his eyes.

"Where the hell you guys goin'?" he asked.

"Looking for you," I said.

"For what?"

Edie and No Legs had become the audience, non-participating. No Legs' enthusiastic welcome had still not been acknowledged. William's question was blunt. I answered as bluntly.

"After your father collapsed there were questions that maybe only you could answer, but you weren't around. After he was killed, there were a lot more questions. Everybody thought you might have some of the answers, but you still weren't around."

Suddenly the radio crackled. No voice, just a crackle. William jumped and stared, now looking both scared and confused.

"That radio open?"

"Yes," I said. "We called Fort Norman detachment when we saw you coming."

"How'd you know it was me?"

"We didn't."

"Better shut it off," he said.

I shook my head. "We might need to raise them again."

He still sat on his machine, motor idling, as if not certain what to do or say next.

I gave him a chance. "I was on the aircraft when your father was shot."

His voice was abruptly passionate and angry. "I know! Hell of a cop you are! Why didn't you stop it?"

I didn't answer that directly. He knew as well as I did that I couldn't stop it, he couldn't have, nobody could have.

I said, "One of the things we thought you might be able to help with is, who'd want to have him killed. Is there anybody you know who might have done it just the way it was done, kill a man, get away by snowmobile, and disappear?"

There was a slight hesitation, then unconvincing bluster. "How the hell would I know? If I'd known, maybe I could have stopped it from happening at all."

While William and I talked, No Legs looked from one to the other as if our tone puzzled him. Finally he broke his silence. "I'm really sorry, William. You know what your father was to me."

"I'm more than sorry!" William shouted. "Those bastards killed my father!"

"It was only one guy who shot him," I said.

He realized he'd used the plural, but recovered quickly. "There's no way one guy could have organized it!"

"That's what we think, too," I said. Then I hesitated. There were things I could have said about what we suspected, the theories we had. They might do as bait to get him talking, but depending on where he stood in this thing, might do the reverse—scare him off.

So I didn't mention the downed aircraft, Harold Johns, Albert Christian, Benny Batten, Jules Bonner or anyone who could have been named Billy Bob Hicks or Dave Hawkinsville. Instead, I played it completely straight.

"If you can help us in any way, we oughta sit down where we can talk. That's why I came to Fort Norman. When we couldn't find you and knew you'd come this way, I decided we'd better try to catch up and try to persuade you to help."

I was trying to skate around a little, obviously. But I also was sure that wasn't going to work.

"So how'd you know where to look for me?"

I told him that when he couldn't be found in town, we'd had to look elsewhere.

No Legs obviously couldn't stand the futzing around. "I saw you go, William," he said. "I was comin' in from my trapline and saw you and Smokey . . . Hey! Where's Smokey, somethin' happen to him?"

William turned to look at him, his expression stricken, but he didn't answer. No Legs looked at him hard, even opened his mouth to press the question, but in the end said nothing more.

"Why did you take off like that?" I asked.

He took a little time answering. When he did, his rancor was gone. That didn't mean he was telling the whole truth or even part of the truth. But it was at the very least a social note.

"I just felt I had to get away by myself for a while. I couldn't do it around home. Too many people would want to talk, to tell me what a wonderful man my father was . . ."

He slowed to a stop, then, "Which he was, I know. But there were things I had to figure out and I wanted to do it on my own."

At that point I had some figuring to do, too. William had got away from Inuvik without giving the answers the case needed. He'd got away from Fort Norman, possibly for the same reasons. I didn't want to have to chase him any more. That meant we couldn't leave him speeding away now wherever he wanted to go, while we plodded back along the trail admiring Seismo doing his thing. I felt that wherever he had been was important to know, but I also knew that with the distance he could have traveled at snowmobile speed it might be another day or two away by dog team and that being out two days was Edie's limit; she had to be back in school Monday.

I had to make up my mind, and what I decided was that William should not get away from us again. If I had to, I could come out by snowmobile myself or by helicopter and backtrack along his trail. I also wondered what the hell *had* happened to Smokey, the wonder dog that No Legs had been telling me about. His disappearance just made no sense whatever.

I picked up the radio and said, "Pengelly? Over."

"Yes, sir. Over." That sir was something new.

"You've probably heard us talking to William. Over."

"Yeah, but it woulda been a hell of a lot easier to tape if you'd gathered around the goddamn microphone. Got *you*, all right, and the engine on William's snowmobile, but not a hell of a lot else. What's happened to Edie, she been struck dumb? Over."

I didn't bother answering that one. "I just want to let you

know what the plan is. I think the best idea is for me to come back in with William on the snowmobile. Over.''

''Like hell!'' William exclaimed. ''I'm loaded. I can't take a passenger.''

I spoke to him reasonably. ''You got room. That's a big machine. Your best course is to co-operate, help us any way you can.''

I felt like adding that if he'd helped us earlier, we might be getting somewhere instead of out on a frozen river having dumb arguments. But I didn't. I also thought of pointing out that he could be in trouble otherwise, but didn't. ''Let's get going.''

I could tell he was torn between doing as I asked, which he didn't want to do, or taking off and chancing the consequences. In the end he got off his snowmobile and stamped around the way a man does after a long snowmobile ride.

I looked at Edie and No Legs.

They nodded. Neither of them spoke.

''See you back at the ranch,'' I said.

As I spoke, I moved a few steps and swung myself onto the snowmobile behind William—before he could argue any more. It would be an easier ride, I knew, if I could have held him chummily around the waist in the traditional style of a guy out with his kid or a lover or at any rate someone he liked, but I didn't really feel that was appropriate in the circumstances—so I reached down and clutched as much as I could of the seat cover.

William revved the engine and threw it in gear.

I yelled to Edie, ''Tell Pengelly we should be along in an hour or so.''

At the look of them, events moving too rapidly for them to grasp fully without the discussion they no doubt would have on the way back in, I suddenly felt it was time for a little levity.

''And you two behave yourselves, now!''

At least I'd finally made Edie go goggle-eyed.

As we took off I could see them standing there, apparently

in silence. In my last sight of them, Seismo was on his feet looking majestic, Edie was picking up the lead line, and No Legs was pointing after the odd couple on the snowmobile. Suddenly it seemed to me they were both laughing like hell.

E I G H T

There is a form to any murder investigation. Even in the Arctic, where life is supposed to be more simple, you start out knowing not much except that somebody is dead. Then, unless there happens to have been a witness, you try to determine how the person was done in, and by whom. Except with some poisons, identifying the means of murder usually isn't all that difficult—bullet, knife, axe, hammer or some other form of violence nearly impossible to mistake. When you reach the "by whom" stage in an investigation that is really well-organized, as opposed to some guy flying by the seat of his pants, you start a case book on paper or in a computer or both.

The official case book on this one, no doubt someone else was keeping. I keep mine in my head, where insights, intuitions, wild guesses, daydreams or merry little breezes of any other nature have been turned away. Some of these were of little obvious pertinence, such as my sense even now, bouncing along on the back of William's snowmobile, that No Legs and the formidable Edie might just decide not to try getting back tonight. Of course, that had nothing to do with the murder as such, except it had led to putting two people together who even in this small community didn't seem to have noticed one another much before.

I liked No Legs for what so far had been careful insights, and because in the North a man's warm kitchen might tell you more about him than what he'd read or how many legs he had.

Edie, on the other hand, struck me as one of those women who know what they want and when they want it and aren't shy about directing their efforts to that end. At a guess, I certainly wouldn't place her at the truly objectionable end of that scale. I'd known a few of those, having almost offended one once (or was it twice?) by singing my Paul Robeson imitation of "Pull that barge, lift that bale," while lying there unclothed and ready listening to the detailed instructions on how, and with what, I was to make love.

While thinking these warm thoughts I was jolted back rudely to the real world. A sudden turn almost threw me off the snowmobile. I saw that we'd almost hit the bank at a turn in the river. Obviously William hadn't been paying attention.

"Watch where you're going!" I yelled.

"Fuck you!" he threw over his shoulder.

So I concentrated for a while. Riding the back of a snowmobile behind a reckless, angry, maybe scared and possibly vengeful man quickly joined my list of pleasures to avoid. It was cold. The clear day had slid into an exceedingly frosty twilight. Even with my big mitts, I would sometimes have to hold on with one hand while I flexed some feeling back into the fingers of the other. Then it occurred to me that if I'd had a chance at this kind of ride when I was a kid I would have been yelling, "Faster! Faster!" From there I forced my thoughts back in a warmer direction, just as when long ago I would try to ignore miles of tundra by living in my head.

The fact remained that the sane way with darkness coming on would be for Edie and No Legs to make camp in the shelter of this river bank, let the primus stove warm the tent while it warmed the caribou stew we'd brought along, lay out the bedrolls—with mine as an extra—and then cuddle up. I hoped so, anyway. When two people are especially warm toward one another, as they had so quickly become, it seems a pity to stand on ceremony. William and I must have thundered along for a mile or so while I translated that warming thought into me, a girl I'd known in my youth at Paulatuk, and a nice warm igloo out on the Barrens.

Then there was once when I was jolted again. I was pressed closely against William's back. Couldn't help it. That's all the room there was. And suddenly I had a distinct feeling that he was in the grips of something uncontrollable: his back was heaving the way it might when a man is stifling sobs. It was only for a minute or less, but it shook me, forced my mind back to the main event. Unless I misread the signs completely on our only other meeting, with Gloria at Maxine's, he was one of those unfortunates who couldn't run his own life very well, but probably would have wished to have his father proud of him; could do battle with his father over how he lived his life, but would have given anything to have his father say once, just once, "Good job, son." Or, "Thanks, son." But also was just enough of a fumbler that he could have unwittingly played some part in his father's death that would haunt him to his own dying day.

I kept thinking that Bonner should be picked up again if only because, apart from William, he seemed the only one available who might know something about the murder that I didn't. Yet.

The ride seemed interminable, as well as wild. William had the advantage on me in every respect—the handlebars to hang on to, a sight of what lay immediately ahead. When the terrain was rough he could see a bump coming and be ready while each jolt was a total surprise to me and my spine, which rattled up and down like a pogo stick. I tried craning my neck around him to give myself some warning, but he was too bulky. When I did manage to get a brief look at what was coming up, it was never reassuring. The meagre daylight was failing. In the growing dusk the headlight beam jerked back and forth, up and down, now dissolving into the darkening sky and now flashing across a stretch of river bank or scrubby trees.

The only break I got was that William avoided the stretch of fairly rough bush that had hidden him for a while on the way out two days before. This time he stayed on the river where he could make better time. I finally just hung on and let my thoughts wander on what I didn't know of Christian, Batten and Johns, the three I'd never seen except on that wall of photos and clippings in Gloria's room.

Christian, oddly enough, looked Mediterranean—Lebanese, Greek, whatever. His hair was very dark and fitted his head like a skullcap, close to his eyebrows on both sides, and going down into a moustache and beard. The whole effect was of a poker face framed in dark hair, wide at the cheekbones but narrowing at both the forehead and the chin. Batten was a different bird altogether. He had thick grey or white hair in sharp contrast to black (or at least dark) eyebrows, a round face, a smallish mouth that in the photo was open, as if he'd been talking, showing stained and crooked lower teeth. His eyes were unrevealing but his whole expression was not an attractive one; not mean, just closed.

The photo of Johns had shown a handsome man, dark brown hair falling over his forehead on the right side, brushed over his ear on the left. Thin face, long nose, wide mouth, deepset eyes, and unseen but at least as important, a background that—despite the single outburst of bad behavior that had lost him his job in the east and brought him out here—was geared to traditional values.

They were either down and alive, down and dead, or down with some alive and some dead. In the North that image of a crumpled plane in the bush, or out on the Barrens, or on some lake ice, was familiar. Yet relatively few crackups were fatal. Experienced bush pilots were usually so good, lakes, rivers and open spaces so plentiful, that one would never get into trouble without planning immediately what he was going to do about it.

If they had landed safely, kept radio silence and all three were in it together, the money would be enough reason for not using their radio. Until they were really desperate, and even then, rescue would be a dirty word if it meant both they and the money wound up in custody. But how could they manage to avoid that, without outside help? And who could be the outside help? Did that come back to William?

But maybe the three of them weren't partners. If Johns was as dependable as my old friend Thomas Nuniviak said, he would want to be operating his crash finder. The others wouldn't, meaning Batten and Christian against Johns, maybe in a real battle of wills, strengths, even brutality.

I thought all that, bouncing along at high speed with William on the snowmobile. That one show of emotion was not repeated that I could notice. I wondered if he just didn't give a damn what happened next as long as he didn't have to face squarely what had happened in the recent past.

When we reached the first lights of the town's outskirts I yelled, "Stop at the detachment office where we can talk."

Instead, we zipped past the detachment and on through the nearly empty streets until he braked by a small house. When he turned off the machine, the silence was deafening. For a moment we just sat there. Then a door opened and in the light I could see the tall figure of Paul Pennycook, who'd visited me at Bear Lodge on Thursday night with the advice that William's fuckin' business was his own fuckin' business, which I now was doubting more than ever.

Abruptly, all my other emotions dissolved into anger. I climbed off stiffly, as close to making an unwarranted—at least by the real evidence so far—arrest as I'd ever been. If I'd ever had much sympathy for William it was gone now. I faced him. Pennycook watched us from the door.

"You can walk the rest of the way," William said flatly.

I didn't give my next move any thought, just decided that I wasn't getting anywhere being polite. Maybe leveling with him would produce an effect that nothing else had.

"What I want to know first," I said, "is if you know you're a suspect in some drug dealing in Inuvik."

Of course he knew, if Gloria was right. She was sure his father had challenged him on that point. I believed her.

He looked uncomfortable but he still said, "Like hell I am!"

"I also want to know if you and your father came to blows that night before he collapsed, and what the fight was about, and where he got the bruise on his head that he had when he was brought into the hospital and Doc Zimmer made a note of."

He stared at me with a flash in his eyes of what I took to be deep apprehension. We were standing two feet apart, by the snowmobile. I decided to keep right on.

"I also want to know if you have any idea where Albert Christian and Ben Batten were going along with half a million dollars of drug money when Harold Johns flew them out of there in that Cessna that disappeared."

He glowered. "That's all you want to know, eh?"

"For now."

"Fuck off," he said.

But I had the plug out. I didn't mind Pennycook hearing. Might help. Somebody had to convince William that stonewalling was getting him nowhere. The convincer might as well be me.

I yelled, "You've been treated like a guy who has just lost his father and should be given some breaks! You wouldn't know a goddamn break if it farted in your face."

We were now practically nose to nose, or would have been if my nose had been about six inches higher.

"So I'm telling you that if you don't at least try to help us work on who the hell killed your father, you are going to have to get a goddamn court order even to go to his funeral, and that's a promise.''

For a few seconds I thought he was going to swing at me, but he didn't. It was strange to see in such a powerful-looking man, but his face suddenly crumpled and he fumbled, ''Look, I'm upset, I feel terrible about all this, I'll try to talk to you in the morning.''

He turned and took a couple of steps toward the open door where Pennycook still was listening, but keeping out of it.

I called to his retreating back, thinking that when he seemed to be on the run one more shot was in order, ''Okay, that'll give me a chance to get on the radio and find out whether we've managed to trace Billy Bob Hicks.''

He wheeled slowly and carefully, now really looking like a man who was trying to avoid acknowledging a telling blow.

''Who the hell is Billy Bob Hicks?'' he asked, without conviction. He was bushed, confused, beset. I almost felt sorry for him.

''You know who he is and what he's like. You know he's a friend of Christian and Batten.''

''But what's he got to do with me?''

''You tell me.''

''So you don't know nothin'!''

I hesitated. I thought I'd given him enough. He would have some drinks and do some talking, maybe brave talking, maybe sad talking, but I thought maybe that all through his long evening and night, he might have to pause now and again and wonder if he was playing his cards right.

Pennycook had stayed back through this but now he walked a few steps toward us with what almost seemed like a shy smile. ''Hey,'' he said to me, ''you were just on TV.'' He turned to William. ''The guy might help, William,'' he said. ''Jesus, he's supposed to be awful good, according to the piece on the CBC.''

Imagine that, the CBC making me credible to even one guy in Fort Norman.

William just turned away. I let him go. As I walked slowly back to the detachment, I racked my CBC-endorsed brains for the key to unlock what he knew but wasn't saying.

Maybe the thought of a key abruptly made me wonder again about his dog Smokey. If No Legs hadn't made such a point about the way William felt about that dog, I might not have thought of him again. Which, as it turned out, would have been a mistake.

By then it was deep dusk. Soon it would be pitch dark. I figured that if and when Edie and No Legs came in, she would head for the detachment. But given the relative speed of dogs versus snowmobile, that couldn't be for two or three hours. They had powerful flashlights. If they had kept going, William's trail was fresh enough that even a mediocre lead dog would have a chance. If that big Seismo was as good as he seemed, they'd get here sooner or later.

It turned out to be sooner rather than later. Around 7:30 I could see her coming, driving her team hard. I went to the detachment door just in time to see her go past. No Legs, riding the komatik, waved. She didn't even look my way, let alone stop to tell me thanks for an excellent day in the open air or any other appreciative things that might have occurred to her. In fact, she didn't even slow down. In a few minutes she drove past again, going in the other direction, toward her own place. Her outfit no longer included No Legs.

"Well, well," I deduced shrewdly (the CBC would be proud of me), "somehow I have offended Edie."

I walked the few hundred yards to where she lived. She was hard at work. She knew I was there but chaining six rambunctious dogs takes concentration. She didn't look at me until she had all six securely tethered far enough apart that they couldn't eat one another in the night.

"Have any trouble getting back?" I asked, for openers.

"Obviously not," she said.

"I want to thank you for your help. It didn't work out the way I thought it might, but—"

"Never mind," she snapped. "Better pick up your stuff." She stomped into her house and firmly closed the door.

I picked up the tent and survival gear. It was what they call a lazy man's load, no second trips, I thought, as I staggered back to the detachment. No Legs was parked outside on his sled. The office had no ramp for the disabled, and rather steep steps. The bulb over the door didn't throw much light but at least we could see one another.

"What's Edie mad at?" I enquired.

He looked at me with his lips pressed together the way a person might do if recalling some action that he was beginning to regret.

"She thought we oughta make camp and come back here in the mornin'. I said I thought we could get back in all right, with that fresh trail for the dogs to follow. She said of course we could get back all right, that wasn' the point." He allowed himself a small smile. "So we came in. She didn' talk on the way."

I had an idea he wasn't telling me everything, but then he might not wish to give it in detail. I don't imagine the detail included any consideration that the news would have swept through the town like wildfire if it were known that he and Edie stayed out all night in a seven-foot tent when they didn't really have to. Neither of them, it seemed to me, would have done other than what they felt like doing at the time, if they'd happened to agree on it. Obviously, they hadn't.

"Maybe you missed your big chance," I said.

"I thought of that, don' think I didn', but"—ruefully—"I figured I should come back and get my sister and maybe have William over for dinner, so we can talk. I mean, the poor guy . . ." He stopped.

"Is that what's going to happen?" I was pretty sure from his expression that it wasn't.

"Well, Cecilia is at the Pennycook's with quite a few other people but what is goin' on there is mainly drinkin', right now. Which ain't my favorite pastime anymore."

"Do you think the main trouble with William is the business about his father, or something else?"

He didn't answer directly. He was choosing his words carefully. "He didn't have to go as far out as he did, wherever that was, just to be alone for a while." His eyes were troubled. "I just can't figure what happened to Smokey."

That bothered me, too. Maybe there was an answer. I couldn't think what it would be, but tried a few on No Legs. "Of course, the dog could have got hurt, or lost, or chased a caribou, say, and never came back, and William figured he'd make his way home somehow in time, a smart dog like that."

No Legs just looked at me.

When he left, poling off slowly toward his own place, I had an idea of the questions he was beginning to face. The one about missing a camp-out with Edie would be the least of them.

I went back into the detachment office. Nicky Jerome had come out of his room at the back and was sweeping up, tidying desks. He looked up with a grin. "When you were out just now the corp'ral phoned and says he still has some of that rum and that Bertha has thawed some more caribou, steaks this time. They're expecting you."

That was the best news I'd heard lately. I stood there, considering things I might do first. Meaning, before the rum.

I thought of calling Buster but decided against it. If I called anybody it should be headquarters in Yellowknife, but if anything big had happened they'd have let this detachment in on it for sure.

I thought of calling Lois, but I decided against that, too. Her unusually friendly attitude the other night had been unsettling. It was so much like the times of long ago, when I'd been studying to be a white man and giving her more breaks as a woman and a wife. If that kind of thing went on, I might find myself rethinking other matters that I didn't have time in my head for, right now.

I called Maxine. She was just home. She said that Jules

Bonner was around town, had been questioned and released, apparently unscathed, but had stayed away from Gloria totally.

"But he's not a worry to her for a while, anyway," she said.

"Why not? He become a born-again nice guy?"

She laughed. "What I mean is Gloria left on the afternoon Canadian for Yellowknife. They're having a service there for Morton, you know."

"No, I didn't know. When?"

She said CBC news hadn't been able to get a straight answer yet. "The people running it hadn't been able to get in touch with William, last I heard, but when they can find him they want to do it fairly fast. A lot of the big wheels are due in Ottawa for some parliamentary committee or other. They've already had the thing postponed a week. Morton was supposed to go, you know. Lead the delegation."

I wondered about the kind of shape William was in for an emotional memorial service, which this one sure as hell would be.

Maxine suddenly giggled. "There was a piece on TV about you." She had a really nice giggle. She could laugh at a guy without sounding mean. It's a gift not everybody has. "The mighty Matteesie Kitologitak, scourge of bad guys from Pangnirtung to Herschel Island. Almost made me proud to know you."

"Almost, but not quite, eh? Because you know how weak I am in the middle of the night."

She giggled again. "Oh, I've never thought that."

"Yeah, yeah. Well, I'm firing blanks these days."

I told her, without details, that I'd hooked up with William finally, but to hold the applause. This memorial business in Yellowknife was a complication I had to think about.

"You going?" she asked. "Quite a few people from here are."

"I haven't had time to decide."

It had some angles, but they didn't include any pluses for

me in going to Yellowknife. If William was gone from here for a couple of days he'd at least be within surveillance distance of the North's greatest concentration of Mounties. If the weather held, and the forecast was okay, that would give me a chance to get back out on the trail to find out where William had been for the last two days. Maybe I could even hunt for a lost dog.

"Where's Gloria staying?" I asked.

"She's at the Yellowknife Inn," she said.

That's where Natives usually stay in Yellowknife. The attached Miners' Mess cafeteria is where all visiting Natives congregate eventually, Inuit at one table, Dene with several tables together, Metis tables here and there. All peoples separate.

Eventually we told each other to take care, and said goodbye. By now the powers that be in Yellowknife must have got to William. Even phone messages to the band council's office would mean he'd know about it by now at Pennycook's. Well, he'd said that he'd talk to me in the morning. I didn't count on learning much but it was always a possibility. Maybe I should have kept on pushing when I had him on the run. I found myself hoping that William wouldn't be too hung over to catch a morning flight. The odds were that he would go as soon as possible, partly to leave me behind. Also, the sympathetic support he was getting in Fort Norman was about the best he could hope for anywhere right now. If he didn't go to a memorial service for his father, a lot of people might start wondering if the presence of the paunchy little Mountie from the Barrenlands who was harassing good old William might make more sense than they'd been willing to admit.

But the main idea I had, which kept growing, was that with William gone to stand bareheaded listening to eulogies for his father from his own people and politicians of all colors and stripes, I might get lucky around here. Or south of here.

I still hadn't made up my mind when I walked down toward No Legs' house to ask No Legs what he knew about the country farther south than we'd traveled today. But passing the Pennycook house I saw his sled at the door. He could move short distances just sliding, using his arms and his leg stumps. Or maybe somebody had carried him in. All lights were on, upstairs and down, but the place seemed fairly subdued. Maybe I'd see No Legs later. Hunger and thirst had taken over. I turned towards Pengelly's, looking forward to food, drink and uncomplicated people.

I was there a couple of hours later when Nicky Jerome relayed two messages. One was that No Legs was home and wanted to talk to me if I had a chance. The other was that Gloria had been trying to get me. I walked back and knocked on the door at No Legs' place.

I heard him call, "Come in," went through the dark little coats and boots room and opened the inside door to the warm and bright kitchen. No Legs was on the chair where he'd been that first morning I visited him. On the table beside him were a pot of tea, tea bags, mugs, the electric kettle, an extension cord plugged into a wall outlet, his lighter and cigarets. He looked up at me.

"You heard about the memorial service for Morton?" he asked.

"Yeah, just heard."

"That's what I wanted to talk to you about," he said. "There's somethin' strange goin' on. I'd just got back to Paul Pennycook's when somebody got him on the phone from Yellowknife to tell him about the service and ask if he could be there Monday for sure."

He stopped as if not sure whether to say what he had to say.

"What he done right away was say that he couldn' go, couldn' they pos'pone it? Then everybody started tellin' him William, you have to, but he kept sayin' he couldn'. Just that he couldn'. He was so upset that it was hard to make out what he was sayin', except once it sort of come out like somebody cryin', that he had things to do aroun' here, no use goin' when Morton was dead anyways.''

I waited. He put a tea bag in each mug and poured in boiling water. ''I'm goin','' he said. ''So are some others. We're flyin' Nahanni.'' He took a deep breath. ''William is goin'. I think he really knew all along he had to. But he ain't happy about it. I mean, somethin' else is sure as hell on his mind. He was talkin' real wild—''

''Like what?''

''Like that he'd get a flight back as soon as the service was over, even if he hadta charter it.''

''Do you think it's anything to do with the trip he just got back from?''

''That crosst my mind.''

I went back to the detachment. It was starting to look like a long night. I had to make the call to Gloria, and others I had decided upon.

Nicky came out of his room when I went in. I was just picking up the phone book. ''Whose number you want?'' he asked. I told him. He had it written down, including her room number.

''You know Gloria well?'' he asked, while he poured me a coffee I hadn't asked for. Rum and ginger, tea, coffee, I'd be getting up every two hours all night to go to the can.

''Fairly well,'' I said.

''I used to know her here when she was a kid, before she went to live with Maxine. Nice kid, then. I often wondered how she's doin'. She in Yellowknife now?''

''Just for the service for Morton.''

A message had just come in noting that the service would be at ten a.m. Monday, day after tomorrow. So William would be able to get back here on the noon flight, if he wanted.

''Gloria okay?'' Nicky persisted, as I took a swallow of coffee and dialed.

''As far as I know. Why?''

He shrugged. "Sounded as if she'd had a few too many, is all."

While I had the phone to my ear, waiting for the hotel switchboard to answer, I wondered what exactly had been in Gloria's mind in going to Yellowknife so early for this service. It meant she'd have to spend an extra day or two there. Of course, only a few, if any, would know her relationship with Morton. And there'd be enough from Inuvik and other places in the North, people from this committee or that, band chiefs, people Morton had worked with or against, that she wouldn't be all that noticeable. Unless she made it that way herself. Yet as flaky as she sometimes could be, she wasn't the type to go getting her name in the tabloids under the heading of *Mystery Beauty Throws Self on Coffin*, or some such. The fantasy she'd been living out with Morton hadn't seemed to have much more to it, really, than just an affair between a young woman and an older man. But who knows? Maybe he was nice to her, respectful to her, a gentle lover instead of the string of grunts she'd had before in her life.

"Hello?" Gloria was in her room, and she did sound as if she'd had a few too many. Anyway, she wasn't down in the bar having a few more.

"It's Matteesie," I said.

"Oh! I'm so glad they found you. I had to tell somebody."

"Tell somebody what?"

She laughed. It was slightly out of control but still I thought, that's good, she's in good spirits. I couldn't tell on the phone whether she was really loaded or just in that state where a few drinks and a lot of emotion give that impression. There was a kind of spacey elation in her voice. Then she went on, dropping her voice to a confidential level. I guess she was used to hotels with thin partitions.

"I visited him today," she said.

"Yeah?" I couldn't imagine what was coming.

"I sneaked in before the regular visiting hours and they let me see him," she said. "They had him all laid out in a nice suit and . . ."

I couldn't imagine the scene at all. From the last time I'd seen Morton, I couldn't imagine an open coffin. Sure, the shots had hit the back of his head but his face, as I remembered it, Jesus . . .

"How the hell did you manage that?" I interrupted.

"There's no family, you know, until William gets here. I got a young guy who works in the funeral home and told him I was Morton's girlfriend and couldn't stand being there in a crowd during the regular visiting hours, so he let me in by myself, just me and Morton."

I waited. She was crying. It sounded like the edge of hysteria but there was sort of a happiness to her, too. I thought maybe she'd gone off her head, at least temporarily. She sure sounded like it.

"I talked to him," she said. "He didn't look the same."

I thought, bullets will do that to a guy, but didn't say it. I just waited, feeling I was in the presence of some kind of madness, whether drug-induced or alcohol-induced—who could say.

Now she was wailing. "I said to him, 'What have they done to your nice face, painting you all up like this?'"

I've known people, my own people, who talked to their dead, or thought they did; that much I could cling to, even if with great difficulty. I wasn't exactly playing along, but I was caught up in it.

"What did he say?" I asked.

"Just like him. He said it was none of my business."

I could hear her sobbing, the crazy girl.

I talked to her for a while. It didn't have much effect. I told her to phone Maxine right away, it was important. When I hung up I just stood there a while. Finally I couldn't help smiling, with a catch in my throat, when the thought occurred to me that anyway, it was nice that Gloria thought Morton had answered her question. Always the gentleman.

Then I phoned Maxine to tell her to call Gloria. The line was busy. I phoned an old school friend I knew who was an operator for NorthwesTel in Inuvik and asked could she tell me if the call on Maxine's line was long distance from Yellowknife.

She came back on in seconds, "Yeah, it is, Matteesie," she said. "How've you been, anyway?"

I said I'd been great, thanks, really great. "See you soon."

After I'd hung up I phoned the RCMP in Yellowknife and got the home number of the sergeant who'd done the checking for me on Billy Bob Hicks/Dave Hawkinsville. I could hear a hockey game in the background. I told him I needed a light aircraft or helicopter for tomorrow to follow a lead I had and did he have anything there that could fly up and help out, helicopter preferred.

He said everything was tied up in air rescue right now, no sign of the goddamn Cessna, probably never find it now, especially if it had somehow got west of the Mackenzie into the mountains, where the grid search would go tomorrow. But anyway . . .

"What've you got in mind?" he asked.

I just told him I had a hunch on the Morton Cavendish murder, knowing those would be the magic words around Yellowknife right now. I said I needed something that would maybe have to land and take off a time or two, depending.

He didn't ask any more, which is one reason why we'd been friends ever since I was still a special and he was a young constable based in Tuktoyaktuk nearly twenty years ago.

"I can authorize a light charter if you can find what you want around there or Norman Wells," he said. "You get them to phone me about billing," and then added hastily, "in the morning," and explained that with, "I'm watching the hockey game."

I didn't know every outfit that flew around there so I looked in the Yellow Pages. There were plenty of display ads for companies large and small with addresses all the way from Edmonton to Tuk. I picked one that read, "Single-Engine Aircraft, Cessna, Beaver, Otter. Wheels, Skis, Floats." The company name, Pine Tree, was unfamiliar but had a Fort Norman number. The office was closed, the answering machine informed me, but gave an after-hours number.

Ringing that, I heard the same hockey game in the background as a male voice with a slight accent said, "Stothers here."

Then I knew who he was, Ian Stothers, English, a household name in these parts. Had walked away from a few crashes himself. I'd never met him but knew he'd been a pilot in at least a couple of wars, I think the 1948 one in Israel and then in Korea, so he'd be pretty well on in years.

I thought I'd match his crisp delivery, just to see how it rolled off the tongue. "Matthew Kitologitak here," I said. "I'm looking for a charter in the morning."

"You're the Inuit cop, of course. What kind of an aircraft?"

"Something ski-equipped and light, a Beaver would do fine."

"What for and how long?"

I told him I'd need it for at least a few hours, maybe a few days, couldn't be sure of the details right now.

"Cash or Visa?" he asked.

"The Mounties in Yellowknife will authorize it," I said, and told him my name and who to call about billing. "Call him in the morning," I specified hastily.

"Morning suits me. I'm busy watching the hockey game. Wasn't even intending to answer the phone. What time you want to take off?"

"Daylight." I'd have to be able to see William's trail. "I also have to ask that you don't mention anything about this, especially tonight."

"Mum's the word," he said. "Don't know who the hell I'd see tonight, anyway. They're all home watching the hockey game."

I wondered who was playing but didn't ask. When dealing with the English it's important not to sound like an ignoramus. Didn't want to give Inuit a bad name.

"Who's the pilot going to be?" I asked.

"Me," he said. "That okay?"

"It'll be a pleasure." I hoped.

I hung up, thought a minute, then wrote a note to Pengelly and told him what I had in mind and who was flying me, in case he came in before I did in the morning. I asked him to keep it private. On this trip I didn't want surprise visitors.

I didn't have much packing to do. Most of it had been done for the trip with Edie and No Legs. I'd pick it all up in the police van in the morning. Nicky could run me out to the air strip. I tapped on Nicky's open door. He was watching "Dallas."

"Yeah!" he said, swinging his feet to the floor. "Hey, inspector, come in."

He puffed on his pipe and kept one eye on the set while I told him I was going out in the morning on a charter, didn't know for sure how long. Had my own clothing, snowshoes, bedroll, match container and toilet paper but from him I'd need the radio, Thermoses, tea, a kettle, primus stove, fuel, rifle, ammunition, tent. I paused there, figuring. "And food for . . . better make it, ah, food for four days . . ."

"Four days!" Nicky said, laughing. "Where the hell you goin', inspector, Calgary?"

I was on my way out of his room when there was a commercial break. The screen showed a 747 or some other giant airplane filling up at an Esso gas pump. He jumped up convulsively, light dawning, and called after me, "Hey, inspector!"

I took a few steps back into his room. "Yeah?"

"Gasoline! The commercial reminded me! You know the message early in the week about if anybody gets some gas stolen on them, they're to let us know right away?"

I felt a rush of adrenalin.

"Did the corporal ever tell you his story about the Icelander, ah, Oscar Frederickson, beatin' the hell out of his lady friend wit' this guitar, lives out in a shack other side of Bear Rock near the winter road? Well, he was in a little while ago, on foot. Mad as hell. Was supposed to come in tonight and have a few drinks and watch the hockey game, they haven' got TV out there, and he and Delphine got on the snowmobile and went about a hunnerd yards and it quit. Outta gas, although he knew he'd filled it day before yesterday, last time he used it. So they walk back to get a coupla gas cans he has in a shed behind his place and they're gone, too. Jeez, was he mad. Says if he ever catches the sonofabitch he'll kill him.''

NINE

Oscar Frederickson was six feet two or three, with the kind of hair that from boyhood on is so fair as to be almost white. In contrast, his cheeks looked like shiny red apples, a natural fair-skinned ruddiness with an assist, I guessed, from rye whisky. He was waving a glass of that right now. I figured him at around a hard-living fifty. His belly hung over thick woolen pants held up by suspenders of the kind that firemen and police used to wear, and some still do.

Blustering was his style. When I wondered aloud if the guy who liberated his fuel supply could have sneaked up to the house in daylight, Oscar fired back at me as if such a stupid idea was beneath contempt. "Y'nuts or somethin'? No guy is gonna come t'my house in broad daylight knowin' that when he bends over to suck on the hose and get the siphon goin' the next thing he's gonna get is a charge of number six shot up the ass."

That greatly amused his Delphine.

"New kinda hemorrhoid operation, eh, Oscar?" she said, smiling broadly for only an instant before she remembered to hide her mouth. The gesture was almost graceful, raising one hand so that the forefinger touched her upper lip lightly and the other fingers hid her ruined teeth. Black hair hung stringily down her back. When I looked at her a sense of sorrow swept through me. I thought she was not old enough to be so used up. It happens more to Natives than to whites.

We were in their cabin just off the winter road to Norman Wells. Nicky hadn't known for sure where Oscar had been headed to watch the hockey game when he stopped in to report the gasoline theft, but in Fort Norman two or three phone calls usually will locate someone unless they would prefer not to be located.

In minutes I was parking the police van at a house brightly painted red and white, one of an identical dozen or so laid out in the flats on either side of where the street dipped downhill toward the river bank. I knew such houses, had lived in them, played cards in them, argued drunk and sober in them. They and brightly painted others up and down the river and along the Arctic coast came north in sections by barge or on the winter roads, each to be assembled on pilings that had been hammered down to solid permafrost. Not only the colors, shape and size were the same, but so was fuel supply; each had a 200-gallon oil tank on one outside wall. Igloos can be individual. So can teepees, riverbank shacks, hovels, lean-tos. But not buildings that a government provides. When I was walking to the door none of this was going through my head. It was just there in the marrow of my bones.

The hockey game was just over, as was a bottle of rye. I asked Oscar to come and show me the scene of the crime.

"Hell, we can tell you what there is to know right here," Oscar argued, at first. "Don't have to go home to do that."

I said it would help me to see for myself, maybe get an idea of the place and the bush around it, in case there was a place the thief could have hidden while he watched the house until he figured it was safe to come in and steal the gas.

It was only when I said I'd drive them home right now in the police van, save them the walk, that Oscar got up, drained his drink, and laughed, "Let's go."

He came from Manitoba, he told me while we drove out

of town on what led to the winter road. "Delphine here comes from there, too, but farther north, where the government flooded them out."

"How do you mean?" I asked.

"Power development," she said, and seemed about to tell me which one, there's hardly a Native band in the north of the provinces as well as in the Northwest Territories that hasn't had to fight progress and sometimes lose, except that Oscar cut her off. Icelanders I've met are often blunt, direct. He was just plain objectionable. He wouldn't live in this god-forsaken place at all, he interrupted Delphine, except that his wife, who lived in Winnipeg now, would never think of looking for him here.

"She come in the front, I go out the back," Delphine said, looking serious. "That for sure."

Apart from his innate boorishness, Oscar, when addressing me, spoke very loudly, slowly and clearly; a non-nostalgic reminder of my childhood when seismic crews and summer groups of artifact-hunting archeologists and some crew members or passengers on the supply ships usually seemed to figure that if they spoke loudly enough we Natives would understand.

There was no more than a path into their place so I had to park on the road, presumably not far from where Pengelly had been the time he came out to deal with his noted case of the near-lethal guitar.

With Oscar talking and laughing loudly at his own jokes ("You know what we call siphon hoses where I come from? Indian credit cards, haw haw!") we walked maybe two hundred yards into the bush, lighting the way with two flashlights. The snowmobile stood where it had stalled after using the few drops of gas the siphon couldn't reach.

Inside, the log shack was one well-cared-for room. Blankets and patchwork quilts were laid neatly on a double mattress and springs set on peeled poplar logs in one corner. There were two old overstuffed chairs, three or four wooden ones, a table covered with red-and-white oilcloth, a battery radio. Delphine lighted two kerosene lamps and started a fire to heat water for tea. Oscar came outside with me while I shone around with my flashlight.

I couldn't see much except the imprint where the snow-mobile had been parked, halfway inside the woodshed. I checked the sight line. It could have been seen from the road, meaning the intruder would have recognized this as a place where snowmobile fuel almost certainly would be available. Right beside it, Oscar said, had been the two red five-gallon gas containers, one full and one empty.

"The bastard must've come in last night," he said, re-peating himself for the third or fourth time. "I wasn't out here yesterday. Delphine was, to get wood, and she noticed the gas cans weren't here but didn't mention it, says she just figured I'd moved them somewhere else, the dumb prick. So the way I figure, whoever did it siphoned all the gas out of the snowmobile into the gas can that was empty and then took both it and the full one."

"You seen anybody around lately that you didn't know?" I asked.

"Hell, no. I see anybody I don't know I ask their name."

Then a thought suddenly hit him. "The cans have my name on them in black paint. You should be hunting around in town, dammit. That's probably where the guy who took the gas went from here, right?"

"Hard to say," I said.

"Where the hell else could he be unless he came from the bush and went back into it? He'd be in town, and red gas cans with my name on them can't be that easy to hide unless he ditched them somewhere in the snow."

I decided it wouldn't be fair, even to Oscar, not to let him know why we were taking the trouble.

"He might have been someone we're looking for," I said. "You heard about the guy that killed Morton Cavendish at Norman Wells. He got away on a snowmobile that had no extra gas containers."

Oscar's mouth fell open as he got the drift.

"He might have had gas stashed somewhere on the winter road and couldn't find it, or did find it and holed up for a couple of days, then got lost and used up too much gas, and knew if he wanted to get away from here, wherever he was headed, he needed a lot more gas. If it was that guy, he would have been desperate enough to take a chance on stealing some. He had a gun, too, remember. A Colt .45. And knew how to use it."

On Oscar's face as it showed dimly in my flashlight beam, a dramatic change of expression was taking place, from know-it-allness to something I really couldn't read. "Jesus," he said.

I drove back into town. So, this was something. But if it was the first sign of the man who had shot Morton Cavendish, there was still all the bush and tundra to think about in trying to figure out where he'd go from here. From now on I could be looking for two snowmobile tracks, William's and one other.

At noon the next day, Sunday, I was sitting in the passenger seat of a clean, trim Beaver flying south along the Big Smith River. Ian Stothers in the pilot seat to my left was wearing, astonishingly enough, a shirt and tie under a couple of sweaters. I'd liked him immediately, one of those Englishmen whose sharp edges had been rubbed off and was just easy to be with. He had thin longish hair to his collar and a straggly growth of facial hair that started at his cheekbones, flowed easily into his moustache, and seemed untrimmed without being untidy. He wore horn-rimmed spectacles, which he took off occasionally, letting them dangle around his neck on a loose leather thong that looked like a retired lace from an old workboot.

Even more telling, from when we met in the frosty dawn of ten a.m. and minus forty-two he never once said old chap, or old boy, or right-o. Certainly he'd never make it socially among the English transplants I'd observed in Victoria, B.C.

back in the 1970s when I'd been part of security on a Royal Tour.

When we were moving the engine-warming heat-pot and pulling off the heavy canvas cover that kept the heat in where it would do the most good, I even kidded him a little. "I thought the only pilots who wore shirts and ties were flying 747s," I said.

"A nasty habit, I admit," he grinned.

Airborne with the heater going full blast, he in his sweaters and I in my old goose-down vest with Maxine's red nail polish dotted here and there to stop the down from escaping through holes made by pipe ashes, back when I used to smoke more, we were fairly comfortable.

Our parkas were stashed in the back on top of my supplies and his standard emergency gear, including some extra fuel.

At first we flew at around 500 feet. No more than ten or twelve minutes from the airport we'd picked up the heavy double north-south trail of William's snowmobile and Edie's dogteam, easily followed from this altitude. The Beaver could cover in that short a time what had taken the dog team a couple of hours. In another few minutes I pointed down to where we had stopped the dogteam and held our little nature-study session over the wolverine tracks before we saw William approaching. Stothers eased down a couple of hundred feet to circle the place before following again what was now the less distinct single trail left by William's snowmobile.

"I flew down here, y'know, the first day we could fly after the murder," Stothers called over the engine noise. "I thought of this river right away as one place Harold Johns might try to make if he was in trouble. He'd know it. I also swung farther east to Lac Ste. Thérèse and flew south to Blackwater Lake, and Keller, all places you could put down a Cessna 180 on." Those were just names on a map, to me. "But of course it isn't that Cessna you're thinking about so much . . ."

He let that trail off, but looked sideways at me. "Unless maybe young Cavendish was looking for the Cessna, too."

"That's my guess," I said. Maybe I had a valuable assistant, here. "What about landing places farther right, toward the Mackenzie?"

"But we're still following the snowmobile track, I take it?"

"Yes. I was just wondering."

"I think Johns was too good to try over there if he was in trouble. If he wasn't, and knew where he was heading, maybe. I've met him a few times, y'know. He picked up the gen on bush flying a lot faster than some new ones do. The mountains along this side of the river are no picnic. There's one peak not a lot west of us right now that's better than 4700 feet. Not the way anybody with any sense would go, looking for an emergency landing."

I looked off to my right toward the rougher country of the Franklin Mountains, and wondered.

William's snowmobile track ran steadily along the narrowing river. There was really very little to see except the track, and a few animals from time to time. Once Stothers banked and pointed down at a wolverine running across the open tundra. Neither of us had to say the word. There's no mistaking that distinctive humping bear-like gait.

Soon we came upon a herd of caribou, maybe 200 animals, crossing the river diagonally. On the other side of where they were crossing we could see no resumption of William's track.

"We'll circle and see if we can pick it up," Stothers called, and again dropped the Beaver to 200 feet. It was while the Beaver went wide of the caribou herd that I could see the wolves. They'll often shadow a herd like this. If you ever wondered where the phrase wolf-pack came from during naval warfare in World War Two, it would help to fly over a herd of caribou attended by wolves. Stothers pointed down at them, his jaw set in a way quite unlike his normal benign expression.

The wolves, eight or nine of them, perhaps one family or two, were in a mile-wide arc out of sight of the moving herd,

just as submarines shadowed convoys in the Atlantic. If the
herd changed direction and moved toward the wolves on one
side, they would fall back, outwards, to adjust, staying ap-
proximately the same distance away, on all sides. They
wouldn't attack the herd itself but were alert for signs of
stragglers. When a sick or injured or unwary animal fell
behind or wandered off, they'd suddenly move in for a kill,
all the wolves on that side racing in to attack simultaneously.
From the air as we made a complete circle, the scene below
looked like a gigantic target with the loosely-bunched herd
in the middle the bull's-eye.

Stothers pointed down again at a single wolf loping along,
keeping station. Then Stothers lined up the plane with the
course of the wolf and suddenly we went into the Beaver
version of a screaming dive to come at the wolf from behind.
We were hardly twenty feet above the snow when the Beaver
rocked over to the right as Stothers tried to hit the wolf with
the right-hand ski. From my window a few scant feet above
I could see the wolf plainly as it flattened itself the way a
dog will do to avoid a blow, head turned sideways, teeth
bared, as the ski skimmed by.

"Missed," Stothers said.

My breath was coming harder than I generally allow to
happen. "Not by far."

"I rather dislike wolves," he said.

"No kidding."

"I should've warned you." After a pause, "Well, back to
business."

We circled again, wider and wider, but couldn't pick up
the snowmobile trail again.

"Damn strange," Stothers yelled at me.

Not really. A possibility occurred to me that seemed possible, even likely, but needed checking.

"Can you land here?" I yelled. "Right where the herd
crossed?"

"Sure." He went into a shallow bank, landed, and bumped

along a bit to the outside edge of the caribou crossing where there'd be a smoother takeoff run.

I reached for my parka and pulled on my fur hat with the ear flaps down. It was warm in here but outside the cutting northwest wind seemed to be rising. He was unscrewing the coffee Thermos as I clambered out of my seat toward the door just behind me. The jump to the ground was easy enough and I turned and slammed the door shut. It would have been easier walking if I'd thought to grab my snowshoes, but what I wanted to see wouldn't take that long.

I walked along in the thin sunshine with the silence of the North all around me, the moisture crystals from my breath whipped away on the wind in little white disappearing clouds.

Out here somewhere William had been, maybe looking for others not far away.

I wasn't more than a few dozen feet into the churned snow-chunks left by the caribou's passing before I found what I wanted. Caribou droppings are small, not much more than half-inch pellets, quite a bit like those of a deer. Droppings from the herd just gone by were easy to see because their soft freshness slightly stained the snow. When I stepped on a few of these they squished, with only a thin outer crust frozen so far. But mixed among them also were droppings frozen through, as hard as a hockey puck. They could be an hour old, three, five, possibly more. Kicking at the snow I uncovered other frozen droppings of much older vintage. Some were buried nearly a foot. They'd been there for days at least.

I clumped back to the Beaver, climbed in, secured the door and slid back into my seat. Stothers had a steaming cup of coffee in his right hand. The gesture with his left I later came to know. It was what he did when he had a question. He put his left hand alongside his face, the heel of his hand on his chin, the fingers together up towards his left ear, his expression quizzical.

"I guess you found what you wanted," he said. "Old droppings. A regular caribou crossing."

Exactly. William hadn't turned merely so he could enjoy the ineffable experience of bashing along on a highway paved with caribou droppings. When he reached the crossing place two days ago he'd known the odds were good that there'd be more caribou along in the next hours or days, obliterating his snowmobile tracks. Moving caribou sometimes act as if they are going by road maps. "He must've turned on the same course as the caribou," I said. "Either where they were coming from or where they went. He might have been heading for this crossing all along. He lived here long enough to know."

So now we had two possibilities, that he had turned left on the course the caribou followed, or turned right to where they'd come from.

"Let's try both ways," I said. "It might be only a matter of a few miles before he'd branch off. If he branched off."

"You're the doctor."

West toward the Franklins and even into them a few dozen miles to where a winter tractor road ran along the Mackenzie, was rough country. In it were many places where someone flying over would have to be lucky to see what someone didn't want seen. In the absence of any other possibility I could think of, if William had an educated idea that he'd find something or somebody out here, let's say somebody who would prefer not to be found, to the west they'd be difficult to spot from the air. More so than in the big open spaces to the east.

I said, "East."

Stothers looked surprised but said nothing, starting up. The engine roared instantly and we taxied for take-off.

"My hunch is west," I yelled. "I thought if we try east for a while and get blanked, then we turn back and try west until you run out of gas."

"Thanks a lot!" he yelled.

We found nothing to the east except the caribou we'd seen passing, and then stayed on the much older but still visible trail of earlier herds. The course wavered this way and that, depending on the terrain. Every time I thought of turning back west I kept thinking, just a few more miles, but there was never a snowmobile trail leaving the caribou's route. Eventually Stothers raised his eyebrows at me and I said, "Yeah, let's turn around."

When we crossed the Big Smith again it was the same game, but the country more rugged, with the caribou trail winding among gullies, valleys and minor watercourses defined mainly by the few scrubby trees along the banks. By late afternoon, sometimes circling miles to either side, both Stothers and I were beginning to imagine things. The lengthening shadows made errors easy. When a trail seemed to lead off somewhere, he'd point or I'd point and we'd go down sometimes perilously close to the crests of hills to find an animal track, a shadow or nothing.

The Franklins aren't mountains in the sense of the Rockies, but even the foothills that we now were in seemed high enough to two guys in a single-engine Beaver. Time was getting on. The shadows below were getting darker.

The sun had long been on its downward course and now was no more than four or five degrees above the horizon. I was torn, but still I could only go on my guess that William had come out here for some purpose so far unknown, but more specific than assuaging his grief. I was wondering if I should get Stothers to land me. But I really couldn't think why. If there was something to go on, being out here on snowshoes might have some merit, but for all we knew William might have gone east all the way to the Johnny Hoe River south of Great Bear Lake, or west all the way to Blackwater Lake. Somewhere, there had to be a break.

"We're going to have to turn back in a few minutes," Stothers said. "Too dark on the ground to see anything clearly now anyway."

I nodded. "Could you raise Fort Norman and ask whether William got on that plane to Yellowknife today?"

He did so, and got the reply: "Affirmative."

"What are you thinking of?" he asked.

"Coming back out tomorrow. Can you do it?"

"Sure." He gave me that sideways quizzical look. "I'm starting to get interested."

"Okay," I said. "Home, James."

He banked the Beaver around the crest of a hill to head north. I think both of us saw at the same time the flash of a snowmobile headlight a thousand feet below. We saw it only for as long as it would take a watchful man to hear a sudden noise above the sound of his snowmobile, glance up, see the Beaver, and switch off his headlight and maybe his engine.

With the dark shadows below, the headlight beam gone, he was invisible. He could have stopped, could have steered into the meagre cover. Anyway, the sign of him had vanished.

"I had a thought I could turn off my engine and see if we could still hear his," Stothers said. "Then I had another thought. This machine is not a real champion at re-starts in the air."

"Can we get back right here tomorrow?"

He was making marks on his map. "So young Cavendish is in Yellowknife, which means this is someone else."

"Yeah," I said, thinking of Oscar Frederickson and his missing gasoline.

T E N

The flight took longer going back. The northwest wind that had been on our tail outward bound had grown through the afternoon and was now a substantial headwind. We were being buffeted, bounced around. Some of the buffeting was going on in my head, as well. That snowmobile whose light we had glimpsed so briefly might be the missing piece in the jigsaw puzzle. If it belonged to the man who had murdered Morton Cavendish, had hidden somewhere for a few days, then had stolen Oscar Frederickson's gasoline—the intention could only be to make sure of enough fuel for a substantial trip—how did we manage to be out here with a dog team through most of yesterday, fly along more or less the same course and more today, and never see a sign of it? The answer obviously was that it had not been in any of the territory we had covered.

When we landed and the Beaver was tucked away for the night, still loaded for tomorrow, Stothers offered to drive me into town. We'd gone scarcely a half mile when he said, "My place is just ahead—feel like a drink?"

"I thought you'd never ask."

He glanced sideways at me and grinned.

"Line I picked up in a movie," I said. "Has no Inuvialuit equivalent."

He turned almost immediately in to park beside a long, low log house. The windows were dark and the wind had filled his path to the side door with snow and scoured it into ripples and peaks and bare spots. He grabbed a snowscraper from a drift by the door and cleared the way with about three scoops and gestured me in. The door wasn't locked and when I was in he reached around me to the light switch.

The house was unlike anything I could remember in the North. On the Quebec side near Ottawa, maybe. Outside blasts of ground-drift snow swirled against the windows but the dining table I recognized as mahogany, with high-backed chairs set around it. The rest of what I could see was like a northern adaptation of something in Ottawa's up-market enclaves like, say, Rockcliffe—except that instead of a discreet Tom Thomson or Riopelle hidden away under its own lighting system over your run-of-the-mill deputy minister's fireplace, these walls were hung with photographs of people old, young and in between. The most striking one was over the log fireplace, a young smiling woman in an officer's uniform of the Women's Royal Naval Service. The Wrens, they were called. No doubt there were still Wrens, I'd even met some of them in Ottawa, but if this one had been in the Wrens when Stothers was a young officer in the Royal Air Force, they'd be about the same age and somehow I had an idea that was the case. But he obviously lived alone, so if my guess was right she wasn't here. Anyway, I didn't ask about her or any of the others in the photographs. I figured he'd tell me if he wished. Bookshelves were everywhere. I didn't ask what he read, either.

He poured me a Barbados rum and ginger and himself a Scotch, which he downed quickly and poured himself another.

"Living alone requires rules," he sighed, coming back to his chair with his new drink. It looked darker than the first. "One of mine is two drinks per night. The only trouble is I drink mine too quickly and then have the whole rest of the evening to deal with.''

He sounded slightly melancholy but, perhaps fighting a rearguard action in defence of his second drink, firmly put it down and wandered over to a map of the western Arctic. He slowly trailed one forefinger along the course we'd followed today, then stood and stared at it.

"What do you see?" I asked.

He shrugged and shook his head. "Nothing."

One question had been bugging me, I realized, ever since I saw that snowmobile headlight and tried to fit it in to everything else I knew about this case, its principals, and the shrinking space that had become the action area. Stothers knew the country better than I, better than Pengelly, better than anyone except maybe William Cavendish and No Legs and the friends they'd grown up with. Farther north among my own people I had always used—took for granted—what you might call insider information. I needed the same thing badly, here. How badly I hardly realized until I noticed that I still hadn't finished my first rum.

I asked, "If you were in Fort Norman two nights ago and had just stolen a couple of cans of gasoline and wanted to get to where we saw that snowmobile's headlight without anybody seeing you, is there a way it could be done?"

He didn't have to think about it at all. "That's really why I was looking at the map, trying to remember things. The thing is, I've rarely crossed the Franklins right where we went into them today. Never seemed necessary when I could fly safer inland like we were today, or down the Mackenzie . . ."

He stopped suddenly and commanded sharply, "Answer the question, Stothers!" and then turned his head, shrunk a little, and said obsequiously, "Right, sir," as if re-enacting some long-ago incident in an RAF mess. He was maybe a little drunk. "So okay, I can't say exactly how somebody could get from here to there without attracting attention. But I think it could be done, with a little luck. Or absence of bad

luck—I mean, absence of the bad luck of running into someone who might ask questions, or notice more than you wanted
anyone to know. It would also mean having a definite, probably mapped and pinpointed, destination. In the second or
two, no more, that we saw the light, it was moving west.
That means he was trying to reach someplace over near the
Mackenzie, or even across it.''

"Could he get to where we saw him without running in
the open where he'd be visible?''

Stothers wandered around the room, avoiding the rest of
his second drink as if it were shooting out deadly gamma
rays.

"The key would be two nights ago after he'd stolen the
gasoline. If he's your man, even if he has no firsthand
experience of these parts but still knew where he had to
get to, he'd sit around somewhere in the bush northeast of
Fort Norman until he figured he'd be pretty safe, all the
drunks and lovers home in bed, and then he'd move. There
are lots of snowmobiles that run every day near the town,
so even if somebody out late did see him he'd be pretty
safe. He'd cross the Bear River a few miles east of here,
go south a bit and then head west, again staying in snowmobile traffic areas. Up to there, clear night, there was a
nearly full moon, he might even run without lights. He
wouldn't go too far west, wouldn't want to chance the
winter road with everybody in the North looking for him.
But when he got what he figured was far enough west he
could simply turn south. It'd be slow going, running at
night, no trail broken.''

"And around daylight he'd have to stop," I said. "That
would mean making camp with both his tent—I assume he
has one—and the snowmobile under cover so he couldn't be
seen from the air.''

"Right.'' Stothers stopped pacing and finished his drink,
quickly.

Everything made perfect sense. Out with Edie and No
Legs and the dogs, I'd been fixated on William, forgetting

there was someone else to look for, and, until I learned about the stolen gas, not suspecting he might be this close. Certainly he'd be holed up by day. Maybe he even saw us go by in the open, with the dogs. Then he'd move south again by night and make camp for the day, maybe by then close to the caribou trail. Hidden again, he'd probably been aware of the Beaver. But he'd be anxious to move as soon as he could and, as a guess, with the wind carrying our engine noise away from him, he might have lost us and thought we'd gone home while really we were still fooling around farther south. Add up that and darkness coming on, he must have thought it was safe to move. That would take him to where we saw whatever it was we saw.

While I was going through that, saying some of it aloud, Stothers poured himself a third drink, with a small apologetic smile. "I don't have company every night," he said, as if in explanation. "The thing is, tell me where you think he might have been going. You've got a theory. It's been sticking out all over you. Maybe I can give it an outsider's assessment."

"I think the Cessna is down somewhere between where we saw that snowmobile and the river. It might have gone to a pre-arranged landing spot. Maybe it had been arranged that Morton Cavendish's murderer was to hide out until the first heat of the search was off—after all, there aren't enough Mounties in the world to cover every old trapper's cabin or every snowbank in the bush—and then rendezvous with the people on the aircraft."

"And after that?"

"If they came down at a safe, pre-arranged place, they would plan to take off from there and fly somewhere they'd figured out in advance, maybe even have a car waiting, take the money, ditch or hide the Cessna, and live happily ever after. There's only one piece that doesn't fit."

"Young Cavendish," he said.

"Yeah." I wondered if William had chosen the safe landing place to start with. I still couldn't think of him as part of the deal to murder his father. But maybe I was wrong. Everything else fitted.

Back at the detachment, Nicky was watching the Disney Sunday movie. He gave me his usual cheerful welcome. I read the day's messages, which yielded nothing. Flights west of the Mackenzie in the widening grid laid out by the baffled Search and Rescue people again had come up zero. Nicky came out during a commercial and said, "Hey, that dog-team lady was in lookin' for you. Wants you to call her or go see her when you have a chance."

I thought of her frostiness at our last parting. I'd worry about her later, if at all. I called Inuvik and was patched through to Ted Huff's home. In some respects I'd rather do a thing and explain later. But what I had in mind might wind up with a search party going out for me. If so, Ted, who would have to give that order, had a right to know what I was proposing to do.

"Matteesie!" he said. "Jeez, that was fast!"

I didn't get it.

"Can't be more than three minutes ago I got Pengelly at home and told him to find you for me!"

I didn't tell him that the other phone was ringing and Nicky answering and then looking over at me and grinning while he said in a low voice, "Yeah. They're talkin' right now."

At the same time Ted was saying, and not in any low voice, "We got a screw-up here. Bonner. I think I told you we didn't hold him on the Gloria thing, beating her up."

"Yeah, matter of fact I wondered why."

"Two reasons. One, he might lead us to some evidence in the drug case, not bloody likely, him not being stupid, but possible. Two, the kind of assault charge we had in mind was confused somewhat by the number of stitches he needed from where Maxine hit him with the ski."

I loved that image.

"Anyway, we just told him not to leave town. But he caught the flight out today. Told the agent he was going to Yellowknife for the service for Morton. Didn't even use a fake name. Might even have gone on to Edmonton, the flight isn't in there yet so we haven't been able to check. Or he could have got off at Norman Wells. If so, and where the hell he'd go from there, Charlie Paterson is trying to find out. If we pick him up we'll let you know. Meanwhile, if he shows up there . . ."

It was a lot to take in. It wasn't all bad. Depending on where he did get off, it could have been just a decision to run and hide, or the kind of desperate move Bonner might make if he knew all along where the Cessna was heading and was trying to catch up to his share of the money.

Ted went on, "We've issued a warrant now on him beating up Gloria, so anybody who sees him can grab him."

I thought of another way. "Maybe we shouldn't grab him," I said. "Just watch him, follow him. Even in Edmonton if he gets that far." I was thinking, if Bonner really is trying to get to his share of the money before it disappears, it might be just the kind of break we've been waiting for.

Should I change my plans for tomorrow? I didn't think so. But before I could tell Ted what I had in mind, the original reason for my call, he went on to say he'd heard from Yellowknife that William had arrived and was staying at the Yellowknife Inn.

"Maxine's sister is there, too. One of our people said that she and William had been in the bar together."

That reminded me. Gloria might be one person close enough to William to find out more than the rest of us had. Like what William's snowmobile trip had been all about. After I'd told Ted my intentions, I'd give her a call.

So I told him that, forgetting Bonner until he showed up somewhere, I thought we should go on what I had. He listened without interrupting. When I was finished he still didn't speak for a few seconds. Call it a thoughtful pause. "Well, sounds like you're doing it the hard way, Matteesie," he said finally. "Wouldn't it be better to pick up the search by air where you left off today?"

I said I thought I could do better on the ground.

"Well . . ." I could imagine him thinking I was a stubborn bastard, but then that would be no surprise to him.

He went on, "Then how about I get on to Search and Rescue and have their aircraft comb that district again. If you're on the ground and need help, you could radio. They'd be on you right away."

"I could do that anyway," I said. "I wouldn't need a goddamn air force zooming around right in the area and scaring everybody under cover. The advantage of me being out there—the possible surprise—would be lost. If everything is the way I'm thinking it is, whatever shape that Cessna is in, it's been well hidden and will stay that way until somebody comes at it on the ground. If I can do that, I won't go riding in like the bloody cavalry. I'll hole up myself and report by radio and then you can send in the troops."

"But it'll take you most of the day just to get to where you thought you saw that snowmobile. God knows where that guy will be by the time you pick up his trail, if you can find it at all."

I said it wasn't going to take me a whole day to get there.

"How you going to arrange that?"

"Stothers will fly me in, with the snowmobile, land me as close as he can to where we saw the light, unload the snowmobile, give me a compass course to where we saw the light, and I'm off."

"You're still taking a hell of a chance if that's the murderer."

"I'm willin'," I said. " 'Barkus is willin'.' " I don't remember everything I read in Dickens, but I do remember Barkus, the one who, faced with whatever test of dumb determination, always replied, "Barkus is willin'."

Ted got it. "Yeah, but Dickens never sent Barkus out on

a snowmobile after a murder suspect and two or three accomplices.''

"He would have if the situation had called for it," I said stoutly.

Reluctantly, "Okay. Be careful. We'll keep in touch by radio if we get anything on Bonner or anything else. And you bloody well keep in touch, too. Every hour on the hour would do fine.''

When I hung up I thought very briefly of Edie. She should be warned against anybody, especially a plausible bastard like Bonner, applying for the use of her dog team. Nevertheless, I decided I'd try Gloria first.

She answered the phone in her room. She sounded strained, not much more together than she'd been in that bizarre conversation the night before. "I've been trying to figure out whether to phone you," she said. "I had a couple of drinks with William, I mean I had a couple and he had six, and he was talking real crazy about those other guys . . ."

Her voice trailed off. Then, as if she'd taken a deep breath and decided not to stop now, went on. "Maybe I'm wrong, but I almost got the idea that he'd seen them! Kept saying he didn't blame Harold Johns, he hoped he was okay. And once he said, like mumbling to himself, I mean he was really drunk, 'I fixed those two bastards, though, and I'll get the other one, too.' Those were his exact words. What do you think he meant?''

Well, I had an idea. But it seemed too much.

I said, "Do you know where No Legs is?''

"No. I tried to find him, but he must be staying with friends. He's probably a little short of cash for a hotel."

"One more thing," I said, and told her about Bonner. She listened to that in silence. The question running through my mind was whether Bonner was now desperate enough to be a killer himself.

Edie. Her place wasn't far away. I walked. The wind had died a little but had left a frosty clear sky where northern lights were forming and reforming, audibly crackling. My beautiful North.

I really missed being able to talk to No Legs. Never mind Bonner for the moment. He might never show up. I had an idea we had almost everything we needed to know, if we could just jiggle it around a little: the caribou crossing, the second snowmobile, and William's wild claim, if it was intended as a claim rather than a forecast, to have "fixed those bastards." If anyone could project all these elements into a guess on where the centre of the action was, based on knowledge and experience, it was No Legs. Before, there'd been no way of narrowing the search into one specific spot somewhere between that caribou crossing and the Mackenzie River. Maybe it was right in the middle of the Franklins, a hidden place that William might know and only a few others, natives like No Legs, a place where a plane might land and nobody would suspect it was there.

But if I couldn't find No Legs, I couldn't find him. His sister had gone with him, so I couldn't check with her either.

Edie's dogs set up a clamor when I got close. I knocked on her door. She must have started for the door when she heard the dogs. But if she had any holdover annoyance from the previous night she didn't show it, just looked past me to her dog lines and decided they didn't need her attention, then said, "Come in. Tea? Just made a pot."

Her space was small, neat, everything in place. She was wearing a pink sweatsuit, her hair neatly brushed, and without the bulky winter clothing she'd worn every other time we met, she looked fetchingly feminine. In contrast, I felt sweaty, harried, dirty, and somewhat masculine, oddly enough. She came to the point as soon as she'd poured my tea.

"I was rude to you the other night, Matteesie. I'm really sorry."

"That's okay."

"I was disappointed because it seemed like such a great trip and then got blown to hell."

"I was disappointed, too. I thought it would be sort of nice, you and I and No Legs snuggling up in the tent to keep warm and listening to the wind."

She looked at me for signs of lack of seriousness, but I wasn't showing any.

"Anyway," she said, "I want to volunteer again, if you need me and the team. Today I heard a few things."

"Such as what?"

"About the guy stealing that gasoline maybe being the one who shot Morton Cavendish."

"Who told you that?"

"Oh, hell," she said, "that Icelander talks a lot. I heard him in Bear Lodge saying he wished he'd had a chance to shoot the son of a bitch and, I quote, 'beat the fuckin' Mounties to it, about time there was a little law and order around here' unquote."

"That sounds like Oscar."

The tea was good. I could have used a drink but she didn't offer. I warned her about Bonner and described him to her: "Curly hair, parted in the middle, reddish moustache." I told her about him beating up Gloria and saw the glint in her eyes. She didn't like the beating-up-Gloria story at all. Then, since we were being chatty and I'd been too unchatty with her before, too busy being the steely-eyed man-hunter of song and story, I told her what Stothers and I had done today and what we had planned for tomorrow. I'm sometimes like that with good-looking women. Like them to know that even if I'm five feet six, I think like a giant.

"I'd rather be going out with dogs," I said. "Quieter. Better on the trail." I was laying it on. Besides being true, I figured she'd like that. "But I've got to start a lot closer to the action than I can get by dog team. Anyway, you've got a school week starting tomorrow."

She didn't comment on that, just shrugged. I finished my

tea. It was getting late. She came with me to the door. ''So we're friends?'' she said.

''Sure.''

''I haven't met many men like you, Matteesie,'' she said, and reached over—we were about the same height—and kissed my cheek.

ELEVEN

So I had that much more on my mind when I was flying over the empty tundra the next morning. Because of our load, we'd had to switch planes. "No problem, we'll take my jumbo jet," Stothers said, wheeling out his Twin Otter.

Among other essentials, we were carrying Charlie Paterson's Norman Wells detachment snowmobile and sled, the outfit I'd brought down to Fort Norman. On the sled was loaded what every well-equipped Mountie on a getting-our-man patrol in the frozen North required—extra fuel, watertight match box backed up by three Bic lighters or vice versa, bottle of Mount Gay rum, light block and tackle, tools, spare belts, axe, tent, police strength two-way radio, Verey pistol, signal flares, binoculars, boil-in-the-bag food, primus stove and fuel, kettle for boiling snow, flashlight, tea bags, bedroll, snowshoes, extra socks, spare parka. In the way of guns there was a Colt M-16 rifle which fired .223-calibre ammunition from a 20-shot magazine, and a sawed-off Remington Model 870 12-gauge pump-action shotgun. The shotgun I hoped I'd never have to use (they make a real mess).

I also had what I considered to be a lifetime supply of ammunition, too much, but Pengelly had argued, "You'd

feel pretty stupid swinging an empty at the bad guys and
yelling on the radio for more ammo.''

He'd picked me up at Bear Lodge in the van, and lectured
me all the way to the airport about being careful.

''Nothin' personal,'' he said. ''There just ain't so many
Eskimo cops around that we can afford to lose one.''

It all took a while to load, but after that we made good
time. At a little after eleven, an hour after sunup, Stothers
landed where the caribou had crossed Big Smith River. We'd
estimated that to be about thirty to thirty-five miles east of
the Mackenzie.

In the air he'd yelled that he'd like to take a run farther in,
maybe find a landing place closer to where we'd seen the
snowmobile headlight, but I shook my head. A desperate
man who suspected he might have been spotted could decide
to lie in wait to see what happened next. He'd have to be
nuts, but people do nutty things sometimes. It was chancy
enough without us towing a banner reading, ''Look out, man!
We're on your tail.'' Stothers didn't argue.

When it came to unloading I was glad I wasn't using one
of the heavier breeds of snowmobile. A forklift had helped
load it. Unloading was up to us. Neither of us was Arnold
Schwarzenegger. The heavy webbing holding the Elan and
sled in place reminded me briefly of Morton Cavendish as
he was strapped in on his last ride. We unlashed it, laid a
narrow sheet of one-inch plywood as a ramp from the Twin
Otter's door to the snow below and attempted to manhandle
the snowmobile a couple of feet to where gravity would lend
a hand. At our first, ''One, two, three—heave!'' it didn't
budge an inch. Stothers looked at me with a smile and released the brake. Next heave, we got it moving and then had
to strain mightily from behind on ropes to keep it from breaking the Northwest Territories speed limit even before it hit
the ground.

The loaded tow-sled was easier. I had to remove my mitts
to secure its rigid tongue with its draw-pin attachment to the
snowmobile's hookup. Icy metal and bare hands don't go

together; the sensation is like a burn. On top of the load I added Thermoses, ammunition boxes and the radio. The guns were in light scabbards, one ahead of each knee, rifle on the left and shotgun on the right. The rifle's loaded ammunition clip went in one parka pocket, a handful of shotgun shells in another. Face-mask on, helmet on, goggles ready to be pulled down, I switched on the radio.

"Matthew Kitologitak testing testing, over."

Pengelly said, "Hear you good, Matteesie. Be careful, now, it's a jungle out there, haw haw." Hill Street Blues has a lot to answer for.

I started the machine, waved and headed west. When I glanced back Stothers was taking off with a short run north into a fairly heavy ground drift whipped up by the wind. He made an immediate bank east to lessen the chance of being seen from where I was heading. The sound was another thing; even with the muffling effect of the wind, if anyone was close enough the aircraft would be heard.

I'm not really big on snowmobiles, especially where there's no track to follow, and here there was definitely none. The weather was worsening fast. High above was a cold sun, but on the deck the wind-driven ground drift cut visibility to a few yards in some places.

I followed the course of the caribou herd we'd seen yesterday. It was churned up, the snow in rough icy chunks, like riding a road made out of loose bowling balls. Then I began to see here and there a snowmobile track. One looks much like another, but there were no others. It figured that these were William's. We'd lost him from the air in this stuff, but being on the ground was a new ball game. In one place I might see the mark of the drive belt, about sixteen inches wide with lugs a couple of inches apart. In another I might see the narrow cutting mark of his runners. I concentrated on these signs so much in one stretch that I clean forgot to keep a lookout ahead. I reminded myself that William's track was one thing, okay, he was in Yellowknife right now, but remember the other guy.

From then on I looked down, then ahead, every few seconds. It was very slow going.

Despite my precautions, I was banking on my quarry having hit the trail again last night quickly after we saw him. What else could he do? He was not the type to sit and wring his hands. If he traveled all night, or as much as required to reach his objective, he might be dozens of miles away by now.

I was on William's trail for about an hour when I neared where we'd seen the headlight of the other snowmobile. I stopped, looked around for some shelter, pulled over beside a snowbank with a wind-sculptured flaring crest and took out the chart Stothers had made for me from notes the night before.

It was a single sheet of white cardboard, the kind some shirt laundries use, protected by Saran Wrap or a reasonable facsimile thereof. Near the bottom, he'd drawn an arrow pointed at tiny linked circles denoting the caribou trail. The length of this arrow was marked: "300 yards approx." At the top of this arrow was what looked like two golf balls close to one another. They were labeled "twin-peaked hill." Beyond that was what looked like a big tent labeled "long sharp-topped hill." Between Twin-Peaks and Sharp-Top, Stothers had drawn a rectangle with handlebars, labeled: "Snowmobile." In front of it he'd drawn outward-bursting lines like eyelashes, or a kid's concept of a headlight.

I went on slowly for nearly a mile watching to my right before, more like 400 yards away than 300, I saw a hill with two rounded peaks. I gazed carefully ahead, behind and to both sides. As I looked, I took up the shotgun at my right knee and loaded it, mostly by feel.

The shotgun law when you're hunting is one shell in the breech and two in the chamber, but that's for ducks and geese and ptarmigan. I'd never paid a lot of attention to it anyway until I became a special and had to check other people's guns from time to time. Now, for hunting men, it was back to the joys of childhood: one shell in the breech and five more into the chamber, all it would take. I'd used pump guns a lot and knew I could fire almost as fast as I could pull the trigger. I swung it to my shoulder, sighted on a scraggly tree, let the gun down and was swinging it up again, getting the feel of it, when a big Arctic hare jumped up in front of me. I had the gun on it encouragingly fast but of course didn't pull the trigger.

I put the gun back in its scabbard by my right leg and turned toward the twin-peaked hill. I went slowly and watchfully, the snowmobile at less than half speed. To climb directly over the hill would have taken more power. I figured I didn't need the extra noise, so I turned right to skirt the base of the hill. When I reached the other side I stopped to reconnoitre.

Before me was the long sharp-topped hill, as advertised. In the narrow, winding little glen between the two I could see plainly a snowmobile track—and something else.

I turned off the machine and could hear nothing. I took the binoculars out of the body-warmed front pocket of my parka. They fogged up immediately. I waited a minute or two to let their temperature adjust to the minus thirty-five or whatever we had out here. Meanwhile I wasn't as interested in the snowmobile track below me, as back along the glen to a place that even to the naked eye was noticeably not just right. When I could use the binoculars I saw that someone had made camp there and hadn't done much to make it look as if he hadn't.

At first, extra careful, I didn't move. I turned the binoculars along the snowmobile's trail heading straight west and out of sight. Then I swept the hills around. The sun had gone and it was one of those days when snow blended with sky in a way that made the horizon strictly guesswork. At dead slow I descended through the soft and unmarked snow to where the man had camped.

It was easy to see where his tent had been, a melted place where his stove had sat, a Cameo cigaret package, two Oh

Henry wrappers, an empty pork-and-beans can, an empty corned-beef can, a yellow stain in the snow where he had urinated, and an empty red five-gallon gas container. On its side in black paint was one word: Oscar.

I figured the man couldn't have been more than a minute or two away from his camp last night when we saw his light from the air. He could not have heard us or he wouldn't have started. Maybe our sound was wiped out by his snowmobile warming up while he got ready to move out. After we'd passed he might have thought that he'd got lucky, had been unseen, so didn't bother to clean up traces of his camp. Or, if he thought he'd been seen he might have panicked and zoomed out of there without the cleanup. Or maybe he was just some guy from Nashville who didn't know that the Arctic, while big, is not big enough to leave garbage around even half buried in snow and have it unnoticed. Discards don't go away in the Arctic. He wouldn't know that odds and ends left by weary and starving men a century or two ago are useful now as firm evidence that Sir John Franklin, for instance, spent much of a winter in one place, or Samuel Hearne in another. Admittedly, none of those early explorers left red gas cans around with the name Oscar painted on in black.

It was decision time. William's old trail along the road left by caribou herds was a few hundred yards south of me. But now I had a fresher track, and the conviction that, while moving separately, the two had the same destination—and that whichever one I followed likely would lead me to the same place, where also I'd find the Cessna and, I was convinced more and more, the three men who had been aboard.

I turned on the radio, wondering if the radio in the Cessna, if operational, could scan frequencies and eavesdrop.

So, I thought, what you gonna do, Matteesie, use smoke signals?

"Matteesie calling Fort Norman, over."

"About bloody time," Pengelly said. "Where are you? Over."

I told him, as closely as I could. "Found where a guy camped yesterday and left one of Oscar's gas cans. Over."

"So you're getting close. Want some help? Over."

"No help needed until I ask for it. I'm going to stay on the new guy's trail. Over and out."

After I picked up any debris that I thought might be useful (in court?) and began following this snowmobile trail not much more than half a day old, I jacked up the speed a little. He had moved at night and because he was the one breaking trail, I could travel at close to twice his night-time speed but didn't, for safety. If he had made his objective before daylight, in a few hours I might know a hell of a lot more than I did right now.

The ground drift was getting worse as the afternoon wore on. In places I'd lose the trail, but the contours of the little valleys and frozen streams pretty well dictated where he'd go, or I kept guessing right. If he'd had to make camp again at daylight he couldn't be far ahead. After another hour or so, near dusk, I dropped my speed to dead slow, a walking pace. If I caught up before nightfall when he'd feel safe to move again, I'd really like to see him before he saw me. Prudence is my middle name.

There came a time a little after six, not totally dark yet but with the sun down and shadows filling the hollows, when I began to feel very jumpy. By my machine's trip counter, I figured I was no more than six or seven miles from the Mackenzie. I'd been going all along on the idea that the Cessna's landing place, if there was one, was east of the river. If so, I was close.

Suddenly, well ahead, I could identify where the river was. On the shore south of Fort Norman was the area called the Smoking Hills. These were coal deposits on the east bank that had been burning as far back as recorded memory. Early explorers had seen them. From the river at night the fires on the bank could be seen glowing dimly, like nearly spent coals in a home fireplace late at night. But by day smoke could be seen rising here and there. I could see smoke now.

I stopped to think.

I had one Thermos of hot chocolate left. I drank a cup of it and ate the last of my sandwiches. Maybe it was time to give up for today, find a safe place for the tent, get the primus going, eat, sleep and be ready for the dawn. One thing was pretty sure—nobody was following me. And if I came on my quarry now, the gathering dark would be a help to anyone who became aware of my approach, and a hindrance to me and anyone I might summon to help. In short, it was time to camp. The only thing I didn't like about my present position was that here and there there were clumps of wispy trees. Like all Inuit brought up on vast, treeless, open spaces, I liked to be able to see. Anyway, I'd check in.

I unpacked the radio. "Matteesie here. Over."

"Ted Huff here, Matteesie. No more word on Bonner's whereabouts. Position, please. Over."

I wondered what the hell Ted was doing in Fort Norman. I gave my position as being about six or seven miles east of the Mackenzie and pretty well straight west of where I'd started from this morning, a position they had.

"No sign of anybody," I said. "But if they're around I must be getting close. Easier to handle by daylight, so I'm making camp. I'll report when I move again in the morning. What's doing there? Over."

Ted replied tersely. "William hasn't come back. Didn't catch the noon Canadian. Over and Out." No more than that. So he'd been in Fort Norman hoping to talk to William.

I was still holding the radio, wondering if I should switch it off and have a good sleep, or leave it on in case they wanted to call me.

I still hadn't decided when the radio seemed to explode.

First the radio seemed to explode, then I heard the shot. Naturally. A bullet travels faster than sound. The important thing was that the sound of the shot came from my left and was that of a Colt .45, which meant it had come from probably no more than fifty yards away, from a small hump of scrub and rock.

A lot of what I do has always been by instinct. I dove sideways and to my right to take shelter behind the snowmobile while reaching for the shotgun.

I lay still in the snow with the shotgun now in my hands and parts of the radio scattered around me. My mitts were off. The gun barrel's icy metal against my left hand felt like I was grabbing something red hot. My finger sliding from the safety to the trigger was not any more comfortable but I'd had bare hands on freezing metal before and never found it fatal.

I lay motionless, thinking hard. It might well have been that the way I fell made Billy Bob Hicks figure he'd got me. He'd been shooting at me and the radio just happened to bear the brunt. He probably still had only the handgun. If he'd had a rifle, he would have used it instead of shooting at what was practically maximum accurate range for the Colt. With a rifle he could have shot a lot sooner and could have circled wide now, safer with distance, and be ready to shoot again and again. But I could hear footsteps approaching in a silence of such profundity that each crunch of a foot into the snow sounded louder even than the beating of my heart.

He was coming from the other side of the snowmobile. The thunderous crunching of his boots on the snowy crust sounded closer and closer. I considered what I'd do the instant I saw him. Should I shoot immediately, hoping to beat his shot, or roll once and make him try to hit a moving target?

I've seen gunslingers in the movies do that. But was I good enough to be accurate in mid-roll?

When he rounded the end of the snowmobile about twenty feet away with the same black Colt held ready in his hand, the big edge I had was that I knew he was alive. He wasn't sure about me—and besides, I was in the snowmobile's shadow. I squeezed the trigger, pumped, shot again, pumped and fired one more even after the first shot into his chest jolted him convulsively backwards so that the second and third shots got him on the way down.

The Colt has a device which stops the trigger cold as soon as the handgrip relaxes. This must have happened a split second after my first shot, because his only shot was high and wild, a danger only to low-flying aircraft.

I stayed crouching, listening for other sounds. There were none. Then I walked over for a look at Billy Bob Hicks, or what was left of him after three shotgun hits from a range of about twenty feet. He should have stuck to bartending. That shotgun really did make a mess.

That night I mainly lay awake imagining a lot of things. I didn't want to sleep because I felt I was still in danger, with a lot to figure out. Yet, drowsing once, I thought I heard a wolf howling far away then snapped awake and couldn't hear it and decided it must have been a dream because wolves generally sang in chorus.

I had left Billy Bob Hicks precisely where he had fallen. He wasn't going anywhere. Ground-drift snow soon covered some of the stains of death. Splashes of blood were frozen to the cowl of my snowmobile, which I had not moved. If anyone or anything came upon him and thought of doing something rash, they'd have me to deal with. I thought of those movies where nobody can move the body until the police doctor, usually an old grump, arrives and makes notes about the cause of death and possible time of death, and says things like, "I can't answer that, inspector, until we examine the stomach contents on Monday." Meanwhile the lower classes in the police force are taking photographs and admiring the dear departed's taste in period furniture, kinky sex or whatever. Another guy shows up looking glum. "The murder weapon has no prints on it except Mrs. Thatcher's," he states, and the inspector snaps, "Try the loo."

No doubt about it, I really know my business, but I was preposterously short-staffed. The only regret I had was that dead murderers tell no tales. If I'd got him alive he might have been persuaded to clear up matters still pending, then in jail write his memoirs about an underprivileged life as a hit man. But that was a very mild regret. Leaving him alive would almost certainly have left me dead, an option I always tried to avoid.

Right after Billy Bob died and I lived, I had a few moments of indecision. I could run for the hills to guard against having Billy Bob's clients show up and win the next round. Or I could do nothing and wait for Pengelly sometime tomorrow morning to assume that my radio silence meant I was in trouble, and send help. Or I could keep on doing what I had been doing: trying alone to get the answers in what so far stood at a score of two dead, and counting.

I found myself nodding, even smiling. That last option was it.

For some reason then I thought of No Legs and his account of how to trap a wolf—the basic principle being that you bait the trap with something the wolf finds irresistible, like meat rubbed with beaver castor. What I had for bait was the body of Billy Bob Hicks and if any wolves showed up I'd have to shoo them away, but what I had in mind as possible arrivals was any or all of Albert Christian, Benny Batten or Harold Johns.

So I moved my outfit nearly a hundred yards back on the trail and into a few wispy trees where I could see without, I hoped, being seen. At this distance I'd need the rifle, so I unlimbered it. Then I rigged my tent in such a way that the snowmobile was the anchor wall to windward. The other side stretched sideways to where, parallel to the snowmobile and four feet or so away, the canvas crossed, and was anchored by, the loaded sled, which I'd unhitched and moved for that purpose. Although inside and snug, ground sheet and sled cover and anything else usable between me and the snow, I was somehow without appetite for boil-in-the-bag pemmican. I boiled snow, made tea, and kept warm in my sleeping bag while occasionally peering through a tiny but drafty slit in the flap of the tent. I'd lined everything up so that my sightline commanded any approach from the west.

But I didn't expect any visitors. If anyone was close enough to have heard the shots and had a mind to investigate (which was by no means certain; shots affect different people differently), they'd had lots of time.

Thinking over what I'd do the next day was fairly easy. I hadn't ventured from my position to try to find where Billy Bob had left his snowmobile. I didn't really care. I had to assume that he hadn't reached his colleagues, or clients, or whatever Christian, Batten and Johns turned out to be, or there would have been more of them dealing with me. Somewhere between here and the river I still might find the Cessna and its occupants, alive or dead or some of each. The matter of William's trip out here seemed more and more to be the key to a lot of things.

At the first grey light of morning I did one useful thing. When this was over, I certainly didn't want to be playing body, body, who's got the body. With the axe I cut a spindly sapling and to it tied a blue towel. I stuck the sapling as far into the snow as I could by Billy Bob's now rigidly frozen body and braced it further with blocks of snow, some of them on top of Billy Bob. Then I made morning tea, ate some biscuits, stuck some chocolate in my parka pocket and embarked on Plan B—or was it Plan C? This was to go south slowly. As Billy Bob presumably had got no farther than right here, I was hoping to find again William's snowmobile tracks which I had abandoned the day before.

As I traveled, watching for any human sign, I wondered again how long it would be before someone in Fort Norman—Pengelly or Ted Huff if he was still there—would begin to feel that their continued inability to raise me by radio might mean I was in trouble. Somebody then might make a command decision to send out an aircraft. The thought depressed me. It would be an interruption. The body of Billy Bob was one thing, but not all. I was on to something that I wanted to do by myself.

Like always, Matteesie, I thought.

When I was in my late teens out alone in the Barrens on a trapline, isolation was happiness even when I came back famished, tired, with little or nothing to show.

Or I'd be out alone hoping for a caribou so that I could drive my dogs back into camp with the skinned carcass on the sled and see everybody run out into the open to welcome me, smiling men and women and children dressed in caribou skins yelling, ''Eeee, eeee, Matteesie,'' while I, the great hunter, shared out the meat.

I had gone less than a half-mile south looking for the extension of William's tracks when there they were.

Ground drift had covered many of the signs but they were still easier to find than they'd been when I'd followed them along the caribou trail, which must have turned elsewhere. The greater visibility was because from time to time there were two distinct trails, one going west and the other east. Some overlapped but not all. William had come out here, reached some objective farther west, and later had gone back. I stayed with his older westbound track.

I'd been going slowly for an hour or so when William's track turned at right angles and uphill. The highest hills in the Franklins were behind me now, the land gradually dropping and flattening out the nearer I got to the river. Today I had crossed a half-dozen frozen ponds, some with stumps and skeletons of stunted trees sticking up through the ice. When I came to the crest of this hill, something made me stop.

It was a sound, the clamor a dog makes when it is part wolf, as huskies are.

I couldn't see it but I could hear it. It was nearly impossible that this was the sound I'd heard the night before and thought I'd been dreaming. A trick of the wind might carry it that far, but I didn't think so. I had an eerie feeling that I'd occasionally had before, when premonition had told me something that actuality couldn't. I had been thinking about William's dog not long before I had dozed, falling off into brief sleep and then been convinced I'd been dreaming.

I was still convinced I'd been dreaming then, but I wasn't dreaming now.

Below me was a pond that differed importantly from others I'd crossed in the last little while. This one was maybe two hundred yards long, more like a stretch of river except that its surrounding unbroken hills were not only along both sides, but closed off the ends. It was shaped more like a stadium than some stadiums. All it needed was a football team and a considerable rise in temperature.

Nothing showed on it but what I took to be the usual animal tracks. When my binoculars showed more detail, I could see no break at all in the snow covering. Most lakes or rivers will have a few windswept spots but not this one; it was totally protected by the hills.

I swept every foot of it for signs, however old and snow-covered, of an aircraft's skis. Nothing. Then I moved the glasses carefully around the shores, which had here and there a sparse growth of trees. Again, I saw nothing. The dog howled again. The sound echoed around the hills so that pinpointing its source was impossible. But it was down there and if it was William's Smokey it must be chained or William never would have gotten away without it. Why leave it behind? Even if William was planning to come back, there must be another reason. From what No Legs said, the dog had made trips out and back many times, alternately running or riding William's sled.

I considered going down by snowmobile to investigate, but instead unloaded my snowshoes from the sled, looped the tapes swiftly around my feet and ankles and calves, put the clip in the rifle, more shells in my pockets, slipped the safety catch off, and started slowly downhill.

Going down a steep hill in deep loose dry snow on trail shoes is no cinch. Wider shoes get a better grip, but trail shoes were what I had. Once, putting my right foot into what looked like safe snow the foot started to slide out of control from a hard crust a few inches below the surface. I got my other foot up fast to a parallel position so that when I slid for six or seven feet I was more skier than snowshoer, but kept my balance.

I could almost hear Pengelly yelling, "For Chrissake, Matteesie! You'll give me heart failure!" I went on more carefully.

The dog still was singing its wild song, the howling somewhere between an excited welcome and a threat.

By the time I reached the flat surface of the pond, I was nearly sure where the sound was coming from. Then I saw the Cessna. My eyes went by it and then did a double-take. My first glimpse was only of the shape of a window, barely discernible through the aircraft's cover of branches and whole trees. I could see that great care had been taken to keep it unseen from the air. Even someone flying low might not have seen it, tucked in against the bank and covered from above and from all sides.

I stopped the instant I spotted that window shape. In a few seconds I saw the dog. He fitted No Legs' description of William's onetime lead dog, the dark ruff along his shoulders fading to lighter brown on his flanks, a Greenland husky snout. He was chained to a tree a short distance from the aircraft, as if he'd been left on guard. He was plunging again and again toward me to the full extent of the chain.

Apart from him there was no sign of life.

I yelled, "Hey!"

My voice echoed from the hills around ". . . hey, hey, hey . . ."

"Is anybody there?"

". . . dy there, there, there . . ."

I would have liked a coffee and a camp stool right then, to think this over. I held the rifle ready, my mitted left hand holding it by the stock, flexing my bare right hand constantly to keep it limber if I had to pull a trigger. I yelled again and then started toward the aircraft. I don't mind admitting that I was in a high state of nervous readiness. If anyone had opened up on me right then I would have been shooting yet.

But I heard no sound except the half-crazy dog.

When I got to maybe fifty feet from the Cessna I yelled again.

At that precise instant the dog fell silent and I heard what sounded like the weakest cry in all creation: a faint, faint, "Help!"

I still didn't storm in. It wasn't the situation for "away dull care," and so on. I took one step at a time, cautiously, stopping to check the hills around. I noticed that whole trees, although small, had been cut and jammed into the snow a few feet offshore from the Cessna, part of its shield. It was all so well done that there wasn't even a clear path through to the aircraft. Yet I could see that all this camouflage could have been taken away in a matter of moments for the aircraft to warm up and taxi out for takeoff.

I had to move a couple of eight-foot trees in my careful approach to the door on the pilot's side. The dog was the next problem. He'd be in the way. I turned deliberately and pointed the rifle at him. Any northern dog knows what comes next when a gun is pointed. He whined and slunk back. As I moved forward watching him I heard the faint human sound again, this time a muffled groan. It was definitely from the Cessna.

The dog started up again. Dogs don't get on my nerves normally but I wanted to be able to hear other things right now. I turned and snarled at it in Inuktitut, which it translated as, "Shut up!"

It shut up.

Two or three feet from the Cessna I called loudly, "I've got a gun, safety off, full of dum dum bullets, and I'm coming in."

No answer.

I thought it would be nice if I could do like in the movies, wrench the door open and jump in with my feet spread solidly wide and all ten fingers on the trigger.

On snowshoes, forget it. I laboriously untied the tapes, opened the door and climbed in.

T W E L V E

The primus stove had been going not long before. I could smell it. Two candles were burning, stuck in the necks of empty bottles. It was standard, by the book, winter survival practice. Alone in the rear of the cabin Harold Johns was staring my way from where he lay in a sleeping bag on a pile of parkas and life jackets. Even in the bad light coming from the open door I thought he didn't look any too healthy. His face was thin by nature. Now it was mottled and bruised, his mouth set in a thin line, the tip of his nose split and scabbed. Peering at me, trying to see who I was, his expression was one of fear.

I introduced myself: "Inspector Matthew Kitologitak, RCMP."

At that he tried impulsively to sit up in his sleeping bag. He didn't quite make it but did muster a fervent, "God, am I glad to see you! Can't get up. Got a broken leg." And confirmed, "I'm Harold Johns."

I looked around but still couldn't figure out what had happened. The radio had been trashed, wires everywhere, but there were no other signs of damage. The food box, close enough that Johns didn't have to get up to reach it, was half full.

Then I noticed with a sudden rush of adrenalin that he had one hand on a gun. It was the aircraft's emergency rifle, *Komatik Air* burned into its butt. I must have looked astonished. Johns followed my gaze and said, "William left it for me."

Stranger and stranger. "When?"

"Day before yesterday."

That was Saturday, the day Edie and No Legs and I met William coming back. A day later in Yellowknife had come William's drunken claim to Gloria that he'd fixed "those two bastards" and would get the other one, too.

He'd also said he didn't blame Johns, although obviously his decision not to impute blame didn't quite extend to hauling Johns the hell out of here to safety. Which meant, in turn, that Johns knew things William did not want the world to know. But why leave the dog? Smokey was not only loyal, but not a threat to testify in a court of law. My confusion was mounting. I simply hadn't expected to find only one person; or at least only one in evidence. What I really needed was the truth, the whole truth, the story from the start. But I might not have time now. So I asked the main question: "Where are Christian and Batten?"

I got something then, a roll of the eyes, a grimace, a look of remembered despair. I thought: until just now Johns thought that he was going to die before this thing was over; and that Christian and Batten were the heavies in his nightmare.

"They're gone. I imagine with the money, or a lot of it."

"Gone how?"

"I don't know everything. When William arrived, what was it, Thursday or Friday, there was a lot of screaming, but mostly outside where I couldn't hear what it was about. Then Saturday they all went out early, before it was really light—"

"All?" I asked. I wanted things spelled out.

"Christian, Batten, William and even the dog. I heard the snowmobile, the dog barking, and all that fading into the distance and after a couple of hours William came back and said he'd taken the other two on the snowmobile to where they could catch a ride, I guess on the winter tractor road. It isn't far away."

If he was being selective in his facts, how could I tell? "Then he tied up the dog," I said, "and left by himself, right?"

"Right."

"Did he say he'd be back?"

Johns nodded. "Not only for me, he'd have to come back for his dog."

It suddenly occurred to me that Smokey couldn't have eaten for three days. Rummaging in the food box I found a two-pound can of corned beef, stripped off the lid with the key provided for that purpose, levered the meat out with a knife, went to the Cessna door and threw it at Smokey. Down it went. Two gulps. Plus a tail-wagging vote of thanks and a couple of blood-curdling howls for more.

It seemed a good idea at that point to produce my rum. There were two cups on the floor, and a kettle on the primus with a little water in it. In the Arctic it isn't hardship to do without ice. I poured two stiff ones, left the bottle beside him, and asked, "Is this where you were intending to land all along?"

He took a swallow of rum and let out a derisive snort. "At first Christian said probably Wrigley, south of here. But when we got near Fort Norman, could have landed there, he pulled out a detailed map showing this place. He said William had drawn it for them and that this was where we were going. I was too busy flying to argue or use the radio, even if he'd let me. The weather was bad but I knew if the worst came to the worst I could always land on the big river, it's close enough. You know, at that time this thing was still just a charter to me, a hairy one, but that's what this country can be like."

"I'm aware of that," I said—I believe the word is—drily.

"It wasn't any cinch getting in, just at dusk, but I've seen worse. They told me to taxi in by the bank here, more sheltered. Seemed to make sense. That was the first night. It was the next day when I started asking questions. They were cutting trees and branches for camouflage. At first they just ignored my questions about that but then Batten said he was going to beat the shit out of me and Christian said don't, they needed me sooner or later to fly the airplane. By then I knew I was in trouble. Christian, I thought he was a friend of mine, Jesus, did tell me we were waiting for somebody, didn't say who, and then we'd take off. When William came, I thought maybe it was him we were waiting for, but looks like it wasn't . . ."

He paused. "Days before William got here we heard on the radio about Morton. I was sick about it, I knew Morton, I'd flown him a few times. When I looked at them they were grinning at each other, and Batten said, 'Good old Billy Bob.' Who's Billy Bob?"

"The man who killed Morton. The guy they were waiting for here."

Johns sighed. "Eventually something like that occurred to me as a possibility, but I didn't say anything. I thought if I could ever get out of here, then I could figure out what to do. Sure as hell couldn't do anything until then. I think if either of them had been able to fly a plane, I'd be dead by now . . ."

He paused for a minute and drained his cup of rum. I shoved the bottle toward him again. He poured and drank. Then, despondently, he said what many a man has said, or thought, before him, "I wish I could have been a goddamn hero in this thing. It kept bugging me that I couldn't figure out how. Then we got drinking one night, too much, and I told them they could rot before I'd even try to fly them out. When we were wrestling around that time, I got my leg caught in some webbing just as Batten took a dive at me.

That's when I broke my leg. I haven't been able to move from right here since.''

So things were coming together. As hard-hearted as it sounds, it wouldn't be the first time a son had collaborated knowingly or unknowingly in his father's murder. But maybe all he'd thought he was doing when he told the others about this place, even drew a map for them, was sending them to a good hideout. At that time his father was still alive. William could have been only trying to help keep the money safe, including what he thought was his share, until they knew where they stood. If the report they'd got about their operation being blown was true, they're gone and scattered but their bankroll is intact. Otherwise they've just been on a little trip, they come back, and presto, they're back in business.

Then came Morton's murder, arranged by Bonner in that series of phone calls. If the guesswork part of that scenario is true, William is left with two options: to go after his father's murderer, or to go after money he thought was coming to him. He might not have even guessed at first that the two were linked.

The part I still wasn't sure about was the whereabouts of Christian and Batten. I'd been rather polite with Johns, so far. If Christian and Batten came rolling back in now, I was in trouble. I didn't like that idea. I thought of a lot of other guys I knew, friends, people I'd worked with. This is precisely when they might slap a guy around, stick a gun under his chin and suggest, ''Talk.''

Was I going to just sit here nodding and smiling while some refugee from Upper Canada College snowed me, or at the very least didn't tell me all he knew, and as a result perhaps endangered my life?

What if I took two fast steps and slapped his face when he wasn't ready for it?

The answer to the first question was yes; I was going to sit there nodding and smiling.

But I do have my ways. ''I'll tell you something,'' I said, ''I killed Billy Bob Hicks out in the snow last night.''

That got Johns' attention; his eyes snapped up to stare at mine.

"I think if Billy Bob had managed to get here, after killing me first, he wouldn't have believed you when you said you didn't know where Batten and Christian are. I think he would have done little things like grinding the two parts of your broken leg together, to refresh your memory. I think he might well have ended up killing you and killing the dog, then have gone looking for Batten and Christian. Now I'm asking you a question and if what you tell me eventually turns out to be a lie and people get killed, you'll be the first. I guarantee it."

Then I asked, "Are Batten and Christian still around here?"

He gave the smallest negative head-shake I'd ever seen. Moved about an inch each way. Yet I didn't think he was scared anymore. My threat to kill him seemed to have restored his courage. It sometimes happens that way.

"You can believe me or not, I don't give a damn which," he said. "I haven't seen them for three days now. I've got no reason not to believe William when he said he took them to the tractor road. None of them are pilots. One of the things I told them was there was no way I could fly this Cessna out of here on this short a take-off run with a full load, like there'd be with them plus the guy they were waiting for aboard. I think after that they'd grab any chance they thought might get them away with the money."

While I was thinking that over for angles, Johns repeated what he'd said before. "William told me he'd come back. I've been expecting him. Did he tell you how to find me?"

I was shaking my head. William hadn't done a damn thing helpful, especially that one.

As I was replying, "No, I found you on my own," I heard an aircraft in the distance.

I reached over to grab *Komatik Air*'s rifle from under Johns. A safety precaution. I was beginning to believe him, but no use taking chances. When I pulled at the gun I was in a hurry and did it roughly. His face went chalk white. I stared and then gently slid my hand over the part of the sleeping bag I'd dislodged when I yanked the rifle out. His bent right knee was pointed one way but the toes on that leg pointed in the exact opposite direction. I winced. Moving that setup might make anybody's face go chalk white.

I laid the rifles in the doorway, jumped out of the Cessna, floundered out of Smokey's range to tie on my snowshoes, then went back for the guns. I was still under cover. From the south the aircraft noise was getting very loud.

Then, flying at no more than a hundred feet directly over where I'd left the snowmobile, I could see first that it was a Beaver and then saw Stothers' horn-rimmed glasses on the pilot side. I couldn't make out who was in the passenger seat. Both were staring downward as intently as if my snowshoe trail down that hill and across the pond had been entered in the compulsory figures at the Calgary Olympics.

I ran out in the open and waved. They waved back madly. Then I walked swiftly back, opened the Cessna door, told Johns that the arrivals were friendly, we'd soon get him out to a hospital, and heard him call weakly, "Good."

By the time I got back to where I could see, Stothers was circling the length of the pond in a careful tour of inspection. That done, he banked out of sight beyond the north rim.

On the way back he came over the peak at least six feet above his normal wolf-harassing altitude, then with the way clear below he practically fell out of the sky, flying that Beaver like a kid riding a bicycle instead of an old guy with wars and women and God knows what all behind him. Nobody could have touched down closer to shore than he did. Maybe in some things it's the old guys who do it best.

Considering that there are no brakes on a ski-equipped Beaver, Stothers made a masterful assumption that the deep snow would stop him fast enough that he wouldn't plow into the bank at the end of his run. He stopped just short, then turned and taxied along to where I stood. The passenger was

Pengelly, who got his door open, jumped down, sank up to his knees in snow, and floundered forward.

I expected he'd say something smart-ass like, "Dr. Kitologitak, I presume?" but for once he was out of quips.

"Jesus, Matteesie, who's that back at the blue flag?"

I told him.

"I just got a fast look at him with the binocs when we circled low, afraid it might have been you." Then, deadpan, "I could pretty well see what you did to him. I'm sure he had it coming, but . . ."

"But what?" I asked.

"You still okay for ammunition?"

I said something very rude.

Stothers hadn't even said hello. He was staring at the Cessna and saying, "Well, well." He slogged over closer to look at the coverup job, then walked in and kicked loose snow from around one of the plane's skis.

"Wouldn't be hard to get this thing out of here," he said ruminatively. "Good thing there wasn't some warm weather, a thaw and then more freeze, or this thing might have been locked in here until breakup."

Then he turned to me and scratched his beard on the left side of his face, that habit he had. "What did you find, Matteesie?"

I told him Harold Johns was inside the Cessna with a badly broken leg; that William's dog, chained to a tree, was what was sounding like a whole six-dog team; and that Christian and Batten were not in evidence, one theory being that they'd gone out to the tractor road.

"We're not far from that," Pengelly said.

"How far?" I asked.

"A mile or so. Easy enough on snowshoes, if they had any. Or, of course, William was out here with the snowmobile. Maybe he took them; they're his buddies."

That's what Johns had said. Now I thought seriously about the tractor road. There's a precious few of them through the North, running for a few months in winter where no road vehicles at all can go through the rest of the year. When ice in rivers and lakes is solid enough to take the weight and the pounding, some years sooner and others later, but normally early January, the big rigs eat up the hard miles through Arctic days and nights, plunging through into icy lakes from time to time when they try to stretch the season too far into spring.

Their crews drink hard, sleep little, live lives of high reck-lessness and get paid accordingly. But one thing those drivers would not do is drive past a couple of men on foot in this winter wonderland and not stop. If anyone in that fix had some kind of a plausible story, such as they'd been on the plane that had been lost last week, the big rig crews would make room somehow. Anyway, going south they're usually empty. And one thing we could count on was that if Christian and Batten saw a cloud of snow approaching that meant a tractor train was heading north, they'd stay well out of sight. North would be people waiting.

"How's your radio?" I asked Stothers.

He smiled. "Oh, fine, thanks, Matteesie. Nice of you to ask."

He'd spent a couple of hours with Pengelly, of course. Learning jokey bad habits.

I said to Pengelly, "Will you call Inuvik and ask them to put out an alert on Christian and Batten for Blackwater Lake, Wrigley, Simpson, Providence, all the way along the road. Somebody could check what rigs have been through going south, and did they pick anybody up. Mention they're prob-ably armed and dangerous."

Pengelly looked at me. "You got charges in mind?"

"Conspiracy to commit murder."

"You think Ted Huff will buy that?"

"Yes, if you tell him I've got enough supporting evi-dence."

"Right." Pengelly started plunging knee deep back to the Beaver.

"You got any painkillers in your emergency kit?" I asked Stothers.

"Nothing much."

"Anything to drink?"

"Brandy," Stothers said.

"Good." I explained that I thought we'd get Johns to the drunken stage that some people call feeling no pain, employing for this purpose rapid infusion of either Stothers's brandy or my rum, whichever Johns preferred, to anesthetize his broken leg for the trip. We'd talked for a couple of minutes when Pengelly called from the Beaver, "Hey, Matteesie. The inspector wants to talk to you."

I climbed into the aircraft and reported in.

"Pengelly tells me what you're thinking, these accessory or conspiracy to murder charges," Ted said. "The job you did on the murderer, I'll need something on that now and full report later. We don't want to be caught short on any of this."

"We won't be. I saw the guy kill Morton and I looked him in the eye after I killed him. Same guy. No doubt at all."

I gave him an abbreviated version of the Billy Bob demise, and what Harold Johns had told me about Batten and Christian waiting for Billy Bob. To me, that made them at least accessories. A judge might rule differently, if you could find a judge insane enough, but there was definitely enough to pick them up on if we could find them, plus enough to pick up William on, and certainly enough to pick up Bonner.

"Nobody except Bonner and William had been where they could telephone Billy Bob and arrange that fast take-off to intercept Morton," I said. "I still can't bring myself to believe it was William. And it was Bonner I saw on the phone."

There was no waste air.

"How do you read the reaction in Fort Norman when we charge William?" he asked.

I said, "Well, they won't have long to stay shocked. There's probably a media balloon race on right now to see who gets in there first for the gory details. And non-details.

There'll be enough media flying in to keep everybody in Fort Norman busy talking about what a nice boy William was, and they just couldn't believe he was mixed up in the murder of his own father . . ." I stopped. Luckily, caution sometimes sneaks up on one. "And maybe he wasn't, really. But once it was done he sure as hell could have helped more than he did. Maybe that charge should be obstructing justice, or however that one goes."

From Ted came a sound of relief. "Good idea. Hell of a job you've done, Matteesie." He paused. "There's something else. I hate to tell you, but I guess you should know—they've sent someone else to Leningrad on that thing there."

I hadn't thought of Leningrad for days.

"The deputy minister asked me to pass on to you personally his regrets and to say there'll be other times."

I should even think about a deputy minister, up to my ass in this?

I asked Ted to tell Thomas Nuniviak at Komatik Air that his Cessna was safe and if he wanted, in a few days somebody could bring him down for it. By then we'd be finished with it.

He said he would.

"Oh," I said. "Would you also let the commissioner know that Harold Johns is okay, leg broken and not much else, apparently an innocent bystander, so the commissioner can pass that on to your friend and mine, the finance minister?"

I was wondering, if it hadn't been for Buster's original phone call about Johns, would I be here at all? Probably. I would have been flying out on the same aircraft even if I'd been heading back for Ottawa.

"Will do," Ted said.

After the over and out I sat there in the Beaver for a minute thinking not so much about Leningrad as about how quickly one obsession can be replaced by another, if a guy has that kind of a mind. Which I have, in what I think of as my unobtrusive way.

Stothers had been waiting outside while Ted and I talked,

Stothers being that kind of a gentleman. He climbed in looking rather thoughtful.

"You know we can't take off out of here with much load," he said.

I said I figured that.

He nodded. "I imagine you want me to take Johns back, get him to the hospital, probably straight to Norman Wells, if he's as bad as you say. I'll have to strip right down, leave extra gas and supplies here, everything dumpable. We can get it later."

"Right."

"I'll tool up and down and make a runway for myself."

I'd foreseen that. Soft snow was a help in landing on a short runway, acting as a brake, but could be very dicey on take-off.

"So what are you and Pengelly going to do?" he asked.

I didn't tell him precisely. I didn't know for sure, but had a couple of odd ideas scratching around in my head. "We've got some checking to do around the aircraft. Also, I want to see if a snowmobile can get from here to the tractor road, and if not look for signs of anybody going up to their ass in snow trying it on foot. We'll probably overnight here and pick up the body on the way back."

"I wondered about wolves getting at it," Stothers said.

I shrugged. I really didn't care. Tell the truth, I was feeling rather flat. Maybe a half-eaten frozen body as an exhibit in a murder trial would make the *Guinness Book of Records* and I'd go down in history. "Right now I'll bring my snowmobile down here and we'll get Johns out to the Beaver," I said.

I had taken a step or two, hating to think of being out here with God knows what going on and us without a radio, wishing that Stothers or Pengelly had thought of bringing a spare when they might have suspected mine was kaput (but nobody's perfect) when Stothers called, "Hey!"

I turned. He handed me a plastic shopping bag.

"What's this?" I asked, looking in to see a two-way radio. Good thing I'd kept my criticism to myself. He grinned as if he'd read my thoughts. As I snowshoed across toward the snowmobile, he started his engine. He had been twice back and forth lengthwise along the pond's surface, flattening the snow, before I reached the machine and idled dead slow back to the Cessna.

"Hey, Smokey," I said to the dog. He wagged his tail, still howling.

Inside, Pengelly obviously had been working hard on his phase of the feeling-no-pain project. I'd told him to have no more than one social drink himself, if he had to, just to get the process going. He was chatting up Johns as much as possible, maybe even getting a few angles I'd missed while Johns had been sober. Johns now was slurring his words rather nicely. Every little bit helps.

I told them Johns would go out with Stothers, soon to be in the arms of nurses, doctors, and people with notebooks and TV cameras and tape recorders. Pengelly and I would stay and mop up.

"So it's you and me for the snowmobile," Pengelly said cheerfully. "Tomorrow, eh? A night here. I mustn't give away all the rum."

"That leaves *you* on the snowmobile, at least after we pick up Billy Bob's machine," I corrected. "I'll drive that and of course you'll have the other passenger."

"But there isn't any other . . . I mean, who? . . . Oh, shit!" he said.

I asked if he'd seen Billy Bob's snowmobile anywhere around, when going by.

"Yeah, it's over a hill to the south. Little camp. You didn't see it?"

"Didn't look," I said. "Does it have a sled?"

He said it had. "Must have liberated one somewhere."

"Well," I said, "because I don't know what shape that machine is in, we'll load everything that needs to go back on mine and you drive it. I'll take the other."

I didn't know yet exactly where I was going to take it.

In a half hour, long shadows from the hills to the west

were falling across what Stothers now had looking like something a plane could take off from.

Stothers took his final run and taxied back and gave me a thumbs-up sign. He was ready. Pengelly and I carried Johns out gingerly. I wished we had as a stretcher the sheet of plywood we'd used as the unloading ramp—ages ago, it seemed, but in reality only yesterday morning.

Pengelly drove the snowmobile out to the Beaver. I walked alongside and steadied the groaning passenger. It struck me as sort of funny what was happening in this total Arctic solitude, or what should have been solitude. Here was a snow-covered bowl not much bigger than a football field, surrounded by hills, with a plane about to take off carrying a well-inebriated man who, presumably unwittingly, had flown a couple of drug dealers out of danger. Setting up a howl was Smokey the faithful dog. That shape hidden from most eyes was an aircraft belonging to an Inuk school chum of mine. Back on the trail was a dead man who, one hoped, would still be there tomorrow in a piece large enough to satisfy any lawyer who cried habeus corpus when the trial came up of four others who had been engaged in both drugs and murder. I wondered if I'd forgotten anyone. Didn't think so. I thought of Maxine, Gloria, Lois and Edie; No Legs, Charlie and Nancy Paterson, Bertha Pengelly and others. Meanwhile Stothers was gunning his engine to a high pitch before he let it jump away, yanked it into the air, seemed to hang on the propeller, losing air speed, wings wavering perilously. Then he missed the north ridge by a few feet, and was gone.

"Hey!" called Pengelly.

"What's on your mind?" I called back.

"The cocktail hour."

While I was walking toward him, the radio I was carrying suddenly squawked. I opened it up. "Matteesie here. Over."

"Inuvik here." I didn't know the voice. "We've traced Jules Bonner as far as Calgary and lost him there. No sign of Christian and Batten. Can't find William Cavendish. Over.''

''What do you mean, you can't find William? I know he didn't make the first plane back to Fort Norman after the memorial service but how the hell can he disappear? Over.''

''He went to the airport in time but didn't board the regular Canadian. Instead, he hitched a ride on a light charter that was in, going to Wrigley and Simpson. He got off at Wrigley. Trying to find him there right now.''

Pengelly had been standing in the doorway of the Cessna, listening to both ends of the conversation.

''You know where William will be right now, eh?'' he said.

''Yeah. Heading for here.''

''He won't know that we found this place or anything else that's happened.''

''That's right.''

''So what do we do, get somebody else out here?''

That was the opposite of what I had in mind.

THIRTEEN

"Great goddamn cocktail hour this is," Pengelly yelled over my shoulder from behind.

You pretty well have to yell, on a snowmobile, or not talk at all. I preferred not to talk at all, so I didn't answer. Not that I figured the hills had ears. It is just that taciturnity on the trail is a cultural heritage of great antiquity, which no doubt is why none of the early explorers ever recorded in his diary meeting up with an Eskimo windbag.

"I said, 'Great goddamn cocktail hour this is!' " Pengelly roared again.

I gave the throttle a little twist, upping the speed and shutting him up. Speeding across the snowy wastes at night in a snowmobile isn't all that bad, given the conditions we had. Clear sky, full moon, frosty breaths whipped out and gone. We were both in parkas with the wolverine fringe covering much of the face, heavy pants tucked into kneehigh boots, face-masks, gauntlets reaching almost to our elbows. We'd been lucky. There'd been no snow and not a great deal of ground drift in the last twelve hours since I'd driven in. That made my trail easy to follow in the headlight.

That morning I'd had to be wary, drive dead slow every

time I rounded a bend or topped a rise. Never knew what
was ahead. Now I could drive much faster because I knew
exactly what was ahead: a blue towel on a stake marking a
body.

Only one thing slowed us now and again: the sled bouncing along behind us was heavier than it had been this morning. We'd loaded it only with what we needed, including
extra fuel, but also with everything else that might have given
away who had been in or near what I now was identifying in
my mind as William's Secret Garden. The various tracks
would tell him everything except, who? There'd been an aircraft, a snowmobile, someone on snowshoes—but who?

I remembered the book *The Secret Garden* from childhood, the first one I'd ever had read to me. The teacher read
it to our class in my first school term at Inuvik. I didn't
remember a lot of details, except that it was a place where a
little girl went but nobody else knew about. William had
been coming out here winter and summer since his teens,
No Legs had told me. It was William's place to be alone. I
wondered if Morton had ever come out here with him. More
probably, being a good man, he had simply accepted that
there was a place where his son liked to go, by himself.

I could imagine William coming here in spring or fall,
months when the tractor road was just an impassable cut
through the bush. He'd be trying to miss the worst of the
mosquitoes and black flies, maybe traveling by outboard or
canoe against the slow current of the Big Smith or maybe
close to the east bank of the Mackenzie. Along the shores
and in the walk in from either river the brief summer's flowers would be a gentle, varied carpet leading to his secret
place.

I didn't know where that had been. Maybe it wasn't right
on the pond. More likely, I thought, it was between the pond
and the banks of the Mackenzie. There he'd have been able
to camp and fish and hunt the days away with nothing else
moving except an occasional barge tow on the river or some
of those venturesome couples or families who'd planned for

a year and got themselves outfitted in Simpson or Wrigley to travel downriver, camping at night, taking home movies to show back home in Chicago or wherever.

"Want me to drive for a while?" Pengelly yelled. I knew the feeling. He had a firm grip around my waist, but being a passenger on a snowmobile isn't exactly going first class.

"No. We're almost there." As he'd come in by air, he didn't have the little landmarks I was using. The ride didn't seem as long to me.

Soon we came to where I'd turned away from my camp and the remains of Billy Bob to look for William's tracks. I cut to less than half speed climbing a rise. There in my headlight was the stake with the blue towel on top.

I stopped at the crest of the rise. The idling engine seemed almost silent after the noise of hard driving. Pengelly jumped off, flapping his arms against his body for warmth.

"Where's his snowmobile from here?" I called.

He pointed out the direction and got back aboard. It wasn't more than two or three hundred yards along, north a hill or two from William's trail. The key was in it. I'd figured on that. When I'd searched him there was a fair amount of Canadian and US currency, but no key. When you leave a snowmobile to kill someone, you don't bother taking the key.

"Now we hope it goes," I said, pumping the primer and then pulling the starting cord. The engine burst into life and after a minute idled smoothly. I got on and drove, Pengelly following on the other machine. Near where Billy Bob's body lay we pulled in to park with the headlights focused on the grotesque snowy lump under its blue towel marker.

"We gonna camp here?" Pengelly called hopefully.

This was where I had to start explaining, so I did.

Pengelly was incredulous. "If you're going back there, why the hell didn't we just hide out someplace and wait for him?"

"The dog," I said. "It is a smart dog and he has seen us go and heard us until the sound faded right away. He will believe that we are gone." I could tell that Pengelly didn't share my belief in the necessity to outwit Smokey. "If we were anywhere around there, the first thing the dog would do when William let him loose was run straight to where we were."

"Yeah, but what's going to stop him doing that just because you're back there by yourself?"

I realized we could be there all night debating the capabilities of dogs. Sometime, I wouldn't mind.

"Look," I said, "I'm sorry about this, but I'm going back and you're going on."

"You're pulling rank!" Pengelly said, full of incredulity. "Jesus!"

"Think of it this way," I said, "Bertha will be pleased."

He started to say something that started with an f and had to do with Bertha, but realized it was not applicable in the circumstances, swallowed hard and let it go.

I tried to placate him a little while repacking the sleds. "When William arrives—*if* he arrives—he could stonewall us until hell froze over, or until a plane arrived to take us all out, and we'd be no further ahead than we are now. I'd like a chance to see what he does if he's sure he's alone."

Meanwhile I was loading my tent, sleeping bag, gas, food, primus, axe, guns and everything else I'd need for a few days, onto Billy Bob's trailer and putting everything else on the trailer Pengelly would tow back. Pengelly had fallen silent, helping me, his big jaw sticking out glumly, bereft of wisecracks. Finally we pulled Billy Bob's body out of its snow covering and tied it, in all its frozen-stiff awkwardness, on the top of the load Pengelly would pull.

While doing this I looked once more into the face of the man I had killed. When I'd looked at him the first time, right after those three shotgun blasts, his body was loose and slack with a lot of blood splashed on his face.

Now I could see that the real mess was more from the neck down. I must have stood there for a minute or more looking at him. I was thinking that here was somebody his mother no doubt loved, which goes to show you. Maybe others, too. Still, I was thinking of the time I killed a polar bear so close to me that when he fell dead, he fell partly on me. I was also thinking of a time I'd found a wolverine in one of my traps. He was busy chewing his trapped leg off so he could get away and when I came up on him he turned and tried to spring at me, snarling. I remembered that in killing the polar bear and again in killing the wolverine, both times I'd said something, always said it when I killed an animal or bird. I'd said, "I'm sorry," and felt it. But when I looked at Billy Bob now I was thinking of that instant when he'd placed that .45 against Morton Cavendish's unconscious head and fired. Three times. Same number I'd fired into him. And I knew I would never be sorry.

His sprawled legs and arms made handy places to lash the ropes around and pull them tight.

"I'll keep in touch," I said to Pengelly. "I'll call you as often as I can, but don't you call me. And tell everybody else, Inuvik included, not to call me."

He got it. I didn't want the radio suddenly squawking just when it would blow my cover, or interrupt (I could only hope) something that would answer all the questions.

"All set?" I said.

"Yep," he said. "How about you?"

"Ready to go," I said.

I could see him in the light of our headlights as he looked at me across Billy Bob's body, and grinned.

"You forgot to pack the ammunition," he said, and handed me two boxes of shotgun shells.

I stuffed them into my parka pockets, laughing, couldn't help it. Trust Pengelly to exit laughing.

An hour later, I stopped and made camp, still miles from the pond. The moon now was playing peek-a-boo with the clouds, but with that and my flashlight, I could see well enough as I unhooked the sled and pulled it around parallel to the snowmobile and lashed the tent between the two vehicles as I had—jeez, was it only last night?—so that I was protected from both sides against wind and weather.

Inside and snug I started the primus. Snow translates into water at the rate of about ten to one so periodically I reached my plate out through the flap and got more. When I had enough boiling water I made tea, dropped in a package of boil-in-the-bag beef stew, drank tea while it got hot, slit the bag with my Swiss Army knife, poured its contents into my plate, dipped in frozen bread, ate ravenously, cleansed the plate with snow and crawled into my bag.

Last thought I had was to hope that William had caught a fast transport going north from Wrigley, or had bummed, borrowed or stolen a snowmobile to bring him here. I couldn't envision any other option he had, having left Johns not dealt with and knowing that by now Smokey would be famished. If I was right, sometime soon he would be arriving at the Cessna, seeing where the Beaver had landed and taken off, signs of my snowmobile arriving and departing, and my snowshoe trails. He'd be trying to figure out what all that activity meant, who was involved, where they'd come from and how much they knew. And he'd be thinking that he didn't have much time.

When he came back—that's when I wanted to be either watching, or following. On that thought, I slept like a baby.

It was therefore a very long and disappointing day, the next one. When I woke and was still for a minute or two I thought that only a week ago Morton was alive and none of this had happened; I'd wakened in Maxine's bed with the sound of the shower running and thought I'd walk down with her in the dark and then loaf around until I had to catch the plane.

I rolled over and looked outside. Heavy grey cloud seemed to fall right to the deck, off to the east. A little wind was blowing, a little snow falling. The temperature, I guessed, was maybe ten below, practically sweltering.

I must have had some kind of premonition that morning. Otherwise why would I start thinking about William's dog? Let's see, I thought, William was here Saturday with, at least in the very early stages, Christian, Batten and Johns. Why he left after getting Christian and Batten off to an early start, couldn't say, maybe thinking he had to attend to his father's funeral, but probably he had fed Smokey well before leaving. Working dogs can go days without food. Water supply isn't a factor. They constantly gulp snow. For seven or eight months of the year they never see water as such. But remembering how Smokey had seemed to warm to me a little when I threw him that corned beef, I put a few extra frozen meat-bags into my backpack. The sun was a rosy glow to the south-southeast when I packed the rest of the food into the animal-proof (well, let's not count barren-ground grizzlies) food box, lashed down everything lashable, added the rifle to my backpack, and set off on my snowshoes at an easy trot.

My plans were fairly simple. I was heading for a spot a little east from the north end of the pond. The prevailing wind was from the northwest, meaning I'd be downwind from Smokey. I figured about an hour would take me to where I could edge up into some of the trees overlooking the pond.

My intention was to be well off William's course when he appeared, as I felt was certain, from southwest of my lookout point. With the wind direction and the vast silence all around me, I was sure I'd be alerted by any sound from the tractor road, either a big rig or a snowmobile. I could see through the binoculars that most of the time Smokey was curled up in a snowbank near the Cessna. He got up once in a while to trot the length of his chain and howl.

It all worked, with the exception of William. Hours passed. I heard nothing and saw nothing. I ate chocolate biscuits, drank tea that went from hot to warm to cool to cold, sometimes paced stiffly around for a few minutes out of sight of the Cessna. Around five in the afternoon, temperature falling with the close of day, I had to ask myself, I say, Matteesie, what now? I obviously couldn't stay in this stakeout all night.

The snowshoe run back to my tent warmed me up fine everywhere, even between the ears—giving me time to consider that maybe it was all over, everyone in the bag, and I'd spent that day in the snowbank for nothing. Almost believing that and thinking, Well, I tried, I grabbed the radio.

"Matteesie here. Over."

Pengelly's voice was relieved. "Hey! What's happening? Over."

Even those few words told me I was still in business for tomorrow. Somehow, I was relieved. I don't like to work a thing hard and not be in at the end.

I told him what I'd done, batting zero.

He told me: No sign of William, Batten or Christian. No more sign of Bonner. Inuvik, meaning Ted Huff, was worried about me and wanted to know how long was I going to stay out if nothing happened?

"Not forever," I said. "A day or two more if it's still a dead end."

I could be ordered back, Pengelly said. The commissioner had pressured Ted on that but Ted had said it should be left to me.

Good man, Ted.

Lois had been calling the commissioner and asking when I would be home and did he have any messages for her from me.

Oh, yeah, and Edie had been around in the morning early. Nice woman when you got to know her. "I told her what a hero you were, very good with a shotgun."

"You bastard."

"I meant it! Anyway, she wondered if it would be a help if she took some time off and drove her dogs out there with a lot of hot water bottles and a nice duvet and a few soft pillows and I told her that was a hell of an idea."

"Okay, okay. I got a camp to make."

"One more thing," Pengelly said. "The media. What we got so far is a woman named Rosie from the *Toronto Star* and guys from *Globe and Mail* and *Edmonton Journal* and Janet from *News North*, you know her, the one-woman bureau chief for what it takes us Mounties about sixty people to cover. Also, five separate CBC departments called, including 'The Journal' and Jack Farr in Winnipeg, that wild guy with the Saturday radio show.''

"Thanks,'' I said. "Over and out.''

In the tent again I drank tea, ate, settled in, all the time wondering if I was losing my touch. It wasn't just a hunch that had gone bad, it was a carefully considered plan. I'd been so sure William would show up and that somehow, somewhere, I'd learn something until now hidden from me—what, I didn't know. Something nagged on the edge of my consciousness; something that didn't jibe. In fact, several things didn't jibe.

From what I knew about him, he would not have contemplated leaving Johns with a broken leg to some uncertain fate. And he would not have left his dog chained and likely to starve, barring rescue by someone else. That wasn't all that didn't jibe, but the something else I just couldn't bring into focus.

I knew that night, settling for sleep, warm inside and out, that I had to change the plot tomorrow. To what? I still had a feeling deep in my gut that if I could find the place where William had spent his solitude for so many years, I would get some answers. If I didn't pretty soon, the situation might outwait me. I would become a pervasive Arctic legend like the Mad Trapper, a little old Inuk tottering around the Barrens muttering to himself who didn't have the sense to know when he was licked.

The next day I packed up everything in dawn light, traveled most of the way by snowmobile and then, just in case, went the last half-mile on snowshoes to my vantage point. Nothing had changed. Smokey was pacing less than the day before. I had a decision to make so I made it. I went back for the snowmobile and returned to run it down the hill to Smokey. He bristled and growled until he saw that I was the last man who'd fed him, then whined. I took out a bag of frozen meat. He set up an uproar that could have been heard for miles. I slit the package and tossed it to him. He wolfed it down. I made sure the last of it had disappeared, even the reddish-stained snow where I'd tossed it, then I went in talking softly and released him from the chain.

He bounded up the trail I'd left, presumably to look around for more visitors, then came back.

My idea was that wherever William's Secret Garden, or cave, or hut, or whatever, was, Smokey had been there and would show some kind of recognition, if I could just catch him at it.

I began a dead slow tour by snowmobile around the pond, up and down the hills, in and out of patches of thicket. Then I made the circles wider, each one taking us closer to the smoke from the Burning Hills. Smokey mostly trailed along behind. Once he took off at high speed, me after him, and when I rounded a bend within sight of the tractor road for the first time, I could see he was losing a race with an Arctic hare. He just didn't seem awfully interested in any of the country we'd been covering. Maybe I'd given him too much to eat, I thought, taken the edge off his desire to please, if any—and then thought, Jesus, I've been away too long, to a husky happiness is a full stomach and the chance for more.

Well, I thought, if the way to a husky's heart is through his stomach I'll make him think I'm the greatest thing since the invention of frozen meat. I rummaged in my food box for another bag. He went crazy, jumping around. I thought he was going to rush in and take it from me. I'd seen huskies in that frame of mind, uncontrollable. I remembered everything No Legs had said about how smart this dog was, how easy to train, how he would stay when told to, just like a well-trained sheepdog.

"Stay!" I ordered.

He stayed, tail wagging, eyes on the chunk of meat.

I cut the bag and threw it to him. He caught it in midair and swallowed in three convulsive gulps, then stood there licking his lips.

I could see what a hell of a dog he was, why William wouldn't sell him with the rest of the team. But that didn't make me feel any less frustrated. "Come *on*," I said. "Where is it?"

Smokey looked at me expectantly. As if he was waiting for me to put it in plain English, where was what?

And then I had what, it later became obvious, was the best idea I'd had in a week.

"Go home!" I ordered.

He turned immediately and headed toward the river. He could move faster than I could, because a rock or fallen tree or any other obstacle was just a leap and bounce for him. He even stopped a couple of times and looked back to make sure I was following, and then he'd bound on again. He led me along gullies and over ridges. When we came to the tractor road there were patterns left by big truck tires, I figured from the slight drift in them none less than a day old. He crossed in a few leaps with me after him, close now. A bit of a run through the bush on the west side of the road caused me to lose a little ground but when I came into the open he was waiting alongside a line of haphazard piles of great ice chunks along the Mackenzie's shore.

He turned north there, with me after him. Up the shore a bit he plunged into a small grove mainly of evergreens, a jumble of spruce and willow. It was indistinguishable from other groves along the bank. He disappeared from sight. I couldn't get in there with the snowmobile, so I got off and went in on foot, not even stopping for my snowshoes. I could hear him ahead of me as I broke off willows so I could get through, remembering that time long ago in an igloo near the Arctic shore, the old woman with a few handfuls of willow twigs trying to coax those twigs into enough fire to boil water for tea. It had taken about half an hour, and the tea was warm, not hot.

I had lost Smokey. All was quiet.

I called and heard a whine just ahead to my left. I went cautiously. I would have passed it a few feet away if I hadn't been sure the whine was close. It looked like just another close-knit clump of willows, until back among them I heard the dog again, this time in a low snarling growl that changed to a full-throated howl interspersed with barks, the way a wolf howls and barks at the same time.

I couldn't get through to where he was, standing up. Then I noticed what seemed to be almost like the entrance tunnel to an igloo, a shallow runway in the snow under a cover of twisted willows. I didn't feel real good getting down on hands and knees and starting in, thinking I might meet Smokey coming the other way.

Then I saw a fragment of torn cloth, no bigger than my finger. Beyond it were other threads. Something had been dragged through here, but not in the last day or two. There was an inch or so of soft snow on the bed of the shallow indentation, enough to show Smokey's big paw marks.

It was not a cave, not a teepee, but looked like a little bit of both. Maybe a rock had been rolled out long ago leaving behind a shallow hollow, or a chunk of ice long ago had gouged a hole in the bank. Willows and spruce around it had been pulled in to form a sort of roof frame, which in summer could have been covered with a tarpaulin against the rain, although it was bare jumbled twigs and branches now. In a patch of bush around a city elsewhere in Canada this would have been what the neighbourhood kids called their cave, or their hut.

I pretty well knew it was William's place even before my eyes adjusted to the dim light and I could see what was in it now: the bodies of Albert Christian, I could tell by his black hair, moustache, beard, and of Benny Batten, I could tell by his thick cap of white hair. They were stretched out side by side a couple of feet apart, facing upward into the tangled branches above.

Smokey growled and showed his teeth. I spoke to him sharply and he retreated to a back corner, howling from time to time.

Christian had been shot in the face, three clean holes from his upper lip to his forehead. There was hardly any blood. Batten had been shot from behind, both in the head and the upper body. Those bullets must have spread after entry. Frozen blood was everywhere.

Both corpses were frozen solid, still in their parkas and heavy pants and mukluks, exactly as they would have been dressed when heading out with William last Saturday to look for a ride south on the tractor road.

Somewhere in this case, the story went, there was a half million dollars in cash. It isn't the kind of thing one carries in a wallet. Crouching between them, I searched carefully. It wasn't easy with their bodies rock hard, totally unyielding, but I found nothing in the pockets, no suspicious bulge anywhere. With difficulty, I rolled them over: nothing.

I sat back on my heels, considering. My first thought was of the radio. It was back on the snowmobile. So was my flashlight. I wanted a closer look around this place, in case there was a parcel or bag or knapsack or something that would hold a lot of money.

I started to crawl back out the way I had come when suddenly Smokey started to whine and dashed precipitously past me, literally shouldering me out of the way. I somehow didn't think it was because he was afraid to be left alone, but my head was too full to think about that much at all.

I kept on crawling, hearing his mad barking not far away. I was near where I'd first got down and started to crawl, and was noticing bits of cloth I hadn't noticed before, wondering how far William had had to drag the bodies, when something made me look up and see, not six feet away, legs.

"Keep on comin'," William said. "Just don't do nothin' funny."

FOURTEEN

"I was such a stupid bastard," William said. "I can't believe how stupid I was."

It was night and we were in the Cessna, William in the pilot seat and I in the one alongside. Not that we were going anywhere. They were just the best seats available. Snow was falling so thickly that I could hardly see the tip of the propeller a few feet away. Smokey was on his chain outside, silent at last, once again a victim of the ups and downs of the dog's life; indulgence beyond one's dreams and then back to reality, a chain leading through a blizzard to a snowbank with a dog inside, curled up snug and warm. William had possession of the only gun currently in sight, his rifle. It wasn't pointed at me but was leaning against the instrument panel near his hand. I knew nothing of his intentions, now or ever. We had eaten and had a good shot of rum and snow. With our second drink I had a fleeting impulse to raise my glass to his and say, "To us," but decided to save that for the movie.

"Yeah, stupid," he repeated.

"In what way?" I was really curious about his first choice. He just looked at me.

At first, over by his secret place after I crawled out of the tunnel, he had held his gun on me constantly, so tense that I had a feeling of imminent danger. Finding me there had not been in his plan. The first thing he said after his, "Just don't do nothin' funny," had been to ask how I'd come to find this place.

I gave the brief version, flying out and losing his trail in the caribou herd, then flying out with a snowmobile and finding it again.

The mention of the caribou trail brought his first ghost of a smile, confirming that he'd thought that a pretty bright idea.

Then it was back to the business at hand. He waved his gun at me and said to shut up and start walking. I walked in front of him up the bank to the tractor road. "Walk south," he said, which I did. He stayed watchfully maybe fifteen feet behind me. Once when a big rig could be heard approaching he waved me into the bush. We crouched out of sight a few feet apart while three tractor-trailers thundered past, a storm of swirling snow marking their passage. It occurred to me that if he decided to kill me now, I likely couldn't stop him.

Half a mile on, off the road and out of sight, was a new Skidoo Elan. Still holding the gun on me, he steered the machine one-handed back to the road and drove dead slow behind me back the way we'd come, the gun handy across his thighs, right down to where I'd left my snowmobile. He seemed undecided for a minute, then tossed me my snowshoes.

"Where are we heading for?" I asked.

"The Cessna," he said. At the same time he saw the radio. "Who else knows you're out here?"

"Every Mountie detachment in the Northwest Territories," I said. Then I had an idea that if I told him we had a call-schedule, he might order me to call in and say everything was okay. If I had that chance, maybe I could say something that would alert Pengelly, such as that Harold Johns sent his regards.

Of course, there was always the chance that Pengelly, being Pengelly, would say something incredulous that would tip William to the trick and go boom with the gun. But it was a hope, the only one I could think of offhand.

For a minute or two I thought I was going to get the chance.

"You got a call-schedule?" he asked.

I said yes, looked at my watch, and said, "In about five minutes."

I think he definitely considered the idea of holding the gun on me while I made reassuring noises into the radio, but if so he rejected it instantly. "Forget it," he said. "You could pass some kinda signal. Now shut up and walk."

I walked. He followed on his machine. I thought of the pond as I'd first seen it, the snow empty of any signs of traffic. When we reached the western ridge above the pond, he stopped, staring, and convulsively shoved his parka hood back off his face. Snow had just begun to fall, flecking his long black hair parted in the middle and hanging down both sides of his head. His mouth had fallen slack below the drooping moustache. He turned his gaze slowly from one end of the pond to the other, taking in all the signs of recent activity: the rough runway Stothers had made for his takeoff, the trail my snowmobile had made when I drove down the hill to carry Johns to the Beaver, the path in to the Cessna's hiding place.

After a long, long look he turned his gaze to me.

"Tell me all about it."

Standing there on the hillside in the growing storm of windblown snow, I told him about Stothers bringing me out on Sunday and glimpsing the snowmobile headlight, about coming back in the Twin Otter the next day, following his track and then switching to the other snowmobile track going the same way. Billy Bob's shot at me that got the radio instead. Killing Billy Bob. Camping by his body. Going on the next day to find the Cessna. Stothers and Pengelly responding to my radio silence by coming out to look for me. The airlift of Johns. Pengelly taking Billy Bob's body back.

William took it all in without his eyes ever leaving my face.

At the end he sighed. In another minute he said, "So Billy Bob is dead. I like that part best. And Johns is okay?"

I said yes.

"Jesus," he said.

In silence, we moved the last hundred yards or so through the growing blizzard, made camp in the Cessna, ate and drank, moved to the seats at the front of the aircraft and started to talk. William obviously had been thinking it all over.

"What made you stay around after Pengelly left with that son-of-a-bitch's body?" he asked.

"I figured you'd be back. I couldn't see you leaving Johns with a broken leg, or leaving your dog."

He nodded, even smiled, shaking his head. "That's me," he said. "Stupid. I thought I'd come back here, probably find Billy Bob here, kill him, lay him in with the other two bastards, take the money, and get out of here, somehow, either right out of the North or someplace safe. In a day or two, or as soon as I could, I'd phone Search and Rescue where to find Johns and Smokey. No Legs would've looked after Smokey for me."

I looked across the dark at him. There was a full moon above the snow. Even with the cloud cover the night was not totally dark. "Billy Bob might have killed you first," I said. "And then Johns, to shut him up. He'd figure nobody was going to find the Cessna until spring, if then. He might've shot your dog, too, just for the fun of it."

William shook his head a little impatiently. "He might have thought of all that, even planned on it, but he wouldn't have done a thing right then, not a chance. Not until he had his money for killing my father. I don't know what those bastards were paying him, but all I'd have to say is that they weren't far away, and had the money, and I'd take him to them. Then at my . . . at my place . . . when he was crawling in there I'd get him from behind, no warning at all, like he killed my father. Maybe years from now somebody would find them, or maybe never.''

Thinking of that secret place of his, I'd bet on the never. He'd had it all thought out. He might have gotten away with it. A guy with that much money could get away with a lot.

''How did you manage Christian and Batten?''

''I maybe wouldn't have even thought of it. But when I said they should get the hell out of here, Johns couldn't fly them with a broken leg anyway, Batten said just as casually as anything, 'We're waiting for Billy Bob.' Christian wouldn't have been that dumb. I could tell by his face he thought Batten was an idiot for telling me. He was right. I'd had an idea they'd been connected somehow with my father's murder—who else would want him dead? But I couldn't figure out how. When they said Billy Bob was heading this way, then I knew. I didn't let on, but I was thinking Bonner knew how to get here. He'd been the only one of the three who could know a day ahead that my father was being flown out, the only one who could get to Billy Bob fast and make the deal that he'd kill my father, the only one who could tell Billy Bob how to get here to pick up his money. That's when I made up my mind.

''They were worried about being trapped in here for weeks until Johns could fly. I told them they could make it on the tractor road, stop a rig and get out that way, and that when Billy Bob got here he and I would follow the same way, better two guys hitching a ride than four. I took them over there early Saturday morning. We got to the other side of the road, the river side. Batten had a gun. Christian didn't, but had the money. They were a few feet ahead of me, facing the other way. We were talking about where we'd meet afterwards in Edmonton. I kept thinking, even if they didn't pull the trigger, these two guys killed my father.

''I got Batten from behind, three shots, and when Christian turned I shot him head on. Four shots.''

''Looked like three to me,'' I said.

''I missed the last one.''

We sat for a few minutes. I was thinking that apart from Bonner the case was all wrapped up if I could get out of here alive. I don't know what William was thinking.

"I take it that when you killed Christian and Batten you became, ah, their beneficiary. You wind up with all the money now."

"Except a few thousand I took just in case. Used some of it for that snowmobile in Wrigley," he said. "Walk in, lay down cash. That part felt good, the only part."

"Where's the rest of it?"

He shrugged. "Can't do you any good, knowing. It's deep in the snow right where I fastened Smokey's chain. That's why I left him here."

Another puzzle solved. "Wonder he didn't dig it up and eat it."

"Even a husky can't eat a steel tool box."

So we sat. I still didn't know what he had in mind for me. It didn't really bear thinking about, so I didn't think about it.

Meanwhile, there were still things that bothered me. "What made you tell those guys how to find this place?" I asked. "Even draw them a map how to get here."

"Well, I was part of them then," he said. "And I always thought this was a wonderful place. It started when I was a kid and we were all still at home before my dad became a big shot, and one summer he gave me an old Viking five-horse motor he picked up somewhere and I put it on a square-end canoe we had. That summer I started traveling around in this kicker canoe for a week or two at a time and found that place on the river. Just loved it, fishing, sleeping, fooling around. Being alone. Thinking maybe I'd quit school and be a trapper . . ."

He said that at first he'd stayed close to the river getting his place liveable. When he started exploring a bit, he found the pond. Saw some ducks heading that way and went to have a look where they were going in. "I remembered thinking what a neat place it was, just long enough to get a light plane down and take off again, and if I was ever a pilot and in trouble I'd remember it. And then once months ago in Inuvik we started talking about what we'd do if we were ever going to be busted, and knew about it and could get away—''

I interrupted. ''Did you have any reason to think that might happen?''

''We'd often hear rumors and wonder for a while until they didn't come to anything. Even a couple of weeks ago, we heard one from Edmonton that some woman cleaner in the Mountie office picked up and told her brother, for Christ sake, a dealer, that a hit was coming somewhere in the North. He passed it along.''

Hard to guard against, a woman with a druggie brother, trying to protect him. But if such information, or even rumor, was out and around, that's how it would get to Morton. He was Mr. Metis to a lot of people, the guy with all the connections in the North, nobody knowing at that time that William might be one of those hit.

''Anyway, that time last fall when we were talking about what we'd do in a bust, there was talk about where to go that would be safe, and where we could meet later if we had to separate. I said, 'Hey, I know the place!' They never listened to me much ordinarily, but right away they were all ears. I drew them the map. I remember Bonner copied it, just in case. I could see it all later, that would give him what he could tell that fuckin' Billy Bob. But at the time it was just planning, just in case . . .''

He stopped there. I didn't actually see William begin to weep, but I saw him wipe his cheeks with his hand.

''Then a week ago last Sunday I got this message that my father wanted to see me at the Mackenzie, and I went, and right away he lit into me, insisting that I was part of a gang that was going to be busted—''

''And you were denying it?''

He wiped his cheek again, his face turned away from me.

''I never could face my father when he was like that. Even over small things I never could say, 'Dad, you're right, I'm sorry,' I always tried to bluster it out, but I've never seen him like that. He was crying! He knew! And I was denying it, and he hit me and I tried to hold his wrists so he couldn't, and we were sort of shoving each other, and then he went down and hit his head, and just stayed out. I called the ambulance and got him to the hospital and stayed a while, but then I went, it was one or two in the morning, and told Bonner what Dad had said to me.''

He wiped his eyes another time but his voice was steady enough. ''Stupidest thing I ever did in a life of being stupid. Of course, this was what we'd made the plan for, last fall, a bust. Bonner went right to Christian with it. That night it looked as if Dad was going to die. We didn't know where he'd got the information. If he was the only one who knew about us for sure, it would die with him. I just wanted him to live. If he came to, I'd tell him the truth, I'd ask him to help me, I'd try to be the kind of son he wanted. But Monday noon when Doc Zimmer said Dad was conscious now and again and might recover, others had, therapy, all that, might be flown out to Edmonton, that would be, I guess, when Christian would phone and lay on the fuckin' gunman, just in case he was needed. And I think told Bonner what to do if the worst came to the worst. He'd have it all set up. Christian was that kind, a big deal planner. That's why we did so well, I guess.

''After that Christian and Batten didn't waste any time. Within an hour or two they took the money and flew out of there. All Bonner told me—that's another shit, Bonner, I wouldn't mind killing—was we were to sit tight and they'd be back if it blew over, and if it didn't at least Bonner and I would be in the clear and we'd meet later somewhere and plan what to do next or anyway split the money.''

Another long, long, pause. Snow blowing outside. Smokey howling awhile, then shutting up. The sound of a wolf howling back.

''Like I said,'' William went on, ''stupid. Since my Dad was killed I've had a lot of time to think. I could even have been, maybe not like him, but at least better than I was. I could have said to myself a year ago, 'William, you're wasting your goddamn life,' and told those guys to deal me out. I could have gone back to Fort Norman, even, and married Cecilia Manicoche . . . She and I . . .''

This time he seemed to be finished. He had poured it all out.

After a while I said, ''You know they'll probably be out for me. They know where I am and it's been all day since I checked in. They'll be wondering.''

He just waved one hand at what was going on outside the window. ''Nobody's flying or even snowmobiling in this . . .'' Which seemed likely true.

Then he said, ''I still can't figure out how my father knew. A rumor, okay. There's always rumors. But knowing I was part of it.''

I thought of Gloria, in love with a man who treated her gently, listening with growing despair that early morning at the Finto Inn as he talked big about a drug bust coming up in Inuvik, and finally deciding she had to warn him that unless he could head it off William would be one of the busted.

I pictured that scene as I imagined it, a weeping woman and a man shocked into numbness, but I kept quiet.

The storm was still raging in the morning when William dug up the money and left on his new snowmobile. Within a few seconds he disappeared in what looked like wall-to-wall whiteout. He hadn't asked me to give him a few hours, or a day, or anything, before I radioed for help. He just left.

I couldn't think of anything I wanted to do right then, except make some tea and wait. If I went out in this stuff maybe I could and maybe I couldn't find my way back to the river and get the radio and let the whole ''G'' division of the RCMP know that Christian and Batten were dead, William on the run to God knows where, Matteesie okay. I decided it could wait until I felt more like it.

I was still in the Cessna about noon, the storm dwindling

away. I was thinking seriously about the snowmobile and the radio, when I heard the sound of dogs. Smokey set up a tremendous uproar outside. The other dogs were getting closer. Then I saw Edie's team plunging down the hill, Edie riding the runners at the back of the komatik. She had the brakes on, the lead line loose around her neck. They reached the flat surface of the pond. I heard her yell, "Whoa!"

On the komatik, on his own little sled, was No Legs. I jumped out of the Cessna while Edie's dogs flopped in their tracks, tongues lolling, panting. She ran to me and hugged me, No Legs poling himself along behind, both with parka hoods over their faces, the fringes as well as No Legs's moustache and Edie's eyebrows rimed with frost from their breaths. They'd left Fort Norman the previous morning. Edie's talk with Pengelly about what was happening out here made her decide there was no way she was going to miss the playoffs. She'd arranged a few days off, picked up No Legs, and here they were.

"You mean you ran all night?"

I was sure they hadn't. No dog team could. "You think we're crazy?" she said. "Even *my* lead dog can't trail in that kind of storm."

So they had made camp. They both looked none the worse for wear. Or even somewhat the better for wear.

"Hey!" she said. "You been listening to the radio?"

I told her mine wasn't around right now.

"They picked up Bonner in Calgary," she said.

Maxine's long black hair lay spread out on the pillow. I confess that I felt rather dreamy.

"You really got here fast," she said. "I hear in the afternoon that the mighty five feet six Matteesie has done it again, bodies all over the place, and I get home and who is here but the mighty five feet six Matteesie."

"Unfortunately not five feet six where it really counts," I said modestly. "Anyway, when they sent Stothers out for me they wanted me to go nonstop to Yellowknife for debriefing. I held out for Inuvik."

"Have you been debriefed?"

I held up the covers and looked. "I must have been. Don't see any briefs at all down there."

It was near midnight and we'd had a few drinks and what other amenities seemed appropriate to the occasion.

She didn't ask how long I'd be staying. I always had to tell her on my own.

"I fly out tomorrow for Ottawa," I said. "I'll be back sometime."

She just nodded. No urging to make it soon. That was her way. No heat.

In Ottawa, Lois was waiting for me in the airport. She was wearing her calf-length silver fox coat. I always thought this coat was a little excessive, for a wife of a simple inspector in the RCMP.

She hugged me a lot and got lipstick on me, but I didn't wipe at it. At least when cameras were running. In addition, she'd had her hair done a sticky new way. When my cheek brushed against it, I knew all the trouble she'd gone to.

When we got home the two Siamese cats, Murph and Surf (not what I called them), rubbed against my legs and sniffed suspiciously. As soon as Lois disappeared, I shoved them away with my foot. She came back in a peach-colored negligee and sat on the arm of my chair, this done on purpose, I knew, so that I could feel the silken softness. Which I did and suddenly felt a longing for the way we once had been. I put my arm around her and in a few minutes we were upstairs in her incredibly soft bed. In time my mind kept drifting away, so that the bed became a snowbank, and then the snowbank became a bed again.

In one of my conscious periods I realized that I was holding her in one of those ways that meant I wanted her. I rolled toward her, fumbling for the way in.

She pulled back and looked at me: blue eyes, fair hair, lipsticked mouth, a few wrinkles, a sag here and there as I also had.

"You're not just doing this as a favor, are you?" she asked.

"No," I said honestly.

In the morning I was up early. Among the many things that hadn't changed was that no matter what Lois did the night before, she slept in until I called and said that tea was ready.

While I waited for the water to boil I stood there naked, potbellied, unshaved, unwashed, uncombed, and besides that a little scruffy, and glanced at the piled-up mail.

An envelope postmarked MOCKBA caught my eye.

I tore it open and read laborious printing in blue ballpoint, "Dear inspector! With large sad I hear you not come Arctic Institute this time! Bloody bad! I Sibir Eskimo from Chukchi peninsula on Bering Strait! My people forefathers Eskimo your side! I famous like you! Only Sibir Eskimo anytime, anywhere, who colonel KGB! Looking forwards to get with you together for exchanging lies! Now dammit next time sure come!"

I couldn't make out his signature but someone at the office would have a great bloody file on him, so I could reply. Only Siberian Eskimo KGB colonel—wow! Maybe we could form an association

The water boiled. I put in three heaping teaspoons of Earl Grey tea, filled the pot with boiling water, and turned on the radio.

The top item on the CBC radio's seven o'clock "World Report" was from Ireland, the second through fifth from the Middle East, the next three from Ottawa, then one from Washington, and I was thinking great, next come the weather and sports, when there was one from Fort Norman.

William had given himself up, the announcer said, "along with nearly half a million dollars less what he termed 'traveling expenses.' "

He'd been in the bush somewhere with a cousin from Fort Providence, heading for a trapline in the Mackenzie Mountains where he'd never be found, when he heard about Bonner being picked up. On the spot he'd decided that he badly wanted to be a crown witness, make sure this last survivor of the murder plot did not wriggle free.

A day later, walking into the detachment at Fort Norman, he'd winked at Nicky Jerome, whose mouth had fallen open.

Then William had put the money box on the counter and called to Pengelly, who had his head down over some paper work, "Hi. I'm William Cavendish," and Pengelly looked up, thinking it was a joke.

About the Author

Scott Young has successfully pursued careers as a writer, broadcaster, and journalist. He has won several National Newspaper Awards since 1959, and a number of his early short stories were translated into Russian.

In 1984, Young published *Neil and Me*, the biography of his famous musician son. In 1987, his biography of one of Canada's most colorful and controversial personalities, *Gordon Sinclair: A Life . . . and Then Some*, became a best seller.

This book has been in gestation for many years. Having written often of the true, and famous, Young has now rewarded himself with a book on the fictitious and—soon to be—famous, the Inuk detective of his own creation.